Nick's punch sent Bevin sprawling backward. A sense of accomplishment flashed through him as the occultist tumbled over the tables behind him. But the feeling was short-lived. Suddenly Carl Neff loomed in front of Nick, his large face filled with fury. Before Nick could react, Carl pulled back one of his beefy hands, bunched it into a tight fist and hit Nick squarely in the stomach. He buckled over, gasping for breath, the wind knocked out of him. An instant later, he was hit again, this time in the jaw. His head snapped back with the unexpected blow.

CARE TACTICS

Copyright © 1996 by Elizabeth Manz.

All rights reserved. No part of this book may be used or reproduced in any manner whatsoever without written permission except in the case of brief quotations embodied in critical articles or reviews. For information address St. Martin's Press, 175 Fifth Avenue, New York, N.Y. 10010.

ISBN: 0-312-95792-0

Printed in the United States of America

St. Martin's Paperbacks edition/May 1996

8 7 6 5 4 3 2 1

SCARE
TACTICS

ELIZABETH
MANZ

St. Martin's Paperb

To my mother, Katherine, whose strength and love
have guided my life.

To Norma,
Stay up late one
night and have fun
reading the book.
Enjoy!
Elizabeth Gilman
5/96

PROLOGUE

ξ

A lone figure stood on the snow-swept landscape in the never-ending darkness and smiled. His time was coming.

Closing his eyes, he breathed deeply. The pungent aroma of death hung in the cold night air. He drank it in, savoring each drop. His large hands were clenched at his sides. His muscular body grew taut with anticipation. The need to kill spread through his body like a cancer, washing over him, threatening to overtake him.

Soon. It would be very soon.

In the distance, an animal howled a long, plaintive sound. The man could hear the hunger beneath the cry. They would hunt tonight, many coming for him, hoping this time to win the never-ending battle they fought with the big man and finally bring him down. He flexed his powerful arms, the tattoo that ran the length of his flesh moving over the shifting muscles. The beasts would spill none of his blood. But he understood their need for blood. He shared that need.

The kill.

He would be called upon to kill again and he would

answer with fervor. Watching death as it slowly overtook his prey. Hearing their screams, their pleas . . . He closed his eyes and breathed deeply.

Soon. It would be very soon.

CHAPTER ONE

ξ

"It takes a lot to scare me." The voice of Nicholas Cross boomed through the auditorium. He smiled as a wave of light laughter drifted toward him. "I know that's slightly evasive but it's the truth." He pointed toward another raised hand. "Yes?"

"If you won't tell us what frightens you then let us in on where you get all your ideas," another hopeful writer asked.

Nick's smile faltered slightly. It had been so long since he had given a talk at a writer's conference. He felt awkward, his answers sounding slow and feeble to him. As a best-selling horror writer, he should have anticipated these exact questions. But he had been so nervous about getting up in front of a large group again that he had not anticipated anything but his own fear.

Taking a deep breath, he looked out at the crowd before him. He knew it was taking him too long to answer. His gaze followed one of the waitresses that had served him lunch. She stepped smoothly between the tables, removing plates and refilling glasses. Her easy movement helped give him courage.

"Where do I get my ideas?" Nick repeated the question, still not sure what he wanted to say. He stalled for another few seconds. "Most of my ideas . . ." His gaze stopped at the young man who leaned against the back wall smiling widely, obviously having fun watching him squirm. No one would guess they were father and son. Jeff's light hair and deep blue eyes were such a contrast to Nick's darker looks.

His eyes narrowed as he continued to stare at Jeff. "Most of my ideas have been inspired by my son," he said finally.

Jeff rolled his eyes, the typical, best teenage reaction.

Other hands shot up, grabbing eagerly at the empty air above them, each person looking for that one piece of information that would change them from unpublished hopefuls to published novelists.

Nick glanced at the clock on the back wall. It was nearly one o'clock.

"I'm afraid I've run out of time. But I'll be around the rest of the afternoon." It was a Saturday conference. Nick still had two more lectures to give. The next one focused on writing for the long haul. He'd decided on the drive over that he really didn't feel qualified to speak on the subject. "If anyone wants to talk or ask a question, feel free. I've got an hour to kill."

Polite applause followed him as he left the small stage. Then came the inevitable rush of enthusiasts, some clutching well-worn copies of his books, others carrying large envelopes he knew contained their own stories.

He spent most of the next hour standing beside the stage talking. Slowly, he relaxed. One-on-one contact. That he could handle. That he was good at. His latest novel had only been out a week, but it was already on the *New York Times* Best Seller list and had been since its release. It was his first new novel in nearly five years. The first one without Linda.

As he flipped open a dog-eared copy of his third novel to the title page, he noticed his son only a few feet away. Jeff leaned close to one of the waitresses who had served their lunch earlier and whispered something in her ear. She giggled, shoving him gently away.

Nick tried not to stare, not wanting to inhibit his son, but it was difficult. *Picking up women? When did that start?*

"I just love your books, Mr. Cross."

Nick pulled his attention back to the young man before him. "Thank you . . ."

"Daniel," he filled in enthusiastically.

During the hour as he had talked and signed books, Nick had noticed this young man hanging back and waiting until he was the only one left. Waiting, it seemed, to be the last one to speak to him.

"Daniel," he repeated, scribbling inside the book as he spoke.

"I've read them all."

Nick handed the now-autographed book back. "How much do I owe you?" he said lightly. Daniel's face screwed up in confusion. "That's a joke." The younger man's expression did not change. If you gotta explain it, it's not funny, Linda had always told him. Why did he even try? He never could tell a joke worth a damn. "You've bought so many books that I owe you."

Daniel shook his head vigorously, his eyes wide. "It's me who owes you. Your books . . ." He paused, his eyes shifting from side to side as he groped for just the right way to finish his compliment. "Your books have changed my life."

"Wow. Not often you hear that." Nick couldn't help

but smile. The kid was so serious. "I'm glad you enjoyed them." The conversation was over, at least as far as Nick was concerned. He turned to leave.

"I reread them all waiting for this latest one," Daniel added quickly, keeping in step beside Nick. "Did I tell you I'm the president of your fan club here in Michigan?"

"No, you didn't." Nick did his best to sound impressed.

"I applied to this university as soon as I read that you went here. That's right, isn't it? You did graduate from here, didn't you?"

Nick nodded, glancing at his new shadow. He couldn't help but feel flattered. How many people had some kid pick his school based solely on the fact that you had gone there once a long time ago?

"You still live around here, don't you, Mr. Cross?"

Nick stopped. Daniel nearly collided with him. How much of his personal life did this boy know? "How . . ."

"I've read everything about you."

It unnerved Nick slightly to realize that it was so easy to find out where he lived.

"Dad?"

He glanced toward his son. Jeff walked toward them. The waitress he had been flirting with stood by the doors waiting.

"We've gotta go. It's almost two." He grabbed Nick's briefcase from beside the podium before heading back to his prey.

Nick glanced at his watch. He was scheduled to give another talk in less than fifteen minutes. Looking back at the young man, he said, "Thanks again, Daniel." He hated to admit it, but he was more than slightly relieved at the prospect of ending their conversation.

"I'll see you in a few minutes, Mr. Cross. I'm attending your next lecture."

"Good. See you there." He tried not to sound annoyed.

Daniel nodded, glancing at the signature in his book. He looked back at Nick before disappearing through the door.

The auditorium was now empty except for Nick, Jeff, the waitress, and two other men who sat at one of the lunch tables, still sipping their coffee.

As Nick walked back to his table to retrieve his conference folder, one of the men stood. He moved slowly across the room, as if in no hurry, and stopped directly in front of Nick.

"Yes?" Nick asked when he did not speak. "Do you want something?"

The man seemed to be about Nick's age, in his late thirties. But unlike Nick's, his brown hair was already flecked with gray. The stranger smiled widely, revealing perfect teeth.

"I was wondering if you could join me at my table for a moment?" He gestured behind him, his voice deep and commanding.

Nick glanced at the second man who had remained at the table. His face was hard and pitted, and his long hair was pulled back into a crude ponytail. He watched their every move. Suddenly, Nick was uncomfortably aware of how empty the auditorium had become. His gaze returned to the man before him. He tapped his watch. "I really have to get going. I have another lecture."

"It will only take a few minutes. I have a proposition for you."

"Proposition." Nick repeated the word flatly. So many people wanted to sell him ideas for novels or little known facts to use in his books. He was sure this was just such an occasion.

"My name is Thomas Bevin." He extended a hand

toward Nick. They shook briefly. "That is my associate, Carl Neff." He indicated the big man at the table.

"Nice to meet you," he said, speaking with a courtesy honed over years of book signings. "Mr. Bevin, why don't you send whatever it is you have to my agent. I'll take a look at it when I get the chance." He took a step away, but Bevin moved with him, blocking him in.

"I don't think you understand." His eyes locked with Nick's.

Nick's gaze did not waver as he stared back. "No you don't. I can't talk to you right now."

Not breaking eye contact, Bevin reached into his pocket and withdrew a business card. "I am an occultist, Mr. Cross." He handed the card to Nick.

Great, he's going to read my future.

"I'm the director of a psychic learning center. I think you and I—"

"Listen." Nick cut him off mid-explanation. "I would be happy to talk to you some other time. But right now I have an obligation to the people running this conference." He stuffed the business card with its Old English print into his front breast pocket. "I needed to blow this guy off somehow. "I will call you. We can talk—"

"I came here to warn you," Bevin said, his voice overriding Nick's. "You dabble in dark forces you don't understand." His eyes flashed with sudden anger. "You have no idea how open you are to attack."

"Is that some sort of threat?" Nick blurted out, his own anger bubbling to the surface. "Listen, pal—" He took a step closer to the man. Out of the corner of his eye, he saw Carl Neff rise from his seat. Nick glanced around for Jeff. His son leaned against the exit, smiling, still talking quietly with the waitress, completely unaware of what was happening with his father. In that instant, Nick realized how quickly this could get out of hand.

"He doesn't look much like you," Bevin said.

Nick jerked back to face him. "What?"

"Your son. He doesn't look much like you."

"I'm leaving." Nick sidestepped Bevin easily this time, the man making no attempt to stop him.

"He has his mother's eyes," Bevin called after him.

Nick kept walking, his back stiff.

"Some even say he has her smile."

Bevin's last statement hit Nick like a slap on the face. He turned sharply. "Who the hell are you?"

"Dad!" Jeff yelled from the doorway. Nick glanced toward him. He stood alone, the waitress gone. "Come on. We're gonna be late."

Nick shifted his gaze back to Thomas Bevin. He smiled with a smugness Nick did not understand. "Stay the hell away from us," he said before turning and heading quickly toward his son.

"We will talk again!" Bevin called after him.

"Who's that?" Jeff nodded toward Bevin as Nick approached.

"No one," he whispered.

A moment later, they exited through the door, leaving Thomas Bevin behind.

"I got a date," Jeff said as they moved down the hall.

Nick nodded, not really listening.

Some even say he has her smile.

He could not get Bevin's words out of his head. People did say that, all the time in fact. Even now, so many years after her death, Jeff was still told he had Linda's smile.

". . . listening to me?" Jeff's voice penetrated the cloud in his mind.

Nick glanced at him. "What?" He had not heard a thing his son had said.

"I got a date with Sandy."

"Sandy?" Nick's brow creased. "Sandy who?"

"Sandy. Our waitress. She goes to school here." He smiled proudly. "I'm picking her up here next Saturday. Pretty good, huh. College girl."

Nick eyed him sideways, glad Jeff seemed to be having a good time. "I'm impressed. How'd you pull that off?"

"Easy. I told her I'm the one really writing all this junk. You've just been stealing it from me for years."

"Junk?" His eyes widened. "Junk?" he repeated more loudly.

Jeff clapped him on the back. "It was a good speech."

"That's kind of you. Especially since you've already heard it two other times." He glanced behind them, just to be sure they were not being followed. The hall was empty. The tension in his back eased slightly. He could not let himself get worked up over nothing. He had done that too many times in the past.

Paranoia annoys, he told himself, remembering all too well the long stares and shaking heads of his past.

"Your speech," Jeff continued, his voice growing dramatic, "it's more moving every time I hear it. Your early failures, the sudden success." He sniffed, wiping at nonexistent tears. "Gets me right here." He patted his stomach. "It was either your speech or the chicken we had for lunch."

Nick laughed. "You're so good for my ego."

"There is one thing, though." He glanced at him.

"What?" Nick asked suspiciously.

Jeff shrugged. "Nothing. Forget it."

"What?" he persisted.

"That opening joke is just too lame."

"You don't like the three-legged pig joke?"

"Everyone's heard it."

"They laughed."

"It's old, Dad."

"You always pick on my jokes."

"Because your jokes are never funny. Never. They never have been. They never will—"

"All right. All right!" Nick held up his hands in surrender. "It's out." He laughed, then waited a beat and added, "Didn't I tell you you'd have a good time today?" But as he looked at Jeff, he noticed his son's smile quickly fade and his jaw stiffen. "Oh, come on. Is it that bad?"

Jeff had not wanted to come to this conference. But like so many other times, Nick had managed to bully him into it. The upcoming book signing tour was a whole other matter. Jeff was already loudly protesting. Nick did not think he'd be able to talk him into the trip.

"I still don't see why I had to come today." Jeff did not look at him when he spoke.

"I wanted you to see the school. You know, I thought—"

"Dad, don't start on that again," Jeff cut in. "I've told you before, I'm not even applying here."

"This is a good university." Nick did not want to have the same old argument with his son. Not here. Not now.

"I've got my own plans. I've told you that a million times. You just don't hear me."

Nick sighed. How had the mood between them changed so quickly? "I don't want to discuss this with you now." He checked his watch for lack of anything better to do. "I just don't understand this need you have to go away to school when we live right around the corner from here."

Because he wants to escape you.

The words swept through Nick's mind as they had so many times before. Ever since his wife's death, he had been afraid to let Jeff out of his sight. At twelve, Jeff had been more than happy to be with his dad day in and day out. But he was seventeen now and Nick needed to let him go. He just wasn't sure he could.

"Let's just drop it, okay?" Jeff ran a hand through his hair.

"Fine." Nick could tell from the tone of his son's voice that he was through talking—for now. "But we're not done with this."

Jeff stopped in front of the men's room door. "I gotta make a pit stop."

Nick checked the time again. "Okay. If we're quick." He took a step toward the door.

"I can go alone." The annoyance in Jeff's voice stopped him cold. "You're going to be late as it is," he added, his mouth set in an irritated frown. "I don't need you to hold my hand." His eyes bored into Nick's, a challenge within them.

He's old enough to take care of himself.

How many times had Nick repeated that phrase in his head? It didn't matter. No matter how many times he thought it, the words never seemed to sink in. When he looked at his son, he saw only the small, fragile boy he had been five years earlier.

It's just Bevin, he told himself. If that hadn't happened . . . But Nick knew that wasn't completely true.

"Okay." He gave in, knowing it was the only choice he had. "I'll see you there."

Jeff visibly relaxed. "I'll look for a new joke on the walls," he said, pushing open the door.

"That's where I got the last one!" Nick called after him as the door swung slowly shut.

* * *

Nick hurried down the hall of the university, reading each room number he passed. Room 238 loomed ahead and he sighed with relief as he entered the doorway. Somehow, he had made it on time.

"Mr. Cross." A young woman approached him. Her hair, neatly pulled back in a ponytail, swayed from side to side as she walked. "I'm Nancy Baxter. I'm with the conference committee." They shook hands. "I'll be introducing you this afternoon."

"Great," Nick said, slightly out of breath from his effort to reach the lecture on time. "Let me just go over my notes real quick. I—" He stopped, the words falling away as he realized . . . "My son has my briefcase." He glanced toward the door, then back to the young woman before him.

"Is that a problem?" she asked.

"Yes. My speech is in my briefcase." Going to the door, he pushed it open, hoping to see Jeff coming toward the room. But the hall was empty. Nick turned back to the woman behind him. "I'm sure he'll be here in a minute."

She checked the wall clock. "Well, do you think you could just start without your notes? Maybe just wing it?" There was no missing the note of hope in her voice. He knew she was concerned about the time.

"I'm not really the wing it type of guy." He glanced out the door again. Still no Jeff. A sinking feeling blossomed in the pit of his stomach. "I tend to repeat myself. So unless you want to hear the same speech you just heard at lunch, you'll let me go and get my notes. Jeff's right up the hall."

Nancy eyed the room full of waiting people. It was

packed beyond capacity, and a few fans were forced to stand against the back wall.

"I can explain before I go," he offered.

She shook her head. "No, it's okay. You go. I'll stall."

"I'm sorry." He shoved through the doorway and jogged back down the hall, chiding himself the entire way for his stupidity.

As he neared the bathroom, he was surprised he had not passed Jeff. What could be taking so long?

He pulled the door wide. "Jeff, what happ . . ." The words fell away as he glanced around the small bathroom. Jeff was not there. "Jeff?" Bending down, he glanced under the stall doors.

Empty.

One of the sinks had been left on. The water rushed from the faucet. And beside the sink, on the floor, sat his briefcase. He stared down at it.

What's going on?

Reaching out, he twisted the handle of the faucet, cutting off the flow of water.

Where is Jeff?

And suddenly, without warning, his mind flashed back five years. Memories of Linda's death flooded through him, rocking him where he stood.

Blood. So much blood.

He gripped the edge of the sink to steady himself. Looking at his reflection in the bathroom mirror, he stared into his own haunted eyes and tried to erase the images that burned in his mind.

He closed his eyes but it didn't help. He could not dismiss the dread that now crept up his back or the fear that knotted his stomach. It was not possible, but for an instant, Nick felt as if he had somehow been cast back in time. The events of so long ago now replaying themselves.

No!

His eyes snapped open. He turned away from the mirror. From his image. From the past. He shook his head, clearing away the ghosts that still haunted him daily.

This is not the same. I will not panic.

But where is Jeff?

Grabbing his briefcase, he exited the bathroom and sprinted back to room 238. As he pulled the door open, he was greeted by a smattering of applause and a small cheer from the waiting group.

Nancy walked toward him, a relieved smile cutting across her face. "You found your briefcase."

He set it down, nodding. "Yes, but I've lost my son." Briefly, he scanned the faces in the room before returning his attention to Nancy. "He didn't come back here, did he?"

"I don't think so," she said hesitantly and Nick realized she did not even know what Jeff looked like. "Mr. Cross, he's probably just looking around."

He tried to imagine Jeff suddenly getting the urge to walk through the campus, leaving Nick's briefcase in the bathroom and telling no one of his plans. "No, he wouldn't just take off." He chewed on his lower lip, thinking. "Do you have any security here?"

"Security? Don't you think you're overreacting?"

"I think I know my son a little better than you do," he snapped. "I know he would not have just walked off." The gnawing in the pit of his belly grew stronger with each passing minute. "Something's wrong," he muttered.

Daniel approached them. "Mr. Cross, is everything okay?"

Nick turned toward him. "Did you see Jeff come in here?" He could hear the desperation in his voice and silently told himself to calm down.

Daniel shook his head.

Nick stared at the two people before him, their expressions a mixture of confusion and embarrassment. They didn't know where Jeff was. Worse yet, they didn't believe there was a problem.

"This is pointless." And without saying another word, he turned and pushed through the doorway, heading up the hall at a fast pace. He glanced inside the classrooms as he went. Empty. Each one. Empty. And he realized for the first time just how alone they were in this school. As room after room dropped off behind him, his fear grew and his imagination went into overtime.

He's already gone. I'm too late . . . again.

He pushed those thoughts away, trying to suppress them, telling himself this was not the same situation as before. Jeff was fine.

Passing the bathroom where he had last seen his son, he turned left toward another hall of closed doors.

Where is he? What's happened to him?

He slowed down at each doorway, looking inside and making a cursory scan of each room. As he glanced in the third doorway, he stopped. He had found Jeff. But he was not alone.

"Mr. Cross," an out-of-breath Nancy Baxter called as she jogged to him. Apparently, she had been chasing him since his abrupt exit from the lecture room.

He turned toward her, his hand on the door. "If you have security, call them."

Glancing in the room, she nodded once and quickly moved away.

Nick pulled the door wide open and stepped inside the room. "Get away from my son," he said, barely able to control the rage that boiled within him.

Thomas Bevin turned toward him, an easy smile cutting

across his face. "Mr. Cross, I'm so glad you've decided to join us." He spoke smoothly, his voice chillingly calm. "We're just having a little chat with Jeffrey."

"They won't let me leave," Jeff blurted out. Panic laced each word.

Nick's gaze locked on Jeff. He stared into his son's clear blue eyes so filled with fear.

So much like Linda's eyes.

Linda.

Unwanted images of the past flooded through him again.

So much blood. There had been so much blood.

"You'll leave. Right now. With me." Nick took a step toward Jeff. But just as Bevin had done in the cafeteria, he moved with Nick, blocking him.

"Mr. Cross, just hear me out."

Nick's hands clenched into fists at his sides. His gaze shifted to Bevin. "Get out of my way."

"Mr. Cross—"

"Now!"

Behind Bevin, Jeff took a tentative step forward. Carl Neff reached out and grabbing him by the upper arms, jerked him back into place.

Panic ripped through Nick as the old fears rushed in, crowding his mind, mixing with the present. "Don't touch him!"

But instead of releasing Jeff, Neff took another step backward, dragging Jeff with him.

"You bastard!" Nick started forward.

Bevin grabbed his arm, trying once more to stop him. "We only want to talk. It's for your own good."

Nick wrenched his arm free.

"Mr. Cross, I—"

But he never finished the sentence.

Nick's punch sent Bevin sprawling backward. A sense of accomplishment flashed through him as the occultist tumbled over the tables behind him. But the feeling was short-lived. Suddenly Carl Neff loomed in front of Nick, his large face filled with fury. Before Nick could react, Neff pulled back one of his beefy hands, bunched it into a tight fist, and hit Nick squarely in the stomach. Nick buckled over, gasping for breath, the wind knocked from him. As if from far away, he heard Jeff yell something. An instant later, he was hit again, this time in the jaw. His head snapped back with the unexpected second blow.

He crumpled to the floor, still unable to catch his breath. His jaw throbbed. His ears rang. Jeff knelt beside him. He was saying something but Nick could not understand it. He stared into his son's worried face. Slowly, the words began to sink in.

"Dad, are you okay?"

Nick nodded and reaching up, touched his jaw, cringing as pain shot through his mouth. "Help me up." He put an arm around Jeff's shoulder, letting his son take most of his weight as he stood.

Bevin was already on his feet, leisurely brushing off his suit. He stood directly in front of the exit. His stare locked on Nick as Nick staggered to his feet. "I guess I should have expected violence from you." He smoothed his hair back into place.

Nick ran his tongue over the inside of his mouth, feeling a deep cut where his teeth had sliced into his left cheek. Using the back of his hand, he wiped away the blood on his lower lip. "You will never touch my son again." His voice held an unspoken threat. "Now get the hell out of our way."

Bevin did not move. His eyes narrowed as he stared at Nick as if studying him. "I was offering you an opportunity." He spoke quietly, almost to himself. "You have no idea ..." He shook his head, never finishing the thought. "You will remain in ignorance. But your son ..." His gaze flickered over Jeff. "He could be a different story."

"You son of a bitch." Nick made a move toward him but Jeff grabbed his arm, stopping him.

"No, Dad!" he shouted when Nick continued to struggle against him. "That's what he wants." He nodded toward Neff, who stepped forward, his mouth pulled back into a happy sneer. The big beefy hands which had already sent Nick to the floor once dangled at his sides, clenching and unclenching.

Nick backed off. He could see the unstable look in the big man's eyes. If given the opportunity, he would enjoy beating Nick into a bloody pulp.

Bevin laughed lightly. "My dear boy, I do not want this violence. It's simply what I expect from someone like your father. But if it'll make you feel better." He glanced at his associate, nodding once, curtly. Neff moved away, taking a seat at one of the desks. His eyes never left Nick. Bevin returned his attention to Jeff. "Now, what can I expect from you?"

Behind them, the door opened. Nancy Baxter entered followed by a burly security guard.

And the show began.

Bevin lurched forward, grabbing his side, doubling over. He leaned against the nearest desk as if suddenly needing it to hold himself upright.

"What the hell?" Nick said as Bevin continued to gasp in false pain. Carl Neff rose and going to Bevin, helped him to a seat.

"What's going on here?" the security guard asked, his eyes on Bevin, his face drawn in concern.

Nick pointed toward Thomas Bevin. "This nut has been detaining my son. First he harassed me in the lunch room and now here."

"Is that right?" the security guard, whose name tag read Ken Parr, asked.

Bevin looked up at the guard, his face filled with pain. "I was simply talking to the boy. Mr. Cross came in and just went crazy." He gasped, clutching his side.

"Are you all right, sir?" Parr watched him with obvious worry. "Do you need a doctor?"

"I can't believe this!" Nick's anger flared. "He's fine. He's not hurt."

"Mr. Cross, I think it's obvious this man is in some pain."

"He was fine until you walked through the door. He and his goon," he hooked a thumb toward Neff, "have been preventing us from leaving."

"Please, Mr. Cross, I know you're a writer but really, let's try to be believable at least." Bevin turned to the guard. "If you must know, I was talking to Jeffrey when Mr. Cross attacked me. Luckily, my associate was able to pull him off me before he did any serious harm to my person."

"You son of a bitch." Nick moved toward him but again, Jeff stopped him.

"You see how he is." Bevin cowered away from Nick, putting on the act of his life. "It's lucky the boy is here to control him."

"You lying bast—"

"Enough!" Parr yelled, quieting the room. He looked at Nick, then back to Bevin, trying to decide for himself exactly what had happened. "I'm sorry," he said, his gaze on Bevin. "I can call a doctor for you if you think it's necessary. But I must ask you to please leave the campus grounds."

Bevin nodded. "I completely understand." He turned to Neff. "Can you help me to my feet?"

Neff pulled him up and swinging an arm around his shoulder, supported him.

"What?" Nick blinked several times, stunned by the turn of events. "You're going to just let them leave?"

"Let's not make this any worse than it already is," Parr said.

"Any worse?" Did he really believe Bevin? "I think this guy was planning to kidnap my son—"

"You think," Parr injected.

"I know," Nick corrected. "You can't just let him walk away."

Parr stared at him, his gaze even and cool, saying nothing.

"I want them arrested." He pointed at Carl Neff. "He assaulted me."

"The police would tell you exactly what I'm going to tell you." Parr pushed the hat he wore back on his head, his voice growing annoyed. "This is a matter of your word against his."

"My son can—"

"And his assistant will back his story," Parr said, anticipating Nick's response and stopping him mid-sentence. "There is no real proof to back up either story. From the looks of it, you both got your knocks in before we arrived. So why not just call it even and drop it."

Nick shook his head. "Forget it. I want the police called. I—"

"Dad, it's okay." Jeff stepped in front of him, effectively cutting off the exchange. "Just let them go."

"No. Don't you see—"

"It's not worth it," he whispered. "I just want them to leave." And as Nick stared into his son's eyes, he knew this was taking as much of a toll on him as Thomas Bevin's detainment had.

"Okay." He reached out and gripped his son's shoulder, squeezing gently. "Okay. I'll let it go."

Bevin hobbled forward, still doubled over. "That's perfectly acceptable to me. I'm just sorry about the whole thing. I'm so embarrassed."

"No need to be, sir," Parr said in sympathy. Walking to the door, he held it open for the two men. "I'll escort you to your car."

Bevin glanced over his shoulder, his eyes locked on Nick. He could see the satisfaction in them.

As the door swung shut slowly behind them, Nick felt some sense of relief. At least they were gone.

Nancy Baxter stepped toward him as soon as they were alone. "I'm so sorry. Nothing like this has ever happened before."

Nick nodded at her but his attention was on his son. He had taken a seat at one of the nearby desks and for the first time, Nick noticed how pale he was. "Jeff, are you okay?"

Looking up at him, Jeff attempted a smile. "I'm fine." But as he ran a shaking hand through his hair, Nick knew he was not. The old fear was back. He could see it in his eyes. Silently, he cursed Thomas Bevin for putting it there.

Ken Parr helped Thomas Bevin into his car. "You can still file a police report. I know the guy's famous but that doesn't mean he can assault people and get away with it."

Thomas waved a hand, dismissing the notion. "There's no need. I'll be fine."

Parr nodded. "You know, I expected some trouble with him being here and all." He spoke quietly, confidentially. "He has kind of a reputation for overreacting."

Thomas feigned surprise. "I never knew."

"Yeah," the guard grunted. "I read this article about him. It said he's paranoid, calls the cops all the time for nothing. But he writes all that crap about monsters." He shook his head. "Go figure."

Thomas shrugged. "I can't." He pulled his door shut. "Thank you again. You have no idea how much you've helped me."

"No problem. I'm just sorry you had to be the one who had to leave." He hitched his pants up. "If I had my way, I'd have tossed that jerk out. But I'm not in charge of this thing, you know."

Thomas smiled. Parr could not have been better if he had cast him himself. "I completely understand."

As the car pulled away, Thomas leaned back, his gaze focused ahead.

"He's as arrogant as I remembered," he said as they turned onto the main road. "But he will come to me." Absently, he rubbed the palm of his right hand with the thumb of his left. "Yes," he murmured. "He'll come begging."

Nick steered the car onto the tree-lined street, turning toward the setting sun. Reaching up, he flipped his visor down, trying to block some of the blinding rays. It was almost six o'clock and with winter fast approaching, the days were growing shorter and shorter.

Nick had wanted the leave the conference right after the incident with Bevin. But to his surprise, Jeff had insisted on staying the rest of the day. Nick couldn't help but wonder if his son needed to prove to himself that he wouldn't curl up and die whenever something traumatic happened. To his credit, Jeff spent most of the rest of the afternoon in good spirits.

But now, with their house nearly in sight, Nick realized he and Jeff had made the trip home in almost complete silence.

"What are you thinking about?" he asked suddenly.

Jeff sighed and glanced out his window. "What happened," he said after a time.

Nick's grip on the steering wheel tightened. His gut twisted with anger. He had worked so hard to make Jeff feel secure since his mother's death. In less than an hour, Thomas Bevin had managed to break away some of that security, leaving Jeff feeling vulnerable once again.

"Are you afraid?" he asked, already suspecting the answer.

Again, there was a pause before Jeff spoke, as if he hated to admit it even to himself. "I don't want to be."

"But you are?" he prompted.

"I wish I weren't but yeah, I guess I am a little." He shook his head. "I just can't believe how stupid I was."

Nick pulled into the driveway of their large two-story home and cut the engine. Jeff stared at the house but made no move to get out of the car.

"You can't blame yourself. It wasn't your fault," Nick said, knowing his words would not alleviate his son's doubts but needing to say them anyway.

"I was stupid, though." Jeff looked at him. "That big guy came into the bathroom and told me you collapsed and I just went with him. God!" He slammed his palm against the dashboard. "I'm not a kid anymore. I should have known better."

"Jeff, come on. How could you know?" Reaching out, he gently squeezed his son's shoulder. "You were just worried about your old man. I can't exactly fault you for that."

Resting his cheek against the seat back, Jeff stared at him. "I guess I just wish I could have handled things better. Handled myself better." His gaze dropped to his lap and for the first time, Nick realized Jeff wasn't just feeling afraid. His son was also embarrassed. He had needed his father to come to his aid and that bothered him as much as Bevin's actions.

"Son," he said, groping for the right words, unsure of what Jeff needed to hear. "No one could have handled those two men alone."

Jeff nodded halfheartedly, his gaze still not leaving his lap. "But you were the one who stood up to them. You were the one who got punched. I just stood there."

"Well, if it'll make you feel any better, I'll let the next guy hit you instead." Nick smiled and was relieved when Jeff smiled and then actually laughed a little.

"Deal."

Nick pushed his door open and strode toward the house. A moment later, Jeff followed.

Leaves blew across their path as they walked. Nick glanced at the front of their home. The lawn, a combination of green and brown patches, barely showed through the maze of dead leaves that had fallen almost a month earlier. The bushes grew wild against the house, any shape they might have had at one time lost. The mailbox, which had been hit twice this year, stood at the foot of the driveway at an angle. Nick shook his head at the lack of work he had put into the house. He had never been very big on yard work but he could at least hire a groundskeeper. Or at least that's what half the neighbors told him.

As Nick slid his key into the door, Jeff said, "Let's get a pizza tonight."

He smiled. "Now I know you're feeling better."

Entering the house, Jeff headed for the stairs and his bedroom on the second floor. "You phone it in and I'll pick it up," he called over his shoulder. He took the stairs two at a time, pulling his shirt out as he went.

"Deal," Nick yelled after him. He was relieved that Jeff seemed to be putting the whole Bevin incident behind him.

After ordering a large pizza with pepperoni and mush-rooms—half with green peppers—he noticed the red light flashing on the answering machine. Someone had called.

Sitting on the stool beside the phone, his tie hanging loosely around his neck, he pushed the button to replay the messages.

"Hi. It's Karen." The voice of his agent filled the room. "Just called to see how the book's coming. I forgot you had that conference thing today. I don't know why you do those things." Nick could picture Karen sitting behind her manuscript-stacked desk in New York, puffing on a Pall Mall as she spoke. "Don't bother calling me back. Just write. Talk to you soon."

The machine beeped once after Karen hung up, indicat-ing that there was another message. Nick leaned back against the wall. He closed his eyes as he waited for the second message to play.

No one spoke. Dead air poured out of the machine.

Then, "Nickie."

Nick jerked forward, his eyes wide. The sound of the deep whisper bounced off the walls of the kitchen and echoed through the room.

"Nickie," it repeated.

As Nick looked toward the answering machine, a low chuckle drifted up.

"Long time no see, Nickie."

A chill raced up Nick's back as the man spoke. His voice, so filled with malice and hatred, clutched his heart like a vise.

"Did you miss me? I missed you."

Then Nick realized that there was something familiar about the voice. He strained to remember, his heart picking up its beat.

"I'm coming to visit you, Nickie. I want to—"

"Dad, did you call for the pizza?" Jeff entered the kitchen now wearing his usual jeans and T-shirt.

"Uh, yeah." Nick fumbled with the machine, not wanting Jeff to hear the message left there. "Yes, I did." He looked at the wall clock, wiping sweat from his upper lip. "You should probably leave now."

Jeff nodded. "Any message for me?" He pointed to the answering machine.

"No," Nick said a little too quickly. Calm down, he told himself. There's no reason to worry Jeff.

Suddenly, he did not want to send his son out alone. "Why don't I go with you?"

Jeff shrugged. "Fine with me. But I'm driving and you're paying."

"An offer I can't refuse." Nick slid from his stool. He pushed the button that would erase the messages left on the machine, trying desperately to stop his hands from shaking.

CHAPTER TWO

ξ

Miriam Cramer jolted awake. Her hand twitched and jumped by her side. Her heart beat heavily in her chest. She gulped for breath. Clutching the jerking hand against her body, she tried to still the movement, tried to block her sudden need to draw.

She glanced at her husband. He had not awakened. Bob lay beside her, completely unaware of her current torment. Closing her eyes, Miriam listened to his deep, even breathing, concentrating on the sound, trying to match her breathing to his. Within moments, she could feel herself becoming calm.

Her entire body fell into a relaxed state. Except for her right hand. The hand that had awakened her, the hand that continued to twitch and jump.

Why is this happening again? The question drifted through her mind before she could stop it. Immediately, her body tensed.

No, she did not want to think about it, did not want to remember the cold room and the dark presence. It had been nearly five years since its release. She refused to believe it had somehow returned to her.

But why did she feel the need to draw so desperately?

Even after nearly thirty years of using the "gift," as her grandmother had liked to call it, Miriam still did not understand it.

By simply touching a hand, Miriam could feel the presence of a loved one who had passed on to the other side. Filled with a sudden life of its own, filled with a need to draw, her hand would lurch to a start. A face, feelings, names. It all flooded through her as the drawing took shape. And she talked, revealing her new knowledge as she worked.

As a child, she had shown signs of possessing the gift at an early age. Her grandmother told her it had skipped a generation, missing her mother before being passed on to Miriam.

"Child," she had said one morning after Miriam had drawn a picture of her late Uncle Willie, "you've been blessed with the gift." She'd seemed very old to Miriam then, the wrinkles on her face so deep they looked painful. "You're different because of it. You must help others. It is your fate."

Later, her mother had told her to ignore her grandmother's words, that they were the words of an old woman who was beginning to lose her senses. But Miriam could not. She knew her grandmother had been right. The gift was within her, there was no denying that.

But as the years passed, Miriam did not come to understand her strange ability as she had hoped she would. She only knew how much it comforted people, how happy they felt when the picture began to take shape and they recognized the eyes staring up at them from the page.

Tonight was different, however. She had touched no one, had not even tried to summon the gift. But suddenly, unexpectedly, it had been there. Her hand began twitching spasmodically, waking her in the middle of the night.

Just as it had five years earlier.

And she was afraid.

That fear kept her in bed, refusing to give in to her need, refusing to let the presence that was now within her, be heard. But as her hand continued to twitch, marking the passing seconds like the ticking of a clock, she knew, could feel, that this was not the same as before. She was in no danger this time. Finally, she gave in.

Carefully pushing back the blankets, not wanting to wake her husband, she slipped out of bed, crept quietly to the kitchen and began to draw.

Her hand skipped and jumped across the page, the pencil moving swiftly over the paper. She could not control it, could not stop it. As always, she could only watch and wait for the finished product.

"What's going on?"

Miriam looked up as her husband entered the room, yawning widely. She said nothing and simply continued working.

Bob sat down beside her, running a hand through his hair, trying to smooth it into place. "What's happening?" he asked. Then he added quickly, "Is it the same? Is it happening again?"

Miriam could hear the anxiety in her husband's voice. She knew he too was remembering the destructive presence that had nearly consumed her five years earlier.

She shook her head. "No, it's not the same presence," she said, hoping to reassure him. "But the emotions coming through are just as strong."

Bob stroked his beard, a telltale sign of his nervousness, and stared down at the drawing. "It's a woman," he said, after a time.

"She's desperate to be heard." Miriam attempted to sort through the emotions that coursed through her as the drawing came into focus. "I'm getting fear and a sense of . . . hopelessness. She's afraid she might already be too late." Her hand moved more frantically.

"Too late for what?" Bob asked, his eyes locked on the drawing, completely engrossed by it.

She opened her mouth to answer but could not speak. Suddenly, her mind was filled with the woman, words screaming through her head. Miriam gasped, her hand lifting high off the table before slamming back down again.

"Miriam?" Bob looked up from the drawing. "Are you all right?"

"Help them," she whispered, struggling to get the words past her lips, needing to free them from her mind.

"Miriam, what's happening? Are you okay?"

"Help them," she said again, her pencil jerking up and down, up and down, the line beneath the lead growing darker and darker. "Help them." Her voice grew louder. The pencil lead snapped off. "Help them." The paper tore beneath the pencil. "Help them!" she screamed.

"Miriam, stop it." Bob snatched her hand from the drawing, the pencil flying from her grip. The words continued to pour from her. "Miriam!" He shook her. "Let go of it. Let go!"

Miriam blinked rapidly, the fog in her mind beginning to fade. She focused on her husband, staring into his worried face. "What's wrong?" She looked back down at the drawing of the young woman. Her eyes grew wide as she took in the torn paper. "What happened?" She reached toward it but Bob snatched it up before she could touch it.

"No, don't." He held the picture away from her.

"Bob, what's the matter with you?"

"It happened again. Whoever this woman is," he shook the paper, keeping it away from her, "she had a hold on you. I won't let that happen again."

Miriam touched her forehead, trying to remember. "I don't think she meant to hurt me." Her brow furrowed. "She . . . she just needs to be heard. There's something—"

"I don't want you to draw her again," Bob said, cutting her off mid-sentence.

"She needs my help."

"I don't care." He crumpled the drawing and threw it across the room.

"Bob!"

"Promise me you'll try and block her." He leaned forward, taking her in his arms. "Promise me."

Miriam held him tightly. "I'm fine," she said, trying to dispel some of her husband's fear for her.

"Promise," he whispered.

Miriam thought of the woman. She was afraid but not for herself. She was afraid for someone else, someone she desperately needed to contact, to warn. She could not ignore her. "I'm fine," she repeated, unable to make a promise she knew she could not keep.

Rattle, *thump*. *Rattle*, *thump*.

The sound came from far away, through a large, dream-like tunnel. Nick pushed it aside, slipping deeper into sleep.

Rattle, *thump*. *Rattle*, *thump*.

It tugged at him again, this time louder, more insistent.

"What?" he murmured, rolling over and opening his eyes. The room around him was dark. He reached toward the light beside his bed but stopped before he could turn it on.

He had thought as he pulled himself up from sleep that Jeff was at his door, knocking and asking to come in. But as he lay in bed listening to the sound that had awakened him, he realized it was not Jeff.

Someone's trying to get in the house.

The thought brought him completely awake, his heartbeat doubling in an instant. Pushing his blankets aside, Nick swung his legs over the side of his bed and gently put his feet on the floor, trying to make as little noise as possible.

He tilted his head, listening intently.

Was he already inside?

No. He could still hear the sound that had awakened him. It was as if someone was trying to force open a door somewhere downstairs. Reaching across his bedside table, Nick snatched up the phone receiver and quickly dialed the police. After giving them his name and address, whispering the information as loudly as he dared, he padded across the room and out into the hall. The police had told him not to leave his room until they arrived. But he could not do that. Jeff lay asleep just down the hall. Nick had to make sure he was safe.

Using the wall to feel his way, he moved slowly down the hall, trying to avoid the places in the floor he knew squeaked. He could hear the steady banging below as he approached his son's bedroom.

Jeff's door stood wide. Nick glanced inside, relieved when the familiar form of his son came into view. He lay in his bed undisturbed.

Suddenly, Nick felt very vulnerable, standing in his hallway, wearing only his underwear and robe, with absolutely no way of protecting himself.

"What now?" he whispered, not sure if he should wake Jeff and try to get out of the house or just sit and wait for the police to arrive.

The decision was made for him. In the next instant, the rattle, thump which had been going on since he woke, stopped abruptly. A moment later he heard the crash of glass breaking. Nick froze where he stood, staring into the darkness around him. His heart and mind raced.

Do something!

Reaching forward, Nick closed Jeff's bedroom door. Then moving as quietly but as quickly as he could, he stepped to the hall closet.

This is taking too long!

Yanking open the door, Nick fished around for a minute before pulling out a nine iron. He had never golfed a day in his life; the clubs were a gift from a friend with good intentions. He was glad he had finally found a use for them.

Holding the club high over his head, Nick moved slowly toward the stairs. The sudden quiet of the house unnerved him.

Where are you?

Reaching the railing, he looked down into the darkened living room. Nothing moved. He cocked his head to one side, listening, straining to hear. But the night was silent. Not even the annoying sound of his neighbor's bug zapper, electronically ridding them of every insect within an acre and a half, reached him.

He moved to the staircase and pressing his back against the wall, began his descent. Maybe the guy had given up? That thought was running through Nick's mind even as he heard glass break again somewhere down below. He stopped, one foot hovering over the next step down.

What if the guy has a gun?

"Shit," he breathed, regripping the club, his hands so sweaty he thought it might simply slip from them.

"The police are on their way!" he shouted, hoping to discourage the intruder. Silence. Squinting into the blackness below, Nick strained to see something . . . anything. The stairs behind him squeaked. He cried out in surprise and turning, raised the club high, ready to strike.

"No, Dad, it's me." Jeff threw his hands up to protect himself.

Nick lowered the nine iron. His hands shook as he realized what he had almost done. "Goddammit, Jeff," he snapped, his teeth clenched with tension. Jeff opened his mouth to speak, but before he could say anything, loud hammering sounded on the door below. Both men jumped.

"Police!" a strong voice called out an instant later.

Jeff glanced once at his dad before hurrying past him and throwing the front door wide open. He flipped on the lights as he went, making Nick blink as the sudden brightness blinded him.

"I think he was inside." Nick told the police officer that stood on his front porch. "I don't know if he left or not," he added, moving down the stairs. He shivered slightly as the cold of the room hit him.

Within moments, a second patrol car pulled into the driveway, the lights washing the street red, then blue. After quickly explaining the situation, Nick and Jeff waited on the couch while the officers checked their house.

"Whoever it was is gone now, Mr. Cross," Officer Denten said as he strode back into the living room. He had a young face but in contrast, his mannerisms were that of a seasoned professional.

"Did he do much damage, Officer?" Nick asked.

"Damage?" Denten's brow knit in confusion.

"I heard glass break." Nick rose and moved toward the kitchen. "I thought it came from in here." He stopped as the room came into view. No glass littered the floor. Dishes remained stacked where he had left them. Everything looked normal.

"Maybe it was the study?" Jeff suggested, looking over his father's shoulder at the neat room.

"We checked every room, Mr. Cross. We didn't find any sign of forced entry," Denten said from behind them.

Nick turned. "But I heard glass break."

"I don't know what to tell you, Mr. Cross. There was nothing. No foot prints outside. No stomped down grass around the doors or windows." He shook his head, tapping his pen on top of his notepad. "Nothing."

"There was someone here," Nick said, realizing what he was getting at.

"You say you were awakened from sleep?" Denten asked, his voice sounding as if he were testing the water before jumping in.

"I was awake. I didn't dream it."

Denten turned his attention to Jeff. "What did you hear, son?"

Jeff glanced at his father, his face clearly showing his distress. "I didn't hear anything," he said. "But I believe my dad," he added quickly.

Denten nodded. "I don't know what to tell you, Mr. Cross."

"I heard someone. I know someone was here."

"I'm sure you thought you heard something. But a lot of times when people are awakened—"

"I'm not some hysterical person who jumps at every shadow," Nick cut in. "I know what I heard."

"Of course you do." But Nick could hear the patronizing tone in his voice. He knew that Denten doubted the entire story. "I'm just glad no one got hurt." He turned to leave.

"What if they come back?" Jeff said suddenly.

Denten stopped. "They? I thought you said you didn't see anyone." He looked at Nick.

"I didn't . . . We . . ." He paused, glancing at his son. "We had some trouble earlier." The officer continued to stare at him. "I was speaking at a writers' conference." Nick spent the next few minutes telling Officer Denten about his encounter with Thomas Bevin.

"Did this Bevin threaten you in any way?" Denten asked. They were now seated at the kitchen table, Denten taking notes.

Nick glanced at Jeff, then back to Denten. "No, not really." He hesitated, reluctant to tell him the rest. "There was also a message on our machine when we got home. It was a man's voice but not someone that I recognized." He paused. "The message was a little weird."

"Why didn't you tell me?" Jeff said immediately.

"Can I hear that message?" Denten asked a moment later.

"I erased it." He looked at his son. "I didn't want you to worry."

Jeff stared at him. "That's why you went with me to get the pizza," he said, realization dawning. "I knew something was wrong."

Nick opened his mouth to speak but the angry expression on Jeff's face stopped him. What could he say? He had no real excuse for his deception.

"You should have told me," Jeff finished, his voice barely a whisper.

He looked steadily at his son. "You're right. I should have told you and I'm sorry. It won't happen again." But this was a promise he had made before, a promise he had already broken several times. It was for his own good. At least that was what Nick always told himself when he kept something from Jeff. It was for his own good. But as Jeff turned away, Nick could see the hurt in his eyes and he felt momentarily ashamed.

"Well, Mr. Cross," Officer Denten said, breaking the uncomfortable silence that now hung in the air between father and son. "I think I've got everything here." Standing, he replaced the pad of paper in his breast pocket.

Nick stood with him. "I wish I could have been more help. I wish I hadn't erased that damn message."

Denten strode out of the kitchen and toward the front door. "Well, we'll run Bevin through our computer. Who knows? Maybe the guy has a history of this sort of harassment." He stepped out onto the front porch. "We'll be patrolling this area heavily the rest of the night. That should keep them away if they're still in the neighborhood." And seeing the look on Jeff's face, he added quickly, "But I'm sure they're gone. From what you've told me, it sounds like this Bevin has been around the block. I don't think he'd be stupid enough to try anything else tonight."

Nick nodded. "Thanks again." He watched as the police car backed down the driveway and headed up the street.

Closing the door, he turned both locks.

"You don't have to worry about me so much."

Nick turned to face Jeff. "It's not a conscious thing. I can't just switch it on and off." He realized now how much he had hurt Jeff by concealing the truth. Going to him, he draped an arm around his son's shoulders and steered him toward the stairs. He left some of the lights on in the kitchen and living room. It made him feel more secure somehow.

"I'll try and be better in the future," he said as they climbed the stairs together.

"It's been five years, Dad. I'm okay." Jeff took a deep breath before continuing. "What happened, happened. We can't change it but we have to get past it." He looked at his father. "You have to get past it."

They stopped in front of Jeff's bedroom.

"I think you're too smart," Nick muttered. He released Jeff's shoulders and stood facing him. Raising his hand and holding three fingers up in imitation of the Boy Scout pledge, he said, "I promise to try and do better next time."

A grin broke out across Jeff's face. "Well, I know I feel better."

Nick dropped his hand. "Good," he whispered and leaned back against the wall, staring at his son. Jeff tilted his head slightly to the left and the hall light hit one side of his face. In that moment, Nick saw his wife again. The expression on Jeff's face, the way his eyes crinkled— it was all Linda. But then Jeff dropped his chin against his chest and the moment was lost, the look gone.

"I'll see you in the morning, Dad."

"Right." They stood there for a moment, staring at each other. Nick wanted to take Jeff in his arms and hug him, hold him close. But he did not. He knew his son would stiffen in his embrace and he did not want to feel that distance between them, not tonight.

"Good night," Jeff said and turning, stepped into his room. His door shut quietly behind him.

Nick stood in the hall, staring at the closed door for a long minute. Jeff was in the next room, just behind that door but to Nick, it felt as if there was a vast span separating him from his son. Regrets, that was all they seemed to share now. With a sigh, he turned, heading toward his own bedroom. As he passed the bathroom, he stopped, his brow furrowing. Backing up, he glanced inside the small room.

Is someone in there?

For an instant, it seemed there was. But he then realized it was just his own reflection in the mirror. He stood in the dim light of the hall, staring at his face in the glass. He could see the fear behind his eyes.

Will it ever leave me?

It was a question he'd asked himself every day since his wife's murder. Will I ever feel safe again? Will every noise that awakens me in the night bring immediate terror?

He turned away from the man in the glass. Tonight was further proof of just how far he had to go.

The lone man stood at the window, staring out at the snow-swept landscape. Heavy white powder drifted high against the house. Tree limbs bent at dangerous angles to the wind's harsh demands. But he saw none of it. He stared ahead, waiting, his eyes unfocused.

Moments earlier he'd sensed a presence, felt it near. His body tensed as he waited for it to return. Then like a whirlwind, it swept through the room. He closed his eyes. His breath caught in his throat. It swirled around him. Brushed past him. Whispered dark promises in his ear.

Your time is near.

Soon you will kill.

He strained to hear more. But once again the night was silent. Except for the wind. It pushed its way through the walls that surrounded him, invading the house, howling through the rooms, placing its icy hands on his flesh.

He did not notice.

His arms hung at his sides. His powerful hands

clenched and unclenched. He grew impatient. The kill. He had waited so long for the kill. He opened his eyes. How long had it been since he left this place and made the journey to the other world?

He did not know. For him, time did not exist. This place, this world he lived in, had no beginning, no end. It was the place of forever night. Eternal darkness was his constant companion. Dawn never came, the sun's warmth never touched it.

But he remembered the other world. He remembered the warmth and the light.

And in that moment, as he stood staring at the endless snow and night, his mind filled with memories, memories buried deep until the presence returned, whispering its dark promises.

It was close now.

He would leave this world, just as he had before. Leave the darkness and cold, the animals and their constant hunger.

And he would kill.

But this time would be different.

This time he would not return.

CHAPTER THREE

ξ

Thomas Bevin pushed open the glass doors, swinging them wide. The late morning sun flooded through the windows, warming the Bevin Institute for Psychic Learning in its soft glow. He whistled tunelessly as he walked swiftly down the hall, the heels of his shoes clicking loudly on the linoleum floor, marking each step.

He went straight to his office. Sandy Parker, his secretary for more than a year, looked up sharply as he entered. She ground her cigarette out in an ashtray already overflowing with butts and glanced at the wall clock.

"You have a lecture in less than an hour." She sorted through his messages, handing him only the most important ones.

"Cancel it."

"This will be the third one I've cancelled this week." Her voice, deep and gravelly sounding from years of too much smoking, grated against his nerves.

Thomas looked at his secretary. She was an irritating woman, rude even to him. He had almost fired her after her first week on the job. But he soon came to realize that her curt manner worked in his favor. She intimidated people with her brusque attitude, easily managing to keep out the ones he didn't want to see. That quality alone overrode all the rest.

"In fact," he said, flipping through the messages, not planning on returning any of the calls, "cancel the lectures for the next week or two. I have some personal business I must attend to." His gaze fell once more on his secretary. "Has Ginny Lambert arrived yet?"

Sandy nodded, looking more than a little irritated. "She's in test room one with Connie."

He smiled. Everything was coming into focus. "Good. Locate Mr. Neff. I need to see him immediately. And tell him to bring the file on Ginny." As he walked into his office, the phone rang on Sandy's desk. He heard the familiar answer: "Bevin Institute. How may we guide you?"

Going to his desk, Thomas sat down. The leather of the chair crackled with his movement. The color was a perfect match to the mahogany desk. He dropped the messages in the garbage can beside him. They could all wait. Nothing was as important as this.

Leaning back in the plush chair, he spun around, staring out the large glass window behind his desk. The grounds of the Bevin Institute for Psychic Learning were immaculate as usual.

The institute spread itself over twenty acres. The main two-story, glass building reflected back the sculptured landscaping that surrounded it. Water gurgled gently from the fountains in each of the man-made ponds, colored lights reflecting off the water, turning it red, green, and blue. He glanced at his watch as the sprinkler system turned on, the small green water jets gently spraying the lush lawn. It would run for exactly twenty minutes and then turn itself off. In four hours, it would turn on again and run for another twenty minutes. Exactly as he had requested. In fact, everything at the institute was to his specification.

Ten years earlier, when he started the organization, he'd had little more than a hope and a prayer. But he had gotten lucky. He had met Mary. She had been so enthralled by him, captivated by his charm and good looks. It had been easy to win her over. After they were married, she gladly built the institute for him. She believed in his abilities and wanted to help him prove them to the world. She died less than a year later, her failing health one of the many things that had attracted him to her in the first place. He inherited everything, just as he had planned to.

The phone on his desk buzzed. He pushed the intercom button. Sandy's voice came through. "Mr. Neff is here."

"Good. Send him in." And a moment later, the door opened. Carl Neff strode in, Ginny Lambert's file, as requested, tucked under his arm.

"You wanted to see me?" He sat in one of the two chairs that flanked Thomas's desk. His face was eager and Thomas knew he would do anything he asked of him.

"Could you please get me a drink of water first?" Thomas indicated the bottled water dispenser in the corner.

Carl stood obediently and drew him a cup of the cool liquid. Thomas liked to use his authority over Carl. It made him feel powerful knowing he could control the big man so easily. Most people did not believe in his institute and the things he taught.

But Carl did.

Carl believed so deeply that he would do anything to help Thomas fulfill the visions he had. They had meet only three years earlier. Thomas was lecturing to a group of prison inmates, asked by the prison warden to try and inspire the men. Carl had been captivated and upon his parole, he had looked up Thomas and offered him his unique service. He was not only a bodyguard for Thomas but also a spiritual learner who wanted to absorb everything he could from the man he thought was so gifted.

"Thank you," Thomas said, accepting the water. He downed the cool liquid in one gulp before crushing the paper cup and dropping it into the garbage can beside his desk. "Before I speak with Ginny, I wanted to get a progress report from you. How is the testing going?"

"She's remarkable," he said, smiling widely. "Connie says she's one of the most gifted psychics she's ever worked with."

"And her personal life. What can you tell me about that?"

Carl flipped through some of the papers in the file. "Her only known relative is the grandmother. The story seems to check out. The girl was in a car accident with her parents. They were both killed; she was seriously injured. She was in the hospital for," he ran his finger down the page, "a total of six months. Half that time she spent unconscious."

"As far as you could find out, she had no psychic abilities before this accident?" He'd read about people who had experienced a trauma to their bodies and come away with new abilities. Ginny was the first person he'd actually met who fit that profile. He found the situation ideal. Ginny looked to Thomas for answers to her many questions, believing everything he told her, never questioning his judgment or the decisions he made regarding her welfare.

But the grandmother was a problem. Evelyn Lambert never let the girl out of her sight. She was over-protective since the death of her son and daughter-in-law. The fact that Ginny was only eleven didn't help matters. But Thomas was beginning to gain her trust. He needed to see Ginny alone and he was confident that he could convince Evelyn Lambert to allow him that opportunity.

"Up until the accident," Carl continued. "She was just a normal kid. Her grandmother told me they have nothing in their family history either. No uncles who could read minds or bend spoons."

Evelyn Lambert had brought her granddaughter in months earlier to be tested. Thomas ran a continuous ad asking anyone who thought they might be psychic to come in for testing free of charge. He needed to find someone with the abilities he required to carry out his plan. The ad had brought him several prospects. But none were as gifted as Ginny Lambert. She was the one he'd been waiting for.

"I'm going to take a walk down to test room one," he said, rising from his seat. Carl rose with him, his eyes never leaving Thomas. "I want to check on Ginny's progress."

He was not sure if Ginny had the strength and endurance he would require. But the exercise he had planned for today would tell him. He was confident she was the one. Then he could begin again. But this time, he would be in control.

Ginny Lambert sat at the table, one leg tucked under her, staring at the deck of cards before her. She reached forward but then stopped. She was supposed to be separating the deck into two sections, black and red, without seeing the face of each card. But she was tired and hungry and she just plain didn't feel like doing it anymore. Grabbing the ponytail on the back of her head, she wound her fingers through her hair and began twisting. She reached for the cards again, and again, she hesitated.

"Don't force it, Ginny," Connie Elliott coaxed. "Just relax."

Ginny looked up at the woman who had been working with her for the past three months. She liked Connie. She was never really angry. Just impatient sometimes. But even then, she was nice. But she preferred to work with Mr. Bevin. The first time she met him, she thought he looked a little like her dad, the way he smiled at her, the color of his hair. He made her feel safe. But now it seemed she never got to see him. In fact, she had only seen him three times since she started coming to the institute. Her grandmother said he was too busy to bother with everyone who was being tested. But Ginny had thought she was special. That was what he had told her the first time he met her. She was special. Now, sitting at the table, staring at the cards, she was ready to go home.

"I'm kinda hungry," Ginny said. "Can't we get some lunch soon?" She glanced back at her grandmother, who sat behind her, silently watching.

Evelyn Lambert nodded, glancing at her watch. "In a little while, dear. It's still a little early."

"As soon as we're done with this deck, we break," Connie said, tapping the cards with her fingers, drawing Ginny's attention back to them.

Ginny smiled. "Great!" And picking up the deck, she began sorting the cards, one left, two right, three more left.

"Ginny." Connie watched her hands move. "You have to be serious. This is not a game."

"I am being serious." She set the last card in the pile on the left and said, "Finished."

Connie looked skeptical as she scooped up the first pile. But as she laid the cards out on the table, each one showed red in color. Ginny's score was perfect.

"I told you I was doing it." Ginny twirled her hair once again. "Can we go now?"

The door to the test room opened and Thomas Bevin walked in. Ginny tensed slightly, her heart picking up its beat. "Hi, Mr. Bevin," she said, unable to contain her excitement at seeing him. Like every other day, she had been hoping he would stop by. She knew she had done well on this latest test and she wanted him to see.

"Good morning, ladies." He nodded at each one. "How is my favorite psychic doing today?" He sat down beside Ginny, his gaze locked on the cards displayed on the table. "Is this your work?" he asked, moving them around, checking that all the faces were red.

Ginny nodded, her eyes locked on Thomas. "I just did that."

"We were about to break," Connie said. "Unless you want to do more work."

He glanced at his watch. "No, you're right. It is closer to afternoon than morning."

Evelyn Lambert rose, gathering her purse and the book she was reading.

Ginny hesitated in her chair. Mr. Bevin had just arrived and now they were leaving again. "I can do a little more," she said, pulling the cards back into a pile. "I want to show Mr. Bevin how I separate them."

"I'm sure Mr. Bevin has other things he needs to do right now," Evelyn said, coming up behind her.

"Actually, I wouldn't mind staying." He glanced at Connie. "Why don't you and Mrs. Lambert head to the cafeteria and get started. I'll have Ginny join you in just a few minutes."

Ginny's stomach did flip-flops. Alone. *She was finally going to be alone with Mr. Bevin.*

Evelyn hesitated. "I don't mind waiting."

"Gram." Ginny turned around in her chair to face her grandmother. "Go ahead. I'm starving. You can get my lunch so that when I get there, I can just eat."

"We can go over Ginny's schedule," Connie said, taking the elderly woman by the arm and leading her toward the door.

"All right." Evelyn glanced once over her shoulder before disappearing through the exit.

Ginny waited until the door was shut before turning back around in her chair. "I'm glad I get to show you how good I've been doing, Mr. Bevin."

Thomas gathered up the deck of cards and began shuffling them. "Now I've told you before, Ginny," he said, the cards moving swiftly through his fingers. "Call me Thomas."

"Okay." She blushed. Until she came to the institute, she had never called an adult by his first name. It felt strange to her but she liked it. "Do you want me to separate the cards for you, Thomas?" The blush deepened.

He set the deck down. "No, I don't think so." Picking up her file, he flipped quickly through it, stopping to read passages here and there.

Ginny watched, fidgeting in her chair. What if he gave her something to do that she couldn't do? She didn't want to disappoint him. "I'm good with the cards," she said, leaning across the table, grabbing for the deck.

Thomas reached out and took her hands in his, stopping her. "You've tested so well," he said, holding onto her hands, "that I think you're ready for some harder work here." He squeezed gently, his blue eyes locked with hers. "Do you think you're ready for some real challenges?"

Ginny felt a rush of excitement as his hands held her own. She liked Mr. Bevin—Thomas—a great deal. Liked doing the testing and the talks they had together. "I'm ready," she said, wanting to please him.

"Okay. Good." He got up from his seat and pulling her to her feet, led her to the couch in the corner of the room. "I want you to lie back and close your eyes." She did it without protest. "Now concentrate on your breathing and just relax."

"Is this another meditation exercise?" she asked.

"Yes." His voice, softer than it had been only a moment earlier, washed over her. "I want you to try and go into a deeply relaxed state." She felt his hand take hers, his grip soft yet firm. "Now Ginny, I want you to picture a field." His voice was so relaxing, the words almost melodic in tone. Her breathing became calm and even as she slipped into a deep state of relaxation.

Picture a field.

And in only a moment, she was there.

She stood in a snow-swept field, surrounded on all sides by trees. It was night. The moon reflected brightly off the white ground. She looked down and realized she was standing on top of the snow, not sinking in. The wind blew around her, causing the trees' branches to sway to its harsh demands. But she did not feel its biting cold.

Observe your surroundings.

She heard the words in her mind, gently pushing her to do their bidding. Ahead in the darkness she could see the outline of a building. Before she could move toward it, she found herself there, staring at the structure. It was a small two-story brick house. The dark windows revealed nothing. She glanced back over her shoulder at the place she had somehow left.

Look inside.

And even as the thought crossed her mind, she was in the house. The room was sparsely decorated, with only the most essential items. A table with a lamp atop it, a chair, a couch. Her gaze stopped on the couch.

Someone was there.

And for the first time since she started doing any of the tests with Thomas Bevin, Ginny Lambert felt afraid.

Unable to stop herself, she drifted toward the figure who sat so quietly, staring ahead, never once turning to look at her. It was a man. She knew that the first moment she saw him. He was large, powerful looking, the muscles in his shoulders outlined beneath the white T-shirt he wore. She squinted in the darkness, trying to see the tattoo that ran the length of his sizeable arms. A snake. The head started on the right arm, wrapping up and around each muscle before disappearing under the sleeve of his shirt. She leaned forward, trying to see his other arm, wondering if the snake reappeared there.

And he moved.

Pushing himself up from the couch, the man turned toward her. His face was lost in the shadows of the dark room. She could see only the tattoo writhing and squirming with even the slightest movement.

He walked forward. Ginny could not move, could not find her voice to scream. She felt paralyzed with a fear unlike any she had ever felt before.

The man reached forward, his hands touching her. A rush of cold sank deep into her chest. She cried out as pain coursed through her body. She crumpled to her knees, gasping for breath.

Her eyes snapped open. She jolted upright, struggling

for air. She felt arms around her, pulling her. She cried out, resisting the strong embrace.

"It's all right," Thomas said, managing to hold on to her. "You're fine." His familiar voice soothed her.

She clung to him, tears standing out in her eyes. She shivered uncontrollably, the ache of the cold that had surged through her body still shaking her from head to toe.

"Tell me what you saw," he whispered. Holding her at arm's length, he stared into her eyes. "Tell me everything." And his eyes flashed with an excitement she had not seen before.

Nick walked down the stairs, yawning loudly. He had slept later than he had wanted to. As he reached the bottom of the steps, he could hear voices coming from the kitchen. Jeff was up, eating and watching TV—as usual.

"You could have shut off the lights, Jeff," Nick called.

He turned off the lamps he had left on the night before, the whole thing seeming so long ago now.

"Dad." Jeff entered the room in a hurry, moving directly to him.

"Trying to rub it in, huh." Nick eyed his son sideways. "I can see the headline."

"Dad—"

"Nicholas Cross, famous horror writer, leaves the lights on at night." He crossed his arms over his chest. "Just try and prove it."

Jeff shook his head. "No, Dad, that's not it."

"Oh, sure." Nick headed toward the kitchen. "I hope you at least made me coff—"

"Dad, would you listen to me for a minute?" Jeff

slipped in front of him, cutting off his sentence and his path. "Daniel's here."

"Daniel?" Nick's brow furrowed. "Daniel who?"

Jeff made an exasperated face. "Daniel from yesterday."

Nick shook his head. "Gotta give me more than that."

"He was at the conference. You signed some books for him."

"He's here?" Nick said, finally remembering the young man in the rumpled clothes who had been so enthusiastic. "Where?" he whispered. "In the kitchen?" Jeff nodded. "What's he doing here?"

"He wants to talk to you."

"It's Sunday morning," he said, irritated at the invasion of his privacy.

"Almost afternoon," Jeff corrected.

Nick gave him a sour look. "That's not the point. How the hell did he find out where we live?"

"I don't know." Jeff led him away from the kitchen as his voice rose in volume.

"Why is he in our house?"

"I didn't know what to do. He was just sittin' on the porch when I got up." He nodded toward the kitchen. "Just talk to him."

"I'm not dressed." Nick pulled his robe more tightly around himself. "I haven't even showered yet."

"He won't care." Jeff grabbed his arm, trying to pull him toward the kitchen.

Nick resisted. "I don't know . . ."

"He said he had to hitchhike to get here," Jeff said in an attempt to change his mind. "This is important to him, Dad."

"What's he doing now?"

"Eating."

"He's what?"

"He's eating. I gave him cereal."

Nick scowled at him.

"Well, what was I supposed to do," Jeff said in frustration. "I was hungry—was I supposed to just eat in front of him?"

Nick relented, even managing to smile slightly. The whole thing was just so ridiculous. "Okay, lead the way."

They headed toward the kitchen together.

"Good morning, Daniel." Nick kept his voice light, doing his best to hide his annoyance.

"Morning, Mr. Cross." Daniel sat at the table, his gaze never leaving his now soggy bowl of Cheerios.

As Nick looked at him, he realized why Jeff had let him in. The boy was painfully shy. Nick guessed he was maybe nineteen, only a couple of years older than Jeff. He was thin, his hair in no particular style, his clothes more than a little rumpled. He couldn't help but feel a little sorry for him.

Sitting across from him, Nick said, "My son tells me you want to talk. What can I do for you, Daniel?"

Jeff grabbed his bowl and the box of cereal from the table. He leaned against the counter and pouring another bowlful, continued to eat.

Daniel fidgeted in his seat, glancing up at Nick and then quickly back down. "I just wanted to apologize," he said sheepishly, his voice barely a whisper.

Nick propped an elbow on the tabletop and rested his chin in his hand. "For what?"

For the first time, Daniel looked at Nick. "I heard what happened yesterday. I should have done something. I should have helped you." Nick could hear the shame in his voice as Daniel's attention quickly dropped back to his soggy cereal.

"Daniel, it wasn't your problem. You don't have anything to apologize for or feel guilty about. Okay?" He began to stand but seeing the disapproving look on Jeff's face, changed his mind. "What?" he mouthed to his son, his eyes growing wide. He had no idea what else he was supposed to say.

Jeff rolled his eyes, Nick interpreting the expression as, how can you be so blind. "Isn't there something else you wanted to talk about, Dan?" Jeff prompted, and the rumpled young man made a haphazard movement that could have been a nod.

I haven't even had my coffee yet, Nick thought, his patience growing thin. "Is there something else?" he asked, working hard to keep the annoyance out of his voice.

Daniel reached down and a moment later, produced a large manila envelope. Nick's heart sank. I should have known, he thought wearily. The kid's got a book.

"I know you probably get asked this all the time. I just . . . I wanted . . ."

Nick reached over and took the offering. "I'd be happy to read it," he said politely.

Daniel smiled for the first time. "It's just some short stories and stuff. But it would be great if you could, you know, tell me what you think and stuff."

Nick nodded. "Fine."

"Great," Jeff said, setting his now empty bowl in the sink. "Me and Dan are going over to the campus for a while. Why don't you look at that stuff while we're gone?"

Nick turned toward his son. "Can I talk to you for just a minute?" He rose from his chair and gestured toward the doorway.

Jeff tapped his watch. "I don't know if we have time."

"I think you do." Nick's tone quickly changed his son's mind.

"Yeah, okay." He glanced at Daniel. "Hold on just one second, Dan. I'll be right back and then we're gone."

Daniel nodded weakly as Nick lead Jeff back into the living room.

"What do you think you're doing?" Nick asked as soon as they were out of earshot. He kept his voice low, not wanting Daniel to hear him.

"What?" Jeff said, taking on his patented defensive attitude. "I'm just going to look at the campus. You're the one who's been pushing that school. I thought you'd be happy that I want to go there."

"You're missing the point," Nick said, his patience growing thinner by the second. "We don't even know him."

"Come on, Dad." Jeff ran a hand through his hair in frustration. "You saw how he is. This is his first year at school and he's not from around here. I don't think he has many friends. I just thought . . . I don't know, I just thought it'd be kinda fun."

"I don't like the idea of you going out with a stranger." In reality, Nick just did not like the idea of Jeff going out at all today. After the conference and then last night, he was more than a little afraid, afraid of what might be waiting in the world beyond their front door.

Jeff smiled readily. "I've got at least twenty pounds on the guy, Dad. Don't worry." He began bouncing up and down, jabbing at the air like a boxer. "I can take him if I have to."

"Very funny." But as he watched his son continue his impression, jabbing and punching the air, he realized Jeff did not have many friends of his own. And Nick was sure he was part of the reason. He was too protective.

This was a perfect example. Daniel was obviously no threat, yet Nick felt threatened. "Okay. Go ahead. You're right."

"As usual," Jeff added.

"Don't push it," Nick said, moving back toward the kitchen.

Daniel sat at the table, exactly as Jeff and Nick had left him.

"Okay, Dan. Let's go," Jeff said cheerfully.

Daniel looked up, his face drawn in distress. "I don't want to cause any trouble."

Nick waved a hand, dismissing his concern. "Don't worry about it. You're no problem."

Daniel beamed. "Good." He grabbed his jacket off the back of his chair. "I'm ready, Jeff."

"We'll be back for dinner, Dad."

"You can bring it—and not pizza again!" Nick yelled as the door slammed shut.

Nick removed Daniel's bowl from the table and deposited it in the sink beside Jeff's. He stared down at the bowl his son had used. "You can't keep him hidden from the world," he whispered, trying to convince himself that Jeff would be fine today.

He grabbed the tea kettle from the stove. After filling it with warm water, he returned it to its usual burner and turned the flame on high.

Turning, he leaned against the counter, staring at nothing, thoughts of the night before still tumbling through his mind. Not for the first time, he considered installing an alarm system. Maybe it would give him the peace of mind he so desperately needed. He shook his head, dismissing the idea, telling himself to stop dwelling on it. After all, nothing had happened.

He moved toward the refrigerator but froze mid-step,

his eyebrows furrowing slightly. Did the front door just open and close?

"Jeff?" he called, listening intently, not sure if he had heard anything. Before he could decide either way, he heard another door click shut quietly. He looked up. Someone was on the second floor.

Leaving the kitchen, Nick walked directly to the stairs and began his ascent. "Jeff?" he called again. No answer. Suddenly, he was sure it was not his son who had come so quietly into their house.

He reached the second floor. "Who's there?" he called, his voice confident. The silence answered back, seeming very loud. Nick felt some of his confidence dwindle as he took in the view of the upstairs hall. He had been so sure he heard a door close up there. Yet all the doors stood wide.

"Hello?" he said, his voice now less assured. He did not expect an answer. The house felt empty.

Nick lingered in the hallway, unsure of what to do. Had he heard anything at all? Or was his imagination just going into overtime because of last night?

The whine of the kettle downstairs echoed through the house as the water began to boil. Nick stood in the hallway, staring at the open doors. But as the kettle continued to shriek in protest, the whistle growing louder and louder, he turned and headed back downstairs.

Reaching the bottom of the stairs, he turned toward the kitchen and stopped. There was something else, another sound just below the cry of the tea kettle.

Niiiickieeeeeee Niiiickieeeeeee Niiiickieeeeeee

He spun around sharply as his name whined on and on, growing louder and louder as the intensity of the kettle whistle grew stronger and more insistent.

Niiiickieeeeeee Niiiickieeeeeee Niiiickieeeeeee

Rushing into the kitchen, Nick grabbed the bubbling kettle from its perch on the stove top. As the whistle died down, the house was once again silent.

He stood, holding the tea kettle, listening, for what seemed an eternity. He wanted to hear it again, needed to confirm in his mind that there was something there. But the only noise that greeted him was the slow, deliberate sound of the wall clock ticking off the minutes and seconds.

He released the breath he didn't realize he was holding before replacing the kettle on the stove. Relax, he told himself. You're jumping at every sound. Moving back to his coffee pot, he set a large funnel on top and placed a filter and then coffee inside. A moment later, he poured the hot water over the coffee grinds in the funnel and watched as his morning brew dripped slowly into the pot below.

Nick stared at the coffee pot. It had been Linda's. He had never even seen one like it until he met her. But it was the only kind she had used and Nick had grown accustomed to it. Now he would not think of using anything else. It was a little piece of his wife he refused to give up.

A knock on the front door drew his attention. After pouring more water over the coffee grinds, he headed out of the kitchen.

Reaching the front door, he leaned down, as he always did, and peered through the peephole. His brow furrowed as he realized who now stood on his porch. He yanked the door open. "What the hell are you doing here?"

Thomas Bevin smiled widely, unaffected by Nick's apparent anger. "I know I was wrong yesterday," he began.

"You're damn right you were," Nick snapped. "And

you are today too. Get the hell off my porch." He began
to shut the door.

Bevin moved forward and putting a hand on the door,
stopped him. "I must speak with you. I know you don't
believe me, but you and your son are in grave danger."
His voice was rushed, frantic. "There are dark forces at
work here."

Nick glared at the man, then turning, looked at the
hand that was pressed firmly against the door. "Get your
goddamn hand off my door." He spoke in a low whisper.

"Who was that with your son just now? He could be
a threat."

Nick's eyes grew wide. His heartbeat quickened. Taking a step forward, he gripped Thomas Bevin by the shirt
and swinging him to the side, slammed him into the door.
It banged against the inside wall. "You keep away from
my son!" he shouted.

"I pose no threat to your son." Bevin pulled at Nick's
hands, trying to release their grip on him. "I'm only trying
to help avoid another tragedy in your life."

Nick slammed him into the door again. His hands shook
where he held his shirt. "You stay away from us." He
shoved the man roughly away. "If I see you again, I'm
calling the police and you better hope they get to you
before I do."

Bevin stood on the front lawn staring at Nick, casually
straightening his shirt back into place, his demeanor calm.
He was completely unaffected by Nick's attack. "You
will see me again, Mr. Cross." And just before he turned
to go back to his car, Thomas Bevin's normally brown
eyes flashed a brilliant blue.

CHAPTER FOUR

ξ

Miriam sat at the table, and the two women who sat next to her were completely engrossed by the picture that was quickly coming into focus.

"She liked to bake bread," Miriam said as she worked. "But she liked the smell of the bread while it baked more than the bread itself."

Anne Travis smiled widely, her round face growing even more full from the slight movement. "Yes. That's right." She looked at her sister. "Barb, do you remember Grandma's bread?"

Barbara Lang shook her head. "Barely." She kept her gaze on the drawing, chewing nervously on her thumbnail. "I was too young."

Miriam had been doing drawings for people professionally for nearly fifteen years. Most were skeptical when they arrived at her modest home in Chicago for their scheduled sitting. Nine times out of ten, a friend had talked them into seeing this "psychic artist": the woman who could draw the dead.

But as the picture began to take form and the information was released, there was always a visible change in attitude. The unbelieving were suddenly transformed. Miriam was still waiting for that transformation to happen today.

"You were her little mop," she said, her pencil working on the detail around the eyes. Barbara's head came up sharply.

"Yes," she said, her voice breathless. She glanced at her sister. "I remember that. She used to call me her little mop."

"Because of your hair," Miriam and Anne said in unison. "She liked your hair," Miriam added and Barbara smiled widely.

Miriam turned back to her drawing. A moment later, she felt a tug within her hand. Something was interfering, threatening to stop her drawing of Sarah Whitford before it was complete. She hesitated for a moment, her hand trembling slightly above the page. But then the sensation was gone, leaving only a strange tingling feeling in its wake. Sarah was now back with full force and Miriam concentrated on her.

"When she was younger," Miriam continued, her voice not as confident as it had been only moments earlier, "she liked to dance. She once entered a dance contest but she didn't win." She was done now. Setting the pencil down next to the drawing, Miriam slid the picture toward the two sisters.

Anne reached out and touched it gently. "I never knew that," she said quietly.

As Miriam watched the women admire the picture of their grandmother, a woman who had been dead nearly twenty years, she knew they believed.

"Is she happy?" Anne asked, and as Miriam nodded, the young woman's eyes grew moist. "Good," she whispered.

This was the last of four appointments Miriam had

scheduled for today. She was glad she was nearing the end of her day. It wasn't that the sessions tired her, in fact, they seemed to give her more energy. But something was happening to her and she needed to discover what.

She would not discuss this latest encounter with Bob. Last night, after she finished the first drawing, they had stayed up late, arguing until the early morning. It did not matter to him that Miriam was sure this woman meant her no harm, that in fact, she desperately needed her help. He was afraid, memories of her last encounter still too fresh in his mind. Instead, he kept telling her to push the feelings aside, to try and ignore them.

But Miriam could not.

The woman was with her now. She could feel her like a constant tugging from within. But the feelings were vague, undefined. Miriam sensed a message, a warning the woman needed to get out. And Miriam had to listen.

She turned her attention back to the two sisters. They had asked her another question and she had not heard it. "I'm sorry. I didn't sleep well last night," she said. And as they repeated their question, Miriam wondered if tonight's sleep would be undisturbed.

Jeff and Daniel entered the house together, each carrying a bag from Kentucky Fried Chicken. As promised, they had brought dinner.

"Jeff, I'm glad you're back." Nick glanced at the clock, hoping Jeff would catch the look. He and Daniel had been gone much longer than Nick had expected. You could have called, he wanted to say, but did not. Instead, he said, "Do you remember Mr. Carver?"

A slightly balding man in his late forties stood, extending a hand toward Jeff. "Ed Carver."

"The alarm guy," Jeff said as they shook.

"You got it, kid." Ed winked at him.

"Yeah, I remember you." And Nick could hear in his son's voice the aversion he had for this man. Ed Carver had a tendency to be a little patronizing and it was obvious that Jeff disliked it. "You helped my dad out with some research stuff."

"That's right, kid."

"What's goin' on, Dad?" Jeff tossed his jacket on a nearby chair.

"We're getting an alarm."

Jeff laughed. "Yeah, right." He dropped down into one of the chairs and dug into his bag. Pulling out some french fries, he stuffed them into his mouth.

"We are," Nick said.

Jeff stopped chewing. "Why? I thought you didn't think they really worked." He glanced at Ed. "No offense, man."

"None taken," Ed said, but his voice was cool.

"I changed my mind. I think we need one, especially after last night." And this afternoon, although he didn't say that.

Jeff shrugged. "I guess." Getting up from his chair, he headed toward the kitchen. "Come on, Dan. Let's chow." A minute later, they disappeared through the doorway.

Nick turned his attention back to the alarm specialist. "So Ed, when can we get all this installed? The sooner the better, you know?"

Ed nodded. "You people are always in such a hurry once you decide to get the system."

Nick smiled weakly, Ed's statement making him feel like a child being scolded by his father. "Yeah, well, you got me there."

Reaching inside his briefcase, Ed withdrew a folder. He flipped it open and scanned the pages inside. "You

got lucky. We can be out as soon as next Wednesday."
He looked up.

"Next Wednesday. Not tomorrow?"

"Got jobs scheduled already. Hey," he said, that same
knowing look on his face, "I'm squeezing you in as a
friend. You call anyone else and it'll be weeks before
they can get out here."

"Okay," Nick said reluctantly. "Wednesday it is."

Ed wrote inside the folder he still held. "Now, it takes
two days to install all the equipment."

"Two days?" This whole thing was more than Nick
bargained for.

"Gotta hide the wires, ya know. People want security
but they want to look good too." He winked at Nick and
Nick could see why Jeff did not care for this man.

After finalizing the details of the installation, Nick led
Ed to the door, happy the visit was ending.

"I appreciate you coming over on a Sunday, Ed."

"No problem. I'm just glad you're finally doing the
right thing."

"Yeah," Nick said and without warning, the whining
sound of his name rang through his mind.

Niiickieeeeeee Niiiickieeeeeee Niiiickieeeeeee

He still wasn't sure if he had really heard anything.
But even if it was just his imagination, maybe a security
system would quiet his personal demons.

He watched as Ed Carver's van pulled away before
turning and walking toward the kitchen.

Jeff and Daniel sat at the table, each biting into a large
piece of chicken. Nick stared at the scene. A combination
of french fries, cole slaw, and chicken bones spread across
the tabletop.

"What's left? A wing?" Nick was amazed at how
quickly they were consuming the food.

Jeff shook his head, swallowing. "No, you got lucky this time. A wing and a leg."

Nick sat down. "Oh joy! All the best parts." Reaching forward, he grabbed the bucket and fished out a piece of chicken. Spooning cole slaw onto his plate, he said, "What'd you guys do today?"

Jeff shrugged, continuing to chew. "Nothin'. Walked around campus, hung out with some guys, got some chili dogs. Nothin'."

"Great. Cheerios, chili dogs, and chicken. Am I a great parent or what?"

"That you are."

The room fell quiet as they all concentrated on the food before them.

Jeff was the first to break the silence.

"So Dad, what's with this security stuff. Are you really gettin' it or what?"

Nick stared down at his plate, unwilling to look at his son, afraid he might see the fear behind his eyes. "Yes, I am. I just feel it's necessary after what happened."

"Okay," Jeff said, shrugging the whole thing away.

Nick looked at him. Jeff was not taking any of this seriously. "Jeff," he began, trying to keep his voice light, hiding the tension that stiffened his back. "I was thinking that maybe you'd like to spend some time at Aunt Cheryl's. What do you think? Winter'll be here soon. She's right on the lake. I know you've had fun in the past there." After Linda's death, her sister Cheryl had come to stay with Nick and Jeff for a while. Jeff was still very close to her.

"Why? Did she call?"

"No, I was just thinking about it. You haven't seen her in a while. I know she misses you."

Jeff made a face. "Nah, I don't really feel like it. Maybe

during the summer or somethin' but not now. It takes too long to get to school from her house." He continued to eat, never looking at Nick.

"Just a suggestion. I thought maybe it'd be a nice break from the boredom around here," he tried again.

Jeff stopped eating and looked at his father. "What happened?"

"Nothing," Nick said a little too quickly.

"Dad . . ."

"Jeff, I just want you to be more . . . to . . ." He stumbled over his words, caught off guard, not expecting his son to see through him so easily. "I just thought you'd like it, that's all."

"Fine," Jeff said, his voice tinged with anger.

"Now you're mad?"

"Forget it, Dad. I knew when I left here that you were worried. I knew you didn't want me to go out. That was one of the reasons I really wanted to go. I wanted you to see that nothing would happen and nothing did."

"Something could have happened." And Nick immediately wished he could pull the words back inside. They sounded lame even to him.

Jeff rolled his eyes, making an exasperated sound. "Dad, can you hear yourself? You think someone tried to get in our house."

"Someone did," Nick insisted.

"Okay." Jeff held up a hand, stopping him. "Someone did but that kind of thing happens all the time. People are robbed every day. It doesn't mean you have to freak out over it."

"I don't think I freaked out."

"You don't?" Jeff's voice mocked. "What do you call getting an alarm system and trying to ship me off to Aunt Cheryl's?"

"Being careful," Nick said, his voice tight. "Excuse me for caring about you and wanting to protect you."

"Protect me from what?" Jeff snapped.

Nick glanced at Daniel.

Christ, I forgot you were here.

The boy sat at the other end of the table staring down at his plate, obviously uncomfortable with the scene that was being played out before him. "Jeff, I don't want to discuss this with you anymore tonight. Let's just table it until we've both had some time to think about it."

Jeff stared at him blankly. "You just don't think I can handle whatever it is you think is going on. Fine. I guess I can't then."

"Jeff, come on. I just don't think this is the best time." He eyed Daniel.

Jeff's glare intensified. "When is the best time, Dad? When I graduate from college? Of course, the college of your choice."

Nick opened his mouth but Jeff continued, not letting him get a word in.

"I have an even better idea. Save it up and on my thirtieth birthday, you can really surprise me by leveling with me."

"Are you done?" Nick snapped, his anger flaring.

Jeff got up from the table. "Yeah, I am." He left the room. A few moments later, Nick heard a door upstairs slam shut.

"Great." He dropped the piece of chicken he was still holding onto his plate. He had done it again. How many times had he promised not to keep things from Jeff and then gone back on that promise? He did not know. But with each time, each broken promise, Nick was managing to put a wall between the two of them, building it himself brick by brick.

"Mr. Cross?"

Nick looked across the table at Daniel. The boy's face was screwed up into an almost painful look.

"Maybe I should go," he said, already beginning to stand.

"No, Daniel, don't leave," Nick said before he could stop himself. He knew he should go up and talk to his son. But what could he say? Sorry I disappointed you again. No, Nick was not ready for that conversation, not yet anyway.

"I read some of your work while you were gone," Nick said, changing the subject, wanting to discuss anything besides his current problem with his son. "I'll get it and we can talk for a while." He stood. As he made his way to his study just off the kitchen, he realized that he was retreating into the safety of his writing. It was a pattern he had repeated so many times that he now recognized it immediately. Anytime something went wrong, he wrote.

Unlike the job of everyday life, with its constant pitfalls and worries, writing was a safe haven where he controlled the environment around him; he controlled any problems that cropped up.

Grabbing the manila folder from atop his computer desk, he stared at the pages stacked next to the printer. His latest novel. And for a moment, he wished he could sit down and rewrite the scene he'd just had with Jeff. With Nick in control, Jeff would understand; he would give the answers Nick expected and Nick could respond appropriately every time.

He shook his head. "Plug us in and off we go," he

muttered, shutting off the light and heading back toward the kitchen.

Ginny stared at her reflection in the mirror as her grandmother ran the brush gently through her hair. It was their nightly ritual. One hundred times through before Ginny could climb under her blankets and go to sleep. She wished they had skipped it tonight, though. She was tired.

"You're awfully quiet tonight, dear," Evelyn said, her hand moving in a slow, easy manner. "Guess they wore you down a little at the institute today. I'll have to talk to Mr. Bevin about that."

"It was neat today." Ginny smiled, her eyes drifting closed. "I'm just a little tired."

"We don't have to finish," her grandmother said and the brushing stopped.

"No, it feels good, Gram." Ginny waited but the brushing did not return. A rush of cold air swirled over her. She shivered. "Gram?" she said, her voice tentative. Slowly, she opened her eyes. Her grandmother was gone. Ginny's breath caught in her throat. She stared into the mirror at the reflection of the room behind her.

She was no longer in her bedroom.

Behind her was the room from her vision. She began shaking her head slowly back and forth, denying the evidence before her. Squeezing her eyes shut, she willed it to be gone, concentrating hard. But when she opened them again, the room was still there, the cold beginning to chill her to her bones.

She turned around. "Gram?" she said, having trouble finding her voice. "Gram, where are you?" She did not stand. Her legs felt weak and useless. She did not think they could support her.

A black silhouette blocked the moonlight that filtered in through the far window. The man's body loomed large in the small room. Ginny could see the snake even in the weak lighting.

He took a step forward and a gust of wind rustled over her. The intense cold stung her exposed skin, blowing her hair backward from her face.

Ginny screamed, cringing away from him. She fell from the chair she was in, hitting the floor sharply, and began crawling away from the man and his icy touch.

"Ginny?"

She felt hands on her, gripping her, trying to stop her escape. She struggled against them. "Leave me alone. Don't touch me!"

"Ginny, stop it! What's gotten into you?"

She recognized the voice as her grandmother's. Her body went limp with relief. Lifting her face, and trying to see through the tears that were now flowing freely, she realized she was back in her own bedroom with her grandmother. The man was gone. "Gram, oh Gram," she sobbed, throwing her arms around her grandmother and holding on tightly.

Evelyn Lambert hugged her granddaughter, trying to soothe her with gentle words of reassurance, confused by her sudden outburst. But as her hands stroked Ginny's hair, Evelyn wondered why it felt so cold.

"No, Daniel, you just find your own voice and write from it." Nick and Daniel still sat at the kitchen table, the dinner plates gone, the bags and containers stuffed deep into the garbage long ago. Daniel's stories now littered the tabletop.

They had spent hours discussing writing. The skills needed, the luck involved. Jeff had not come out of his room since his abrupt departure and Nick felt guilty. The longer he waited to go up and talk to his son, the harder it had become, until, finally, it was too late. He was not looking forward to the confrontation he knew lay ahead.

"Mr. Cross," Daniel began, pulling him away from his thoughts. "Can we go through that last story one more time?" He sorted through his pages.

Leaning back in his chair, Nick rubbed his tired eyes. "What time is it?" he muttered, glancing at the wall clock. "Two o'clock?" The time had slipped by without notice, and it was now the middle of the night. His gaze fell once more on the boy seated across from him. The boy who had hitchhiked to get here. What the hell was he going to do with him now? "Daniel—"

"You don't have to say it, Mr. Cross." Daniel stood and began to gather his work. "I've stayed too long. I'm going right now." He stuffed the papers haphazardly into the manila envelope he had brought with him, bending several in the process. "I'm sorry I kept you up so late." Grabbing his jacket, he strode out of the kitchen at a quick pace, leaving Nick sitting at the table, his mouth hanging open.

"Daniel," Nick said, getting up and following him. "Where are you going?"

"Back to the dorm." He reached the front door but Nick stepped in front of him, stopping him. Daniel stared down at the floor, seemingly too embarrassed to look directly at Nick.

"How are you getting back?"

"I'll walk," Daniel whispered, still not meeting Nick's gaze.

"You can't walk." Nick stared at the boy, mulling over his choices, realizing he had very few. *What the hell? What was the harm?*

"Daniel, it's the middle of the night. If you haven't noticed, this house is very large. You can stay here."

Daniel looked up, his eyes growing wide. "Really?" His voice was filled with astonishment.

Nick smiled. "Of course." And as he led him down the hall next to the staircase toward the spare bedroom, he wondered if he had invited Daniel to stay as another way to avoid his son. He stopped before a closed door. "I'll leave a note for Jeff. He can drive you back tomorrow on his way to school."

Daniel nodded. "Okay." He reached for the door but stopped. "This is so great, Mr. Cross," he said turning to face Nick again. "You don't know what this means to me."

Nick stared at him. He had never met anyone in the past that so openly admired him. It made him feel slightly uncomfortable. He didn't think he deserved all the fuss.

"Well, I'm glad, Daniel." Reaching out, he opened the door to the room. "There's a connecting bathroom. You should have everything you need."

Daniel stepped inside. "I'll be fine. Great!" He was still beaming.

Nick nodded and closing the door, walked back to the kitchen. Grabbing the remaining dishes off the table, he took them to the sink and quickly rinsed them before stacking them in the dishwasher. He was exhausted but did not want to go to bed yet. He knew he would not sleep. He had too much on his mind.

He walked to the message pad beside the phone and grabbing the pen, wrote a quick note:

"Jeff. Daniel stayed over. Please give him a ride in the morning on your way to school."

Nick reread the note and then added quickly,

"Sorry about last night. We'll talk when you get home from school. I was wrong. Dad."

Placing the note on the refrigerator, he held it in place with a magnet made in the shape of a banana. Nick shut off the lights. As he walked up the stairs, he felt like a coward. He had taken the easy way out. He knew that Jeff would read the note and that it would help dissolve some of his anger so that when they did talk, he would be more forgiving than angry.

As he passed his son's room, he stopped just outside the door. Leaning closer, he listened. Silence. He opened the door and looked inside. Jeff was asleep, his blankets twisted awkwardly around him. And once again Nick felt guilty. Had Jeff been tossing and turning in his sleep, disturbed by the argument they had had?

"I hope not," he muttered, his breath fogging out before him. His brow furrowed. Why was it so cold in here? His gaze locked on the open window across the room. He hadn't realized that the temperature outside had dropped so dramatically.

Hugging himself for warmth against the steady breeze that seemed to blow all around him, Nick stepped inside and moved quickly toward the window. He reached out, ready to close the glass against the world beyond but stopped. The wind blew over him, ruffling his hair, sending a chill down his spine. Still he did not move.

Had he heard a voice whispering softly somewhere nearby? Maybe just in the corner, or outside in the hallway?

He listened intently, waiting to hear it again. No, he

decided, it was just the wind blowing through the eaves, sounding more human than it actually was.

Pulling the window down, he shut and latched it. As he padded back toward the door, he glanced again at his son. Jeff slept undisturbed. As Nick closed the door, he thought the room already felt warmer.

CHAPTER FIVE

ξ

Thomas Bevin was not in his home. His body lay on his bed, his breathing soft and even. But Thomas Bevin was not within that body. He floated above himself, moving through time and space, able to travel anywhere and everywhere with just a thought.

Earlier he'd watched as Nicholas Cross argued with his son. And when the boy stormed to his room, Thomas had gone there with him, drifting above his bed, keeping him company.

He knew the layout of their home, the habits they kept. For months, he'd studied them, father and son ignorant of the intrusion. It gave Thomas the upper hand. He was quickly able to learn exactly what it would take to drive a wedge between them. And slowly, he was accomplishing just that. He planned to tear their relationship apart piece by piece before taking the boy away. Because that was Nick's worst fear. It wasn't just losing his son, but losing him when they had unresolved feelings between them.

Just like his wife.

She had been angry with Nick the night he left, the last night he saw her alive. And the guilt of allowing her to die with that anger still between them ate away at Nicholas Cross with every passing hour. He carried it with him like a rock around his neck. It weighed him down and kept him afraid. And Thomas knew it. He knew Nick's worst fear better than Nick did himself. And with Ginny Lambert in his control, Thomas was ready to make that fear a reality.

Now, as he watched Nick move toward his bedroom, he knew it was time. With a single thought, he left the house, moving swiftly toward the one person who could help shape the destiny of Nicholas and Jeffrey Cross.

Ginny lay in her bed, staring up at the dark ceiling, struggling desperately to stay awake. She was afraid to close her eyes, afraid that when she opened them again, she'd find herself back in the house, back with the tattooed man.

She must have done something wrong.

Thomas had told her he was going to challenge her. She must have made some kind of mistake and that was why this was happening now. Thomas would help her. Thomas would stop it.

But not until tomorrow. For now, she needed to stay awake. She rolled on her side.

The cold washed over her.

She was no longer in her bed. Somehow, within an instant of time, she was back at the house, back at the dark place within her mind. She lay on a couch, a sour, filthy smell drifting up from the cushion her cheek rested on.

"No," she whispered, the word fogging out in front of her, echoing through the empty house. She sat up, unable to continue breathing in the foul stench of the couch. She wore the pajamas she had gone to bed in, the light material no protection against the bitter cold around her.

Scanning the familiar room, she realized she was alone. The man was not there, hidden in the shadows, waiting. Her gaze drifted to the window. She could see snow falling outside. Pulling her legs in tight, she curled into a ball on the couch and began rocking back and forth.

"I want to go home," she muttered over and over. She concentrated on her grandmother, her bedroom, her home. And tried desperately to will herself there.

Daniel woke with a start, his body racked with chills. His room was ice cold. As he sat up, the blankets falling away from his bare chest, he was momentarily confused by his surroundings. But as the evening played out in this mind, he realized where he was and smiled. He still couldn't believe it. He was actually spending the night at the house of Nicholas Cross.

Pulling the blankets back up, he turned toward the window. He had opened it halfway before going to bed less than an hour earlier. But as he shivered again with the cold, he wished he had not.

He had gone to sleep in only his underwear, and now he regretted his lack of clothing. Gathering the top blanket around his shoulders, Daniel padded toward the window. A sudden gust of air shivered over him, stirring the bottom of his blanket with force. Daniel stopped. He stood directly before the window, staring out at the black night before him.

"That's not possible," he whispered, as he realized that the breeze blew from behind him, not through the still-open window before him. He shook as icy fingers probed his flesh, the wind feeling deliberate in its movement.

"Daniel." His named drifted on the breeze, brushing coolly against his ear.

Closing his eyes, he told himself to wake up, that this was only a dream; the wind had not suddenly taken on a personality of its own, able to control its direction and intent. But when he reopened his eyes, he was still standing before the window, the breeze continuing its silent assault.

"It's just the wind," he whispered.

But was it? Hadn't Mr. Cross and Jeff been arguing about being careful? Hadn't he been talking about additional security? And what had he said about a break in?

His gaze darted around the room, his eyes now adjusted to the darkness around him. He saw nothing.

Turning and moving quickly toward the door, Daniel stepped out into the darkened hallway. His body was covered in goose bumps despite the blanket that he clutched around his shoulders. He rushed toward the stairs but stopped halfway there.

What am I doing?

Standing in the hall, listening to the silence of the house, he suddenly felt foolish. Here he was in his idol's home acting like a child afraid of the dark.

He smiled. Nicholas Cross had invited him to stay overnight. He was sleeping in the same house as him. He walked down the hall, looking at the pictures on the walls. Many were of his wife. Daniel had read about her murder but knew very few details.

Reaching the living room, he turned toward the study. That was where he wrote. Tiptoeing, not wanting to wake anyone, he moved toward the door. It was not locked, and as he stepped over the threshold, he felt his excitement rise. Beside the computer, stacked very neatly, were manuscript pages. Daniel felt giddy. He could get a peek at the pages and know what Mr. Cross's next book was going to be about before anyone else.

Glancing at the door to make sure no one was coming, he crossed to the desk and began flipping through the pages. It was too dark to make out the words, but he was too afraid a light would wake his sleeping host. Carrying it to the window, he tried reading it by moonlight.

"Is it good?"

Daniel spun around, the pages falling from his hands and scattering on the floor around him. "Mr. Cross, I'm sorry, I didn't mean—". He bent down and began gathering up the papers.

"Don't bother."

As Daniel looked up, he realized it was not Nicholas Cross who stood in the doorway. His breath caught in his throat as the knife the man held flashed briefly in the pale light. He leaned against the doorjamb, his face hidden in shadows. But the moonlight that poured through the window revealed the right side of his body. He was a big man, his muscular build obvious even while partially hidden in the darkness. He wore a skin-tight T-shirt that revealed every muscle in his chest and arms. Daniel stared at the man's bulging biceps and the tattoo that ran up their length. It was a snake, hypnotic in its perfect detail. It coiled across his muscles and disappeared beneath his shirt sleeve.

"I've been waiting so long for this moment," the man said, his voice hushed, quiet. But there was a fury beneath the words, an anger that screamed to be heard.

Daniel did not speak.

The man shifted where he stood. The muscles in his arm flexed, giving the snake brief life. "You will be the first in a long line." He moved slowly toward him, his hand caressing the long blade.

Daniel watched the man approach. The blanket he held around his shoulders slipped from his hands and fell in a pile at his feet. The room around him grew colder with every step the man took.

Nick stood in a long hall staring at the door at the other end.

MORGUE was printed in bold, black letters.

Dread crept up his body, shaking him. He did not want to open that door. He turned, ready to run and hide from the truth he could not face. But no matter which way he turned, the door loomed up before him, huge and impassable, the cold steel halting his escape.

Slowly, his hand trembling, he reached for the knob.

Before he could touch it, the door swept open, disappearing as he moved past it. A brilliant, white light blinded him, washing the room in pale brightness. He could not see but he knew where he was going. Inching forward, he stopped before the stainless steel table. A figure lay beneath bloodstained sheets. He began shaking his head back and forth, denying what he knew was the truth. And then the sheet was gone as if it had never been there, and the body of his wife, bloody and bruised, lay before him. Her dead eyes glared up at him, seeming to focus directly on him, boring into him. Blaming him.

"Linda!" he screamed, not wanting to see her, not wanting to believe she was dead. "Linda," he said again, the word a choked cry.

And her eyes turned and looked into his. "Why did you leave me alone?" The voice was deep and gravelly, liquid sounding.

He tried to back away but her bloody hand, the fingers bent at impossible angles, reached out and gripped his arm. "Why did you leave me alone?" she demanded.

She opened her mouth to scream. But instead of the loud, shrill cry he expected, the noise that assaulted him sounded more like . . . ringing.

She sat up, reaching out to him, wanting to smother him in her dead embrace. He backed away. The ringing pounded through his mind. He covered his ears and . . .

. . . jolted upright in bed. Sweat covered his body, his heart slammed against his chest.

The Dream.

How many years had it been since he'd had the dream?

Seconds later, the ringing sound from his nightmare echoed through his room. He jumped, caught off guard by the intrusion.

The phone rang again.

He glanced sideways, feeling foolish and more than a little embarrassed.

The phone. Of course, it's the phone.

With a shaking hand, Nick reached across the bedside table and snatched the receiver from its cradle just as the answering machine in the kitchen kicked on.

"Hello, we're not home right now," he heard Jeff's voice say, "but if you leave a message, we'll try and get back to you." Beep.

"I'm here, don't hang up," Nick said immediately, his voice deep from sleep. And as he waited for the caller to speak, he realized for the first time that it was morning and that the sun was sneaking through the blinds over his window.

"You're not up?" His agent's voice grated into his mind.

"I am now, Karen. Thanks." He squinted toward the clock. It was nearly noon. Sitting up, he rubbed his eyes.

"I thought you'd be hard at work." Karen spoke quickly, the way she always did, as if she were forever late for something. "You have a deadline approaching. I don't think I have to remind you . . ."

Karen's voice droned on, talking of deadlines and the work schedule he needed to stick to if he was going to get the book to her on time. But Nick heard none of it.

He was frowning, listening closely, gripping the phone tightly because there was something else, another noise. Just below Karen's words and then deeper, past the hum of the phone current, Nick thought he could hear something else. A voice. Muffled, barely audible, but there.

A surprise.

". . . know how that can . . ."

Just for . . .

". . . last time, when I talked to . . ."

you.

". . . starting next week?"

Waiting for . . .

". . . you listening? Nick? Are you there?"

"What?" His voice cracked when he finally spoke. "What did you say?" He had heard none of it.

"Nick, are you listening to me? Is this a bad connection?"

"Why? Did you hear something?" Nick asked, hoping she would say, "Well, yes, Nick, I could hear this whispering, very low but there." She did not.

"You tell me. I don't think you've heard a word I've said." She paused. When she spoke again, her voice held a note of concern. "Are you okay?"

He listened for another moment. But only the quiet hum of the phone line buzzed in his ear. The voice was gone. "I'm fine. You woke me up, Karen. I'm just a little out of it. Don't worry." He rattled off the excuses, trying to reassure himself as well as Karen.

"Well, I don't want to pressure you, but the editor is waiting for that first draft."

Nick sighed. "It's just taking longer than I thought."

"I know it been hard for you since . . ." Karen trailed off, her voice hesitant. "But you managed to write the last one," she finished.

The last one had been nearly impossible, Nick wanted to say. Since his wife's death, he just didn't seem to have the concentration he needed to write a novel. He lost interest quickly, his mind wandering to everything but the computer screen in front of him. He simply no longer had the heart to put his characters through the horrors of danger and death after experiencing it firsthand.

When he finally did manage to finish the last book, he had known when he sent it in that it was not up to par with his past works. But his deadline had come and gone, and he couldn't have improved the manuscript without starting over.

"This latest book isn't getting the best reviews," Nick said.

"And now you're listening to reviews? It was your first one. You'll get better. Besides, didn't you have this one outlined when—" She cut herself off, unwilling or unable to finish the sentence, he wasn't sure which.

"You're right," he said, when the silence grew too long. "I was about done."

"I'm sorry, Nick."

"Don't be. I know Linda would want me to finish it. Trust me, I will."

She laughed lightly. "The day I trust a writer is the day I hang up my hat." Her voice took on a serious tone. "Listen to me, Nicholas Cross, I want you in front of that computer in ten minutes."

Nick managed a smile. "Yes ma'am."

"That's what I like to hear."

"You're a tough woman, Karen."

"Don't you forget it," she said. "Listen, I gotta go. I have a meeting I'm already late for. You tell that kid of yours I said hi." And she hung up abruptly, leaving Nick sitting in bed, listening to the silence of the line.

"Bye, Karen," he said quietly. A minute later, the phone began shrieking in protest, blaring in his ear. He hung up.

Swinging his legs over the side of the bed, Nick stretched his back, groaning as the muscles protested. He needed to start working out again. He was beginning to feel old before his time. He headed toward the bathroom. But as he turned the shower on, the hot water spraying out, he couldn't help but wonder about the voice on the phone. Had he really heard it? He was sure he had.

Is it me? Could something be wrong with me?

Stepping under the stinging drops of water and letting them wash over him, Nick decided it was not. He could not begin to doubt himself. Something was going on. Something was definitely wrong. And suddenly his own words flashed through his mind.

"It takes a lot to scare me."

Was it possible someone had decided to take him up on his challenge?

He froze where he stood, the water pounding on his back, and stared at the beige bathroom tile of his shower.

My God, is that it? Is that the answer?

Nick now regretted the cocky statement. How many times had he said it? He began mentally to tally the amount of times he had told people he didn't scare easily. More than fifty he was sure. A hundred? He hoped not. No matter the count, it seemed that he had said it one too many times. And in front of the wrong person. The conference. Bevin had heard him say it at the conference.

So did Daniel.

The thought ran through his mind before he could stop it. Daniel? He seemed so harmless, even pathetic. No, not Daniel. After all, hadn't Nick invited him, a complete stranger, to spend the night in his house—something he never did. No, not Daniel.

As he continued his shower, he made a decision. He would call the police, tell them his theory about someone trying to scare him, and see what they thought. Whether they believed him or not, he knew it was the right thing to do. He would also tell Jeff. That was long overdue. He should have done it last night when Jeff stormed off to his room. Nick was just so insecure about it all. He doubted himself so much when it came to his son. He just wanted to do the right thing.

Turning off the water, he wrapped a towel around himself and stepped from the shower. He wiped steam from the fogged-up mirror and stared at his reflection.

"Looking old, my friend," he whispered. But Nick was actually just feeling old. He had been carrying the burden of the last few days on his shoulders and it was beginning to wear him down. Grabbing a comb, he ran it through his still-wet hair. He should have realized sooner that he couldn't solve this problem on his own. He needed help. So far, everything that had happened had been pretty harmless. Just voices on his machine and whispers on the phone.

What about the break-in?

But that seemed almost unreal to him now. He hated the idea of the alarm system. It made him feel as if he were somehow giving in to all of his fears.

"Maybe it's all for the best," he mumbled. But he really didn't believe that.

Depositing his damp towel in the hamper, he pulled on his clothes and made his way downstairs. As he strode into the kitchen, he was surprised to see Jeff sitting at the table.

"You're home?" he said, continuing to move toward the coffee pot, long overdue for his morning cup. He stopped after only two steps and turned to look at his son. "Don't you feel well?" Jeff sat at the table, his face pale. "Jeff?" Nick said, going to him.

"I saw your note but he wasn't in his room." He stared ahead, his eyes unfocused, his voice a flat monotone. "The door was open so I went inside."

Nick's eyebrows furrowed. "What are you talking about? What door?" He glanced at the door that opened to the back yard, then at the sliding glass door. They were both closed and locked.

Jeff turned and looked at him for the first time. Fear, anger, and resentment flashed across his face. "Your study," he whispered.

Nick's gaze shifted to the door leading from the kitchen. Stiffly, he rose. The walk from the kitchen table to his writing room seemed endless. He stood before the half open door, not sure he wanted to know what lay inside. Taking a deep breath, knowing there was no way to avoid it, Nick shoved the door open. His heart constricted in his chest. Blood pounded in his ears.

"God," he breathed as the scene before him came into view. He stumbled two steps forward into the room. "God," he said again, unable to believe the horror before him. He stared dully, his entire body numb.

Daniel sat in Nick's chair, facing the door, both wrists sliced neatly. The arms of the chair and the floor around it were stained an ugly reddish-brown from the massive amount of blood that had drained from the body.

Nick stared at him, his breath coming in short, harsh gasps. The smell of the blood was overwhelming. Maybe he's not dead, he thought crazily. He lurched toward him, not wanting to touch him but needing to be sure. There was just so much blood.

He reached toward the boy and pressed two shaking fingers to the side of his neck. As they came in contact with the cold skin, Nick felt his bile rise.

Ginny Lambert lay in her bed. Despite the warmth of the day, she was freezing. Her grandmother had already thrown two extra blankets over her comforter and she was wearing her warmest pajamas. But nothing seemed to help. She could not get rid of the chill that shook her body.

She had been trapped for what seemed an eternity in the house from her vision. She had been afraid to move from the rancid couch, afraid that if she did, she would never return home. She had no idea how she had gotten there or how she had managed to get back again. But she was deathly afraid that when she closed her eyes tonight, she would return to the desolate house, this time stuck forever in that cold, lonely place.

She was sure Thomas would know what was happening, and more important, he would know how to stop it.

There was a light tap on the door and a moment later, Evelyn Lambert came inside carrying a tray. "How are you feeling?" she asked, her face lined with worry. She set the tray over Ginny's legs and reaching out, touched her forehead. "You still feel warm, but I brought you something that will help you get better."

Ginny's stomach roiled at the smell. "I can't." She turned her head away. "Please, Gram, take it away."

"Ginny, don't overdramatize. It's just chicken broth." She sat on the edge of the bed and lifted a spoonful. "At least try."

Ginny did not want the soup but she opened her mouth obediently and swallowed as the light-brown liquid was deposited inside.

"See, I knew you could do it," Evelyn said, a relieved smile cutting across her face. "I'll have you better yet."

Ginny managed another mouthful. "Gram, I need you to call Mr. Bevin."

The spoon stopped halfway to Ginny's mouth, the broth spilling on the blankets. "Oh dear, look what I've done." She stood and grabbing the napkin off the tray, dabbed at the blankets.

"Gram," Ginny said, watching her clean up the broth. "I need to talk to Mr. Bevin as soon as possible."

Evelyn continued to clean. "Why on earth would you want me to do that?" she asked, making a tsk tsk sound with her tongue. "He doesn't have a cure for the flu now does he?"

"I need to talk to him, Gram." Evelyn continued to clean, shaking her head back and forth, her brow wrinkled. Reaching out, Ginny grabbed her grandmother by the arm. "I think I'm sick because of the work I did with him yesterday."

Evelyn looked at her again. "What are you talking about? You have the flu, that's all." She touched her forehead again. "This fever is confusing you."

"No, Gram," Ginny said, her voice firm. She took her grandmother's hand from her forehead and held it in her own. "Yesterday, after you left, me and Mr. Bevin, we did something new. But I think I goofed it up and that's why I'm sick."

"You're not making any sense," Evelyn said, but the tone of her voice had changed. The disbelief and worry were gone. Her words now reflected a certain anger, and below that, fear. "What could he do that would make you this ill?"

"I don't know. That's why I need to talk to him right away."

Nick sat at the kitchen table staring down into the cup of cold coffee that sat before him. One of the police officers who still milled about his house had given it to him with the advice that he should at least try and drink it. Nick hadn't told the man, but as the mug was placed in front of him, the smell of the strong, black coffee drifting up made him feel nauseous immediately. Even now, he would be glad when he could get rid of the brown liquid.

"So Mr. Cross, you were the last one to see Daniel Taub alive?" Detective Diane Nolan sat across from Nick, her questions seeming endless. Daniel's body had been taken from the house less than a half hour earlier.

"Yes. I guess so." Nick rubbed his eyes wearily. "I've already told you that. I don't know why we have to go over it again."

"Please, Mr. Cross, this is all necessary," she said.

"It's for our benefit," Detective Alan Howarth added. He leaned against the counter behind Nick. "You know the story. It's brand-new to us. We need to hear it again." It sounded like a speech he had repeated countless times. "We would appreciate your cooperation." He picked up an apple from the counter top and began polishing it against his lapel.

Nick nodded, knowing the detectives were just doing their jobs. He was at least grateful that his son didn't have to be put through this ordeal. On the advice of one of the paramedics, the detectives had reluctantly agreed to let Jeff rest. He was suffering from a mild case of shock, the man had told them, and shouldn't be disturbed. Instead, Jeff would go down to the police station tomorrow and talk with the detectives there.

But as Nick thought about his son, the fear that had been with him since finding Daniel deepened.

Daniel had been so close in age to Jeff. Even their height was similar. Was it possible . . . No! He didn't want to think it, couldn't believe it could happen again. Not after so many years. Not . . .

". . . Cross? Mr. Cross?"

Nick turned his attention back to the detective. She had asked him a question and he had not heard her.

"I'm sorry. What did you say?"

"Did Taub call anyone while he was here?" Diane repeated, brushing absently at her dark bangs. "Mention a name, maybe?"

"No, nothing."

"It would help if you could ask your son to make a list of all the people he can remember talking to yesterday," she said. "You can bring it with you tomorrow." She made a quick note on the paper before her. Then flipping backward several pages, she read briefly before looking up at Nick again. "I would just like to clarify that you never met this boy before this weekend."

He ran a hand over his face. How many times did they have to go over this? "That's right."

"And why did you invite him to stay overnight?"

"I don't know," he said in exasperation. "Because he

was such a big fan. Because it was late. I guess I felt sorry for him."

Diane jotted down a note, glanced back several pages again, and then looked toward Alan. "Anything you want to add?"

He shook his head. "I've finished with my examination of the room," he said, setting the now gleaming apple back on the counter. "I'll be back in a few days to release it. Until then, Mr. Cross, I need you to stay out."

Diane closed the notebook in front of her. "Well, I think, for now, that covers everything here."

Nick watched them as they gathered their things to leave. "That's it? You cart the body out and you're gone?"

"For now."

"What if he didn't commit suicide?" he said, finally voicing what he had been thinking all along.

The two detectives glanced at each other, their eyes locking for a moment. In that time, they seemed to exchange some kind of silent understanding. "What are you implying?" Diane asked, her voice tentative.

"My wife . . ." Nick paused. Even now, so many years later, the words were still difficult to speak. "Five years ago, my wife was murdered. She was found the same way," he said, his anxiety building with each passing second. "She was sitting . . . in my chair . . . the same as Daniel." The sentence came out in halting fragments, the horrific memory passing through his mind in crystal clarity with each word he spoke. "Almost exactly the same as Daniel," he finished quietly.

"I'm familiar with your family history," Diane said. "And it's unfortunate that the Chicago police were unable to close your case. But I don't believe what happened here has anything to do with what happened in Chicago."

"You said it yourself," Alan continued. "This kid was

a big fan. More than likely, Taub read about your wife, about how she was found, and wanted to die the same way. Maybe as a weird tribute of some sort."

"We've seen that kind of thing before," Diane finished.

"I'll admit Daniel was a little obsessive, but not suicidal," Nick said. "There's a big difference."

"And you think you should have picked up on it if he were planning on doing that kind of thing," Diane said with some hesitation.

"Something like that, yes. But that's not what I'm concerned about." He paused, taking a moment to clarify in his own mind the worry that now plagued him. "What if the man that murdered my wife has come back? What if he thought Daniel was my son and killed him by mistake?"

"Whoa, Mr. Cross," Alan said, a puzzled look crossing his face. "That's quite a leap, don't you think?"

"No, I don't." He rubbed his eyes. "You don't know everything. No one does," he muttered. He had worked so hard to keep it out of the papers. Had managed to keep it a secret for five years. Even now, he found it difficult to speak the words aloud.

"Mr. Cross, is there something you're not telling us?" Diane prompted.

He nodded once. Then, taking a deep breath, he revealed the secret he had not spoken of in five years. "My son was home when my wife was murdered."

Diane blinked several times. "What?"

"Someone came into our home in the middle of the day and butchered my wife while my twelve-year-old son hid in the attic afraid to move." Nick's chest tightened, the words bringing back the anger and bitterness from so long ago.

"Your son could not identify the man?" she asked, her brow knitting with renewed interest.

Nick shook his head. "He never saw him. But he heard him . . . heard what he did to his mother." He paused briefly, searching for the words to make them understand. "He heard the man's voice," he said finally. "What if this man somehow found out and has come back for him?"

"Mr. Cross," Diane said after a time. "I understand your concern. And your statements will be taken into consideration. But you must realize—"

"That there's nothing you can do," Nick finished for her, disgusted by their inability to help more.

"We understand how difficult this must be for you but let me assure you—"

"Don't assure me of anything," Nick said, cutting the detective off again. "Because you can't. My wife was murdered. No one was ever caught. No one was ever even questioned. And now you tell me again that you can't do anything and I'm supposed to be satisfied!"

"I'm sorry about your wife," Diane said, her voice irritatingly calm. "But we have no evidence to indicate a connection between these two cases."

"Basically, you're telling me to wait around until someone shows up at my back door with a .38 ready to blow my head off."

"I'm telling you to wait until we have more information about Daniel Taub. Once we're able to paint a clearer picture of his life, we might see that he was headed toward suicide. And then you can relax."

"Relax," Nick repeated, his voice harsh. He wanted to laugh at the detective's complete lack of understanding of this situation. "I haven't been relaxed since my wife's death." He stood, unable to remain seated, and paced to the window. Outside, he watched as a crow landed nearby and began pecking at the ground for food. For an instant, he wished he were that crow. Wished he could fly away and leave all this behind. "Okay. Let's assume Daniel did kill himself. Fine. I accept that." He turned to face them again. "What about everything else I told you? Doesn't this all seem to be a little too convenient. The incidents with Bevin, the break in, the phone call, and now this? Come on, what are the odds of all that happening in less than forty-eight hours. They've got to be connected."

"Mr. Cross," Alan began slowly. "I don't know if you're aware of the fact that you have a certain reputation within the department." He pulled out a sheet of paper. "You've called the police out on more false reports than anyone in the history of the department."

"What is that?" Nick snatched the paper from the detective. His name appeared at the top with a list of calls dating back almost three years. "You've got to be kidding. You come into my house with this and accuse me—"

"Mr. Cross, that paper does not lie," Alan cut in.

Nick crumpled the paper into a tiny ball and tossed it into the detective's face. "I haven't called the police in years."

"That's true." Alan bent down and picked up the report. Smoothing it out, he slipped it back into his pocket. "But the first two years you lived here, you called on an average of three times a week."

"I don't understand why I have to defend myself." Nick took a step toward Alan. "This is not a false alarm. A boy is dead!"

"And for all we know, you murdered him!"

"Alan," Diane said, her voice holding a warning. "Let's all just calm—"

"You think I murdered that kid?" Nick reached out and

gripped the front of Alan's shirt. "Then arrest me!" he shouted.

Alan stared into Nick's face, seemingly unaffected by his close proximity. Nick wanted to hit the man, wanted to hit someone. But as he continued to stare into the detective's face, he suddenly felt ashamed. He released the shirt quickly and took a step back, away from the detective and the look in his eyes. Was it anger or just pity?

"I'm sorry," he said, covering his eyes with a shaking hand, trying to calm down, trying to get a hold of himself.

"It's all right," Diane said.

Nick turned toward her, really looking at her for the first time. Her short-cropped brown hair was cut for efficiency, and her clothes were casual but professional. They were here to do their jobs and he was only giving them a hard time. They had not done anything to deserve his anger.

"None of this is your fault." He turned to Alan. "I'm sorry," he said again. "I feel like I need someone to blame. I just ... I don't want this to be happening. I don't understand it." He paced away, going over it all in his mind, trying to think of something that would make them see that he was right to be so worried. "What if," he began slowly, a new thought weaving through his mind. "What if somehow Bevin was connected to my wife's murder? What if he met me yesterday in order to see Jeff? To see if Jeff would know him?"

"Bevin just doesn't make sense," Diane said, her soft voice conveying her doubt.

"Why would he do this?" Alan continued, his voice more callous. "Why not just kill the kid? Why make it look like suicide?"

Nick crossed to the table and dropped heavily into one

of the hardbacked chairs. "I don't know," he said in frustration. He knew he wasn't making sense to these people. Hell, it didn't make sense to him. "I just can't get past the idea that there is some kind of connection to Thomas Bevin."

"Who you assaulted," Alan inserted.

Nick turned to face him. "What?" he asked, his voice incredulous. "Who told you that?"

"He filed a police report on Saturday. Said he didn't want to press charges but he wanted the report on file."

"That bastard," Nick breathed.

"He called again." Alan repeated the facts without emotion. "He wanted to know how to go about getting a restraining order."

"This is ridiculous!" Nick shouted. "He assaulted me. He came to my house."

"Then why didn't you report him?"

"I thought . . ." Nick floundered for an answer. "I didn't see the point."

"Right now," Alan said matter-of-factly. "We have no reason to connect Thomas Bevin to any of this."

"Just talk to him. See where he was last night."

"Mr. Cross, do you really believe this Bevin character somehow came into your house and killed that kid and you never heard a thing?"

As Nick thought about it, he realized how ridiculous it sounded. "No, I guess not."

Diane looked uneasy. "At this point, there's just not much we can do. No one has really done anything to you."

"What about the break in?"

"We read the report from that night and . . ." Diane stopped, seeming to try and think of a way to finish that sentence.

Nick helped her out. "You don't believe it."

"It's not that," she said quickly. "It's just that sometimes when you have something on your mind and then you hear something in the middle of the night . . ." She trailed off. "Well, the mind has a tendency to ad-lib certain things."

"You were half asleep at the time," Alan added.

"I never said that." Nick turned to face him, his body taut, his anger quickly returning.

"You told the officer that you woke from sleep. You heard the noise in your sleep."

"I woke up."

They continued to stand and stare at him and he realized they were not going to do anything no matter what he said.

"We'll have cars patrolling the area," Diane offered.

"Great," Nick said with obvious sarcasm. "I already feel better."

"There's nothing else we can do at this point," she explained. "Not here at least." But she was not able to look at him when she spoke. "Maybe after the lab work is done."

"You should think about getting some private security," Alan suggested.

"After my wife died," Nick began slowly, "Jeff didn't feel safe anymore. Some nights he'd wake up screaming. Others, he'd sleepwalk, actually looking for her, wanting to help her." He stopped again, and it was a moment before he could continue, the memories still so fresh, so agonizing. "Eventually, I brought him back to Michigan. My wife and I both grew up here; I thought we could start over." He closed his eyes and began rubbing his forehead. A headache pounded against his temples. "Jeff felt safe here, safer than I did. Now this happens. What do I tell my son?"

"Mr. Cross, I don't think—"

"What do I tell my son?"

CHAPTER SIX

ξ

Alan and Diane exited the house together.

"Can you give me a ride back to the station?" Alan asked as they crossed the lawn, nearing Diane's car. "Stella's in the shop. I had to drive in with a uniform."

Stella. Diane shook her head. Stella was Alan's name for his department-issued car, an '83 Chevy with over 120,000 miles logged on the odometer. He'd been offered other cars time and time again but he always refused, ever loyal to Stella. He told Diane once when they got drunk together that he called the car Stella because he'd lost his virginity in a car just like it to a girl named Stella. Diane was never really sure if he was telling her the truth that night or not, but she never asked.

"I'm the one that called you in on this," she said. "I guess you're my responsibility."

"Damn right." Alan slid into her car.

As one of the few detectives who was also an evidence technician, Alan was called in on many cases. It was easier than waiting for a tech. Alan could collect the evidence himself and go over it with Diane later.

They drove in silence for a few minutes before Diane finally spoke. "So what do you make of it?"

"Make of what? The dead kid or Cross?"

"Both."

"Well, I know what you make of Cross or should I say, what you'd like to make *with* him." He raised his eyebrows up and down suggestively.

She glanced at him briefly, her expression confused, before turning her attention back to the road before her. "I don't know what you're talking about."

"Right," he snorted. "Come on, usually you're the one who has to be calmed down. I get to be the good guy and you're the villain. Today . . ." he trailed off, shaking his head. "Today I'd have to use the word meek to describe you, looking at him with your big doe eyes."

"I was not."

"I think I know you well enough to know when someone is your type, Dee."

"And what exactly is my type?" She glanced his way.

Alan settled more comfortably in his seat. "Those big brown eyes, the vulnerable look, the dark, thick hair." He paused. "No wait, that's my Irish setter, sorry."

"Very funny," Diane said. But part of her knew Alan was right. He was one of the best detectives she knew, a little scattered at times, but his mind was logical, sharp. He could see an answer before most could ask the question. And he had once again pegged the situation correctly. She was attracted to Nicholas Cross. "Do you think the kid killed himself or what?" she said trying to get the conversation back on the right track.

"I will reserve judgement until we have a chance to look at the evidence."

"Don't give me that double talk bullshit. What do you *think.*"

"Off the record?"

"Off the record. Just between two old friends."

"Well then, amigo, I think it's all exactly as it appears. I think the kid offed himself in his idol's home as some sort of weird tribute to him or something.

"But on the record, I'm reserving judgement. You just never know. Cross could be right and we could be looking at foul play. Or for all we know, Cross did it himself."

Diane turned sharply, his statement taking her off guard. "What makes you think that?"

"What?" Alan asked, looking at her, his face confused, as if he didn't even remember what they were talking about.

"You just said you think Cross could have done it. Why? Did you find something incriminating?"

"No. Just talking." He glanced out the window again, his last statement meaning no more to him than one of the many theories that were now running through his head.

Diane's grip tightened on the wheel. She didn't like the idea that Nicholas Cross was a possible suspect in all of this. She hadn't read the situation that way at all. Was it possible her judgment had been clouded by . . . by what? Nick himself? She did not like the picture of herself that was now forming in her mind. The fickle woman, blinded by a man who was vulnerable and angry, yet still alluring somehow. "Why'd you give him such a hard time if you think he didn't do anything wrong?" She continued to probe Alan, needing to be sure she hadn't misjudged the situation completely.

"I don't know." Alan shrugged, not looking at her. "It just seems like there's something he's not telling us, something he's keeping to himself. I was trying to rattle him."

"That story wasn't weird enough for you?"

"He just sounded so paranoid."

"A kid killed himself in his house. How should he be? Kicking up his heels in joy?" Her voice was more harsh than she meant it to be and she told herself to calm down. Alan was shrewd and if she wasn't careful, he would pick up on her doubts.

"No, that's not what I mean." He stared out the window, his brow furrowing as he thought. "The whole situation is just weird. Cross was right about one thing."

"What's that?"

"This Bevin character is not as innocent as he's trying to look. He's gone to a lot of trouble to make Nicholas Cross look like a hysterical nut."

"You practically called him just that."

Alan nodded. "I wanted to get a reaction."

"And you did."

"But if he were a hysterical nut, he would not have protested the way he did. He would have remained calm. An innocent man protests a hell of a lot louder than a guilty one."

"And Cross was very loud."

"Exactly. But what does it all lead us to conclude?" He glanced at Diane. "I have no idea. But something's going on between those two guys."

They drove in silence for the next few miles.

"I remember when his wife was murdered," Diane said, completely changing the course of the conversation. "I can't believe his kid was there. They did a good job of keeping that under wraps."

"Think about it. Would you let it out that your twelve-year-old son was home? That he could possibly identify the guy who did it?"

"I bet the Chicago police had a hard time keeping

that tidbit away from the press. Do you remember the headlines? 'Best-selling Horror Writer's Wife Murdered.' They played it up as this big ironic thing because of the stories he writes."

"Can you blame them? It's a great angle."

Diane slowed as they approached a red light. "Sure, blame the victim. It's his fault because of his books."

"Maybe to a certain degree, they're right."

Diane looked at him, his face a mask of indifference. "I hope you're kidding, Alan," she said coolly.

"Dee, you can't help but think maybe he brought what happened with this Daniel kid on himself. He draws those weirdos to him with those books."

Diane accelerated as the light turned green again. "Have you ever read any of those books?"

"No. I don't need to though. They're all—"

"I have," Diane cut him off. "He's a good writer. He didn't deserve what happened to his wife or what happened last night. No one does."

As they drew near the police station, Diane was acutely aware of the uncomfortable silence that now hung between them.

"Alan, let's just concentrate on the case and save our personal opinions."

"You're the one who brought it up."

"I know and believe me, I regret it." She parked the car. Pushing open her door, she added, "I'm going to call Chicago. Doesn't Rick Giavani work out of there?"

"Yeah. Why? What're you up to?"

"I'm going to ask him to send me the file on Cross."

"What for?"

"Curiosity, mainly."

"Right," Alan said sarcastically.

"And because of the phone calls he's been getting,"

Diane added, feeling suddenly defensive. "You never know."

"You just want to have a reason to go back there." They walked across the parking lot and headed toward their offices. "Mr. Cross, can I call you Nick?" His voice was a pitch higher as he imitated Diane. "I found out something that could interest you."

"I'm just doing my job, Detective." But she did not look at Alan as he taunted her. She feared that the truth of his statement might be displayed on her face.

Thomas sat on the edge of Ginny's bed holding her small hand in his. Dark circles stood out under her eyes, and her skin had a gray pallor that was cold to the touch yet she was sweating. Overall, she was better than Thomas had expected.

"I'm afraid to go to sleep tonight." She quivered despite the blankets covering her. "I'm afraid I'll go there again and I won't know how to come back."

"Ginny," he began, his voice calm and reassuring. "This is a normal reaction to the exercises we've been conducting. There is absolutely nothing to be afraid of."

"But I wasn't trying to do anything. What—"

"Ginny." He took on a firmer tone, like that of a parent scolding his child. "Your subconscious, the part of you that is awake while you are asleep, is simply continuing with its exercises," he explained. "That's very good. I don't want you to fight this in any way. This is great progress."

"But why do I feel so sick?"

"You're just not getting the rest you need because your subconscious is so busy." He patted her hand. "I'll tell you what. I bet the next time you go there, you won't feel at all afraid. You know why?"

"No," she said meekly.

"Because that house is your safe house. I didn't explain the purpose of the original exercise to you. I was hoping that you'd figure it out for yourself."

"I'm sorry," she said, and he could see the embarrassment she felt at disappointing him.

"That's okay. I don't expect you to be perfect." He paused, giving the guilt time to sink in, hoping it would keep her under his control. "We all need a safe place to go, a place that is all our own. That house is your private, safe place."

"But I don't feel safe there," Ginny whined. "It's cold and dark. That man I told you about . . . he scares me. I—"

"But there's no reason to be afraid," Thomas said, stopping the flow of her words. "I didn't tell you this before because, again, I was hoping you would realize it on your own." He paused for a moment, letting the guilt settle. "The people you meet at your safe house are your personal guides."

Her eyebrows furrowed. "I don't understand."

"Each of us has several guides. These are spirits who help us through life. Now, most people can't see their guides. They're not special like you are." He smiled and she smiled back. "But you're lucky. You can see your guides. The man you met, he's your strength guide so you shouldn't be afraid of him."

She nodded. "I'll try not to be."

"I'll tell you what," Thomas said, his heartbeat increasing as his plan ran through his mind. "The next time you see your guide, you tell him that you're releasing him. That way he can leave and someone new will take his place, someone completely different."

CHAPTER SEVEN

ξ

Nick stood at the door to his study staring into the room. Two pieces of yellow police tape crisscrossed over the doorway, preventing him from entering. They were not necessary. Nick would not have entered if someone offered him money to do it. He didn't know if he would ever be able to use the room again.

It was so much like Linda's death. The taped-off room, the blood covering the floor, left there for him to clean up. And suddenly, long pushed away memories flooded through his mind with crystal clarity. He had gone to the morgue alone, telling everyone he was okay. But he had to keep wiping his hands on his pants because his palms were so sweaty.

As they pulled the long steel tray out of the wall, he'd tensed. But when they uncovered the body, he had almost laughed with relief. This was not his wife, he'd thought. He could not see any resemblance to Linda in the woman.

"Is this your wife, Mr. Cross?" they had asked him.

And he had nodded slowly. Yes. Yes, it was his wife, the mother of his child. Her face was marred and deformed from the bruises and cuts she had sustained. He began sobbing then, and leaning down, he'd laid his cheek against hers. She was cold, her skin clammy against his own.

Until the moment they'd pulled back the sheet and exposed her face, Nick had been able to convince himself that it was not Linda, that they had made some sort of horrible mistake.

Now, it was difficult for him even to picture her face clearly. He needed to look at photographs to bring it all into focus. He had thought all the pain was behind them. He had thought . . .

He shook his head. None of it mattered now.

Leaning over the yellow police tape, Nick reached inside the study and pulled the door closed. As it clicked shut, the front doorbell rang. Nick turned toward the sound, his brow furrowing. What now?

The bell rang four more times before Nick could reach it. His patience worn thin by the constant ringing, he threw the door wide and yelled "What!" at the person outside.

A bright light flooded in the front door, blinding him. He instinctively threw a hand up to block the light.

"What the hell?"

"Mr. Cross, I'm Cathy Lauren from Channel Ten." The woman stood on Nick's porch, her cameraman just over her left shoulder. "I know a body was taken out of here earlier. I realize how difficult this must be for you, but I would just like to ask you a few questions." She smiled kindly, her face filled with sympathy.

"Go to hell." Nick slammed the door in the reporter's face.

"Mr. Cross, this is news. We're the first but we won't be the last," she yelled through the door.

Nick leaned against the hard wood surface, his face

drawn and tired. Linda's death had been a media circus and Nick would be damned if he was going to let that happen again. Maybe if he said nothing, they would simply go away. They didn't know anything at this point. He'd just have to keep it that way.

He glanced at the stairs. He needed to talk to his son. Needed to tell him . . . what? That the man who butchered his mother could be back? That Daniel may have been murdered because the killer mistook him for Jeff?

No, he couldn't tell him that. There was no reason to tell him that. The police had scoffed at the idea. Why scare him?

Going to the stairs, he slowly walked up to his son's room. He needed to know that Jeff was okay.

"Jeff?" he called, rapping lightly on the door.

"Come on in, Dad."

He opened the door and peered inside. "Would you rather be alone?"

Jeff lay on the bed, staring up at the ceiling. "Not really."

Stepping inside, he took a seat at Jeff's desk, across from the bed. "I thought we could talk."

Jeff nodded halfheartedly and sitting up, shifted his gaze to his father. "You know what I thought when I found him this morning?"

Nick shook his head. "No, what?"

"For a minute, I thought it was Mom." He spoke in a flat monotone.

"Jeff—"

"It was real quick," he continued, his voice more hurried now. "I was just standin' in the doorway, staring in at him and for just a second, I saw Mom sitting in that chair. She was covered in blood, just like, just like . . ." He closed his eyes, squeezing them shut tightly. "I can't get that picture out of my head." He pressed the palms of his hands against his eyes. "I keep seeing her over and over."

Nick knelt before him. Gripping Jeff's hands, he pulled them away from his face. "You can't think about it." He held his son's hands in his, wishing he could somehow take all of this pain from him. "You have to make an effort to erase it from your mind."

Jeff wrenched his hands free, pulling backward. "How?" He stared at his father, his eyes red and swollen from the pressure he had applied to them. "You tell me and I'll do it. I've been trying for years." His voice rose in pitch as he spoke. "Dr. Jamison used to give me that same line of bull but she just stared at me the same way you are now when I asked her how."

"Jeff—"

"Don't say anything." He slid across the bed, away from Nick. He stood, his back to him. "I didn't want to think about it. I didn't want to bring it all up again." He began pacing the room like a caged animal. "Why'd he have to do that to himself here? Why in our house? I was with him yesterday. I should have known. I should have done something. I should have done something."

Nick went to Jeff and gripped his shoulders tightly. "What could you have done?" he said, shaking him, trying to get through to him. "What could you have done for Daniel or your mother? What!" he shouted.

Jeff stared at him, his eyes wide.

"Nothing," Nick whispered. "There was nothing you could have done. Nothing would have made a difference. Not then and not now. It wasn't your fault." He pulled Jeff into his arms, hugging him tightly.

They stood that way for only a moment before Jeff pulled away from his grip. "I'm sorry, Dad," he whispered, wiping at his damp face. "I didn't mean to get so upset."

"It's okay." He reached toward Jeff again, but he took a step back, avoiding his touch. Nick dropped his hands to his sides. "You feeling better?"

Taking a deep breath, Jeff nodded. "You know, I'm even a little hungry. Do you think you could make something to eat?" He smiled but it was unconvincing. Nick knew Jeff was simply unwilling to share his pain with his father. Unwilling to take comfort from him.

"I guess so. Yeah," he said, disappointed. For a moment, he had thought they might have a breakthrough and actually begin to deal with the feelings Jeff had regarding his mother's death. But once again, Jeff had pulled back inside and retreated from Nick.

Jeff sat back down on his bed. "Yell when it's ready."

Nick nodded. "Sure." He was being dismissed but it didn't really matter. After all, it wasn't the first time it had happened. They'd played out this scene several times over the last five years.

Leaving Jeff's room, Nick headed toward the stairs. Maybe it was for the best. Maybe what the two of them needed more than anything else was to try and maintain their normal routine. Keep the past in the past.

Setting the burner on high, Nick placed a pot of water on the stove to boil. As he searched the cupboard for the spaghetti noodles, he felt the tension in his back relax. Maybe the police were right and he was overreacting. Maybe Thomas Bevin could really see into the future. Maybe he had somehow known what Daniel was planning to do and had actually been trying to warn Nick.

He shook his head. "Let's not go too far," he muttered. Finding the noodles, he measured out the appropriate amount using his fist as a gauge and set them aside.

Everything would be back to normal in a few days, he told himself. He just had to relax.

Reaching out, he flipped on the small portable television atop the microwave. His eyes widened as the small screen came into focus. The reporter he had slammed his door on earlier was giving a report. A live feed from directly in front of his house. Reaching out, he turned up the volume.

". . . outside the house of well-known horror writer Nicholas Cross." She indicated over her shoulder at the brickwork behind her. Nick stared, unblinking, as the report unfolded. "Earlier today, police removed the body of a young man. His name is still being withheld pending notification of the family. So far the police and Nicholas Cross have refused to comment on the event. Sources close to the investigation tell me that the young man committed suicide. A tribute to his favorite writer? Maybe. But this reporter thinks it may be more." Her voice took a dramatic turn. "Sources in Chicago have confirmed that Jeffrey Cross, son of Nicholas Cross, was home five years ago when his mother was murdered."

"No," Nick breathed, unable to believe what he had just heard. They knew. Somehow they had found out. But how?

"Speculation regarding this latest death seems to indicate that the murderer may be back to finish what he started so many years ago," the reporter continued. "Sources near the invest—"

Nick hit the off button, cutting short the remainder of the broadcast.

For five years he had looked over his shoulder, wondering if somehow the man who had murdered his wife knew about Jeff, knew that he had been home. He no longer had to wonder.

His secret. Broadcast. Live. From in front of his own home.

His gaze shifted to the countertop. The card the police officers had left earlier still sat atop it. He crossed the room in quick strides and picking up the card, dialed the number printed on it.

"Detective Howarth or Nolan," he said when the phone was answered. He paced the floor, waiting for one of them to pick up. Five years—a secret for five years— lost the same day he told the cops.

"Nolan." Her voice came through clearly on the line.

Nick's grip tightened on the phone. "Who leaked it? You or Howarth?"

"Mr. Cross? Is that you?"

"Why'd you tell the press about Jeff? Are you hoping the guy'll come back if it shows up on the eleven o'clock news?"

"What are you talking about?"

Nick almost laughed. She was convincing. "I tell you about Jeff and suddenly I have a reporter here saying she knows the whole story."

"Not from us."

"Right."

"Mr. Cross—"

"Save it. I just want you to know, I know and I'm done cooperating."

"Mr.—"

Nick slammed the phone into its cradle, then lifting it, slammed it again and again and again.

Diane stared at the phone. Leaked the story? Did he really think they would use his son as a pawn to catch the guy?

"Who was that?"

Diane looked up at Alan. "Cross," she said. "He's mad

as hell. Thinks we leaked information to the press about his son."

Alan raised an eyebrow. "Interesting."

"We didn't, did we, Alan?" she asked, just to be sure.

"I didn't but I can't vouch for you." His brow furrowed as he stared down at her desk. Reaching out, he picked up one of several papers. "Find anything good?" he asked, scanning the page he held.

Diane glanced down at the mess laid out in front of her. Rick had come through, faxing her some general information he had on the Chicago case involving Nicholas Cross. He'd also promised to Federal Express the rest of the file. She'd have it by morning.

"I haven't found anything so far," she said.

She had only received the information a half hour earlier, but most of it was just a repeat of what Nick had already told them. Linda Cross had been knifed to death on a beautiful Saturday afternoon. No witnesses. No clues. Just a terrified twelve-year-old boy who didn't speak to anyone for a week after it happened.

Alan dropped the fax back on her desk. "Had to be a tough one for Chicago to put it in as unsolved."

Diane nodded her agreement. "I don't plan on that happening here."

CHAPTER EIGHT

ξ

Miriam sat in the living room staring at the television, Bob beside her. They had been sitting in front of it for hours but she did not recall a single program they had watched.

Her mind was stuck in the other room, with the drawings that were burned into her mind. The image of the woman haunted her every waking moment. Although she hadn't heard from the woman since yesterday, she still felt the constant ache of her need. But she was no closer to figuring out what the woman wanted. Or why she was suddenly invading her life.

She glanced at Bob. She knew he was worried. Knew he suspected that she was not completely blocking out the woman as he had asked her to. Reaching out, she took his hand in hers and squeezed gently. He looked at her and smiled before turning his attention back to the television. She stared at him for another moment, remembering the pain she had put him through five years earlier. She would not do it again. She could not let this consume her life. She would put it out of her mind as Bob had asked.

Leaning her head on his shoulder, Miriam turned her attention back to the TV. But as she stared at the screen, her eyes widened.

"Turn it up," she said, grabbing for the remote Bob held. "Honey, turn it up."

"What is it?" He pushed the button. A moment later the volume shot up sharply.

She leaned forward, her heart picking up its beat slightly.

". . . refuses to give any statement at this point," the anchorman finished. But it was not his words that Miriam cared about. It was the picture of the man they were now displaying in the corner of the screen.

She moved off the couch, closer to the television, trying to get a better look at the man with dark eyes and a brooding expression.

"What is it?" Bob crouched beside her. "What's wrong?"

But she did not hear him. Suddenly her hand was alive with motion. The woman was back, ready to be drawn, ready to be heard.

Miriam snatched up a pencil and looking around, grabbed the newspaper off the coffee table. Setting lead to paper, she immediately began to draw.

"Miriam, what's going on?" Bob's voice held a note of concern.

Help Nick. The curves of her face became defined. *Help Nick.* Her eyes stared up at Miriam. *Help Nick.*

Over and over, the two words swirled around inside her head.

"Help Nick," she said aloud, finally voicing the plea that echoed through her mind. Her pencil slowed, the drawing nearly done. She looked at Bob, the first of her tears just beginning to spill down her cheeks. "Help Nick," she whispered.

"I'm a fan of Nicholas Cross." The words of the news anchor drew both Bob and Miriam's attention. "I hope this all works out for him." He sat behind the desk, his face a mask of practiced concern.

The woman beside him shook her head sadly. "Tragic, Ron. Just tragic." She turned back to the camera, her smile returning. "In other news . . ."

Bob reached up and turned off the television. It was a moment before he spoke. "What does this mean?" he said, and Miriam could hear the apprehension in his voice.

"I have to go," she whispered. "I have to help him."

The phone rang and Nick let the machine pick it up. Cathy Lauren's "exclusive report" had aired less than an hour earlier but already the media was crawling all over him, each station wanting its own exclusive. Nick did not watch the television reports or listen to the radio. He knew what they were saying, knew how it would affect Jeff if he found out what everyone, including himself, now suspected.

But doesn't he have a right to know if he's in that kind of danger?

That was the question that had been buzzing around in Nick's head for the past hour. Should he tell his son what might be happening? Should he shatter the last shred of security he now felt?

Nick rubbed his forehead, a headache just beginning to throb against it.

Not tonight. He couldn't tell him tonight. Not with Daniel's death still so fresh. Tomorrow morning, before they went to the police station, before Jeff saw any of the reports. Nick would get up early, make breakfast for the two of them and then tell him. Then maybe—

Breakfast!

His gaze darted to the stove. He had been making dinner. He stood and quickly crossed the room.

"Dammit," he said, staring into the pot, the water nearly boiled down to nothing. Dumping it out, he refilled the pot and set it back on the burner. He'd make Jeff dinner, take it up to his room, and protect him from the world outside. At least for one more night.

Thomas sat in his office at the Bevin Institute staring at the television, his eyes locked on the picture of Nicholas Cross. He sipped the white wine he had poured for himself almost an hour earlier. It was a small celebration. The look on Nick's face when he opened the door to that reporter was priceless.

Grabbing the remote control, he played back the tape.

"Go to hell." Nick's voice echoed through the office and Thomas laughed.

Rewinding the tape, he played back the entire report, listening to every detail. Reaching inside the cabinet beside the television, he withdrew a VHS tape from inside. He slipped it into the VCR and pushed the play button. A younger version of Nick appeared on his screen.

"Mr. Cross, will you continue to write horror novels?" one reporter asked.

Nick wiped at his eyes. He looked ill, thin, pale, and weak. "I haven't thought much about that. I don't . . . know."

"Mr. Cross," another reporter shouted at the press conference held nearly five years earlier. "Do you feel responsible for your wife's death?"

Nick swayed slightly where he stood. The police officer

beside him gripped his arm, steadying him. "No," he said, his voice low and choked.

"Mr. Cross, was your son involved at all?" someone called out.

"Was he hurt?" another yelled.

Any color left in Nick's face drained away. "My son . . ." he began, but he needed to clear his throat before continuing. "My son is fine."

The institute was closed for the evening. Thomas was alone. Sitting in the solitude of his office, he rewound the tape, watching it once more.

"My son is fine," Nick said again.

Thomas raised his wine glass toward the screen. "He is for now," he whispered, emptying the glass in one swallow.

Miriam lay in bed, staring up at the bedroom ceiling, wide awake despite the late hour. "I'm going," she said, her voice strained. She was tired of arguing with Bob. Tired of trying to explain herself to him. He couldn't feel what she felt. Could not understand her obligation to this woman. "I have to go."

Bob did not answer. He lay with his back to her, not moving.

"I can't just ignore what's happening."

Slowly, he rolled over onto his back. "You don't know Nicholas Cross. You don't even know how you can help him."

"But the woman does," she said, trying to make her point. "Honey, don't you see. She's been trying to warn him all along. I know that now, I'm absolutely sure of it. If I can just touch him—"

"Touch him?" he snorted. "I'll be surprised if you can get within fifty feet of the guy." He turned to face her.

"I have to believe Nicholas Cross will not be easily accessible."

"Then I'll have to make him accessible," Miriam said. For the last hour, he'd been throwing obstacle upon obstacle in front of her, hoping one of them would stop or deter her in some way. "I think," she said, jumping his latest hurdle, "if I touch him, I'll know who this woman is. She's connected to him in some way and when I contact him, I contact her."

"Then at least wait until we can go together. Two days." He put an arm around her and pulled her close. "In two days, I can go with you."

She snuggled against his body, feeling safe and protected. "It can't wait," she whispered and immediately felt his body tense. "Bob," she began, wanting his support but more importantly, needing him to understand. "Tonight when I saw that picture of Nicholas Cross, the woman . . ." she paused, unsure of how to explain the emotions that had coursed through her body in that instant. "She's desperate, frantic to reach him—"

"You've been saying that for days," he interrupted, pulling away from her before sitting up in the bed. "I don't understand how things have changed. I don't understand why you can't wait for me."

She sat up, twisting around to face him. "Because I think it'll be too late."

"What will be?" he said, his voice exasperated. He leaned against the headboard, arms crossed over his bare chest, glaring at her, his mouth set in an angry slit.

Looking into his eyes, she reached out and ran a hand along the side of his bearded cheek. Then, leaning forward, she kissed him. He did not respond, his lips stiff beneath hers. She pulled back, feeling the sudden distance between them. "Tonight," she began, "I felt much more of her emotions. She loved him very much." Touching her fingers to his mouth, she traced the outline of his lips. Slowly, they softened beneath her fingers. "She's afraid for him."

Her took her hand from his lips and kissed it gently. "I'm afraid for you," he whispered. "I came close to losing you once. I don't want to risk it again."

"I'll be fine," she said, moving in close to him. He held her, wrapping his arms around her, engulfing her body in his strong embrace. She returned the hug. But as she continued to hold him, her body enveloped by his, she felt the anxiety behind the embrace. He was afraid to release her. "Honey, it's not the same," she whispered, close to his ear. "I know this woman won't hurt me."

He increased his grip on her, his face lost in the thickness of her hair. It was a moment before she realized he was crying.

Nick bolted upright in bed, panting, sweat covering his body. He threw back his blankets, ready to flee from the too real images that still haunted his mind.

The Dream.

"Damn." He fell back against his pillows, breathing deeply, attempting to slow his pounding heart. Squeezing his eyes shut, he tried to erase the bloody images of Linda that still raced through his mind with crystal clarity. "Damn," he said again, wishing he could somehow end these nightly terrors.

"Dad?"

Nick cried out, his eyes snapping open. He had not heard Jeff come in. He sat up, staring at the dark silhouette blocking his doorway.

"What's wrong, Jeff?" Getting out of bed, he moved toward him.

"Dad, Mom's hurt." Jeff stared ahead, focusing on nothing, his voice an emotionless drone. "She needs your help," he said in that same flat tone.

"What . . . ?" And then it hit him. Jeff was sleepwalking, something he had not done in years. Nick's heart sank. "Everything's fine, Son," he said. Taking Jeff by the shoulders, he turned him gently around and steered him back to his own room.

"But I heard Mom. She's calling for you. Why don't you go to her, Dad? Why aren't you helping?"

Nick's hands trembled as he helped Jeff back into his bed. "Everything's going to be okay," he coaxed, trying to get Jeff settled down again.

"Where were you, Dad?" Jeff muttered, closing his eyes as his head hit the pillow. "Where were you?"

Nick sat on the edge of his son's bed, staring down at him. Jeff's eyebrows were furrowed together, his eyes moving rapidly under the lids, his hands balled into tight fists. Reaching out, Nick ran a hand through his son's hair, whispering quietly, reassuringly to him. Soon Jeff's face relaxed, and his breathing became deep and regular. Nick pulled the blankets up close and tucked them under his chin. But he did not go back to his own bed. Instead, he pulled himself up beside Jeff and stretching out, settled back against the headboard.

Where were you, Dad?

The accusation rang in Nick's ears. Jeff still blamed him. Nick had thought he was past it, but now he knew he was not.

"Linda," he whispered, choking back the pain and guilt that threatened to strangle him. "I'm sorry." But he was not sure who he was apologizing to. His wife, who had died so brutally? His son, who still blamed him for the loss of his mother? Or himself?

Nick looked down at Jeff and gently ran a hand across his cheek. Five years. Five long, lonely years and still Linda's death haunted them on a daily basis.

Sighing, Nick leaned back against the headboard. He was just so damn tired. His eyes drifted closed. His breathing deepened.

Beside him, the mattress shifted ever so gently, bringing Nick back from the brink of sleep. He pulled himself upright. He couldn't sleep here. He'd be stiff as hell by morning.

Nick opened his eyes and swinging his legs to the floor, dropped his head forward and rubbed the back of his neck.

"One night," he murmured, wishing aloud for the peace that eluded him. "One undisturbed night, please."

Jeff stirred again. Nick glanced at him, wanting to be sure he was settled before going back to his own room. But it was not Jeff in the bed beside him. It was . . .

"Linda!" he yelled, flailing away.

One bruised and bloodied hand shot out, gripping his.

"Where were you, Nick?" Her dead eyes bore into his as she yanked him closer. "Why did you leave me alone? Why!" she shrieked.

And Nick came awake all at once, barely able to suppress the scream that threatened to break free. Sitting upright in bed, his gaze darted around the room, panic flooding his veins.

Where am I? Where am . . .

But as the haze in his mind cleared, he realized where he was. Jeff's room. He had fallen asleep in Jeff's room. He glanced toward the window and was shocked to see morning light peeking past the blinds.

"Damn," he muttered. He had slept the entire night yet

it had seemed like only seconds. Exhaustion tugged at his limbs.

Standing, he placed his hands at the base of his back and stretched. His back made a loud popping noise. He groaned as he glanced at the bed. It was empty. Jeff was already up.

Already up!

"Shit." He hurried toward the door. He had intended to get up before his son, needing to talk to him before he saw any of the reports on television.

But as he rushed down the steps, he realized he could hear Jeff moving around in the kitchen. Nick relaxed, his pace slowing. Jeff was home. He was even cooking. The enticing aroma of bacon filled the air, making Nick's stomach growl. Until that moment, he hadn't realized how hungry he was.

"Smells good," he said, entering the kitchen. Relief flooded through him as he glanced at the small portable television that sat atop the microwave. It was off.

"I was just getting ready to get you." Jeff stood at the stove, spatula in hand, mixing eggs around in a pan. He did not look at Nick, his gaze locked on the chore before him. "Dad?" he said, continuing to stir the eggs. "Why were you in my room this morning? Did you sleep there all night?"

Nick was taken off guard by the question but was more surprised by the embarrassment he could hear in Jeff's voice. It was obvious to Nick that Jeff suspected another sleepwalking episode and he was ashamed. "Most of the night," he said, watching his son closely.

"Why?" he asked, not able to meet Nick's gaze. "What happened?"

"I had a nightmare," he said, not exactly lying to him.

"I went to check on you and must have just dozed off. Sorry if I crowded you."

"That's okay. It didn't bother me. I was just curious." He glanced at his father, his smile relieved. "I think I'm about done here." He turned off the flame beneath the pan.

Nick filled a plate with slightly soggy scrambled eggs, very well-done bacon, and perfectly toasted bread. Glancing at the coffee pot, he cringed. Jeff had attempted to make a pot of coffee and like always, he had overfilled the funnel containing the coffee grinds with water. The resulting overflow of grinds and water covered the counter. The pot, half full of a light-brown liquid Nick assumed was his morning brew, sat in the middle of it all.

Jeff stood next to him, his own plate in hand, staring at the mess. "I had a little problem with the coffee," he said, taking a bite of his bread. "But the toast came out great." He took a seat at the table and a moment later, Nick joined him.

"Dad?" Jeff said, taking a bite of a particularly crispy piece of bacon. "Why are there so many reporters on our lawn this morning?"

"Reporters?" Nick repeated, but he could see the tension in his son's face. "I hadn't realized there were," he lied.

Five years ago, they had been hounded by reporters, never able to leave their house without someone following closely behind, asking how they were dealing with their loss, how they were getting on with their lives, whether they thought things would ever get back to normal. So many pointless, unanswerable questions.

"It'll settle down in a couple of days," Nick said, hoping to reassure his son.

Jeff nodded. "But why are there so many? Just because Daniel killed himself here?" He looked at his father, watching him, waiting for an answer.

"It's more complicated than that," Nick began.

"More complicated?" Jeff set his fork down. "Dad, what's going on? What aren't you telling me?"

Nick cleared his throat. "The reporters are outside because some of them believe that Daniel's death may not have been a suicide." He paused briefly. "Somehow they found out . . . they know that you were home when your mother was killed. They think . . ." He stopped, unable to say the words.

And in those few moments of silence, Jeff's expression changed. He stared ahead, his eyes focused on nothing. His mouth pulled downward with slowly dawning realization. When he spoke, his voice was a flat monotone. "They think he's come back."

"Jeff, they're wrong. They're . . ." He groped for something more to say. "They're making assumptions based on nothing."

Jeff's gaze cut to Nick. "Did he kill Daniel?"

"Jeff, you can't—"

"Did he kill Daniel!" he shouted.

"I don't know. I hope not."

"You hope not." Jeff stared at his father. "Why didn't you tell me?" His voice was soft and confused.

Nick sighed. "There was nothing to tell. The police have said nothing about it being the same man or even murder. In fact, when I brought it up to them, they scoffed at me."

"When *you* brought it up." His face screwed up into a mixture of anger and astonishment. "You were worried about it?"

Nick hesitated. "Jeff—"

"God, Dad," he said, cutting him off. "How could you not tell me?" He stormed out of the room, ending the conversation.

"Jeff." Nick followed him. "We need to talk about this."

Jeff headed toward the front door but stopped before he reached it. "The goddamn reporters." He paced like an animal in a cage, back and forth, marking a path in the carpet. The stairs. The door. The stairs.

"Jeff—"

"Don't talk to me!"

The door. The stairs. The door.

"I'm trapped," he mumbled. "Can't get out. Don't want to stay." His voice rose in volume. "I can't stand this!" He slammed a fist into the wall.

"Jeff! Don't!" Nick shouted.

Jeff pulled back, hit the wall again, pulled back, and prepared to strike a third time.

"Jeff!" Nick rushed forward and threw a bear hug around him, locking his arms down at his sides.

"Get off me!" Jeff twisted in his grip.

"Stop it!" Nick shouted, holding tight. They grappled with each other for several moments before Jeff finally gave up and stopped struggling.

"Are you going to stop?" Nick asked, still holding on to him, afraid that if he let him go again he would go back to his destructive behavior.

"Just let go," Jeff hissed between gritted teeth.

Nick loosened his grip. Jeff shoved away from him, pulling his shirt back into place.

Nick grabbed for his hand, wanting to see what kind of damage he had done to it.

"Don't!" Jeff shouted, backing away.

"Let me just look—"

"Go to hell." Turning, he ran to the stairs and started up them.

"You're being ridiculous," Nick said, chasing after him.

Jeff stopped. He stood on the stairs, three steps from the top. Slowly, he turned to face his father. "How can you say that?" His face reflected the anguish he now felt. "It's my *life*. You should have told me."

"I couldn't," Nick said, before he realized he was going to speak.

"Don't tell me that," Jeff said, his voice cracking. "I don't want to hear that anymore." His emotions welled up inside him. Nick could see him struggling to hold them in. "I can't trust you."

"That's not true." Nick moved up two steps, wanting to close the gap between them. "I was trying to protect you."

"Protect me." A single tear escaped his eye, making a slow trek down his cheek. Jeff wiped it away. "The way you protected Mom."

The accusation struck Nick like a physical blow, stealing his breath, making him weak at the knees. "Your mother—"

"No more!" He jabbed a finger at Nick, his face contorted with a mixture of anger and grief. "You weren't there. You didn't hear her . . . she begged . . . she . . ." He choked on the words, unable to finish the sentence. Turning, he fled to his room, the door slamming shut behind him.

Slowly, Nick sank to his knees, no longer able to stand. His body shook, overwhelmed by the sense of loss that filled his limbs and made him feel sick to his stomach. In the instant Jeff stood before him screaming his frustration and rage, Nick felt something die between them. And he knew, with a certainty he had never felt before, that things would never be the same again.

Ginny was relieved. She had gone through an entire night without returning to the house. She was sure it was the visit from Thomas that had helped. He had explained it all to her and now she could control it. Her grandmother had kept her home from school one extra day just to be sure and she was glad. It gave her extra time to practice her meditating before her next session with Thomas. She wanted to go in and impress him, make up for disappointing him earlier. As she closed her eyes, concentrating on her breathing, she thought only of him.

Alan waited in the outer lobby of Thomas Bevin's office. Diane knew nothing of this unscheduled visit. He had done some preliminary background work on Bevin and felt there was much more to him than they knew. He wanted to talk to the man face to face to try and get a feel for what he was really all about before he pulled Diane in on it. He was working from instinct, and until he had more than that, he would do this alone.

"Detective Howarth." Thomas Bevin walked toward him, hand extended, a warm smile across his handsome face. "I'm sorry you had to wait. I was meditating."

Alan stood, shaking hands with the man. "No problem."

"Let's go into my office, where we can talk more comfortably." Bevin led the way into his plush office. He sat down in one of the two chairs that flanked his desk, offering the one beside him to Alan. "Now, how can I help you?" he said, his face open and relaxed.

Alan began feeling his pockets, looking for the notepad he was always forgetting. "I'm just doing a routine follow-up," he lied. Then, unsuccessful in his search, he added, "Do you have some paper I could take notes on?"

Bevin nodded and rising slowly, moved to the mahogany desk. He returned with a small pad of paper with the Bevin Institute insignia across the top. He handed it to Alan. "With my compliments."

"Yesterday we talked with Nicholas Cross and he mentioned your name," Alan began.

"He's a very disturbed man," Bevin inserted.

Alan strained not to smile. This was going to be easier than he thought. "Really. Now, what makes you say that?"

"I have tried talking to him twice and both times I was violently rebuffed."

Alan nodded, pretending to be deeply interested. "And what was it you wanted to discuss with him?"

"As I am sure you have already deduced, I am an occultist. Mr. Cross does not realize how open he is to evil. It can be drawn to him because of the books he writes." He talked slowly, as if explaining to a small child. "I simply want to help him."

Alan fished around in his pockets again, looking for the information he had brought with him about this man. "It's funny because Cross seems to think you're harassing him." He found what he needed and pulling it out, scanned the printed page.

"I fear the man is delusional," Bevin said, shifting uncomfortably in his seat.

"You know how it is. We have to check these things out." He refolded the paper and slipped it back into his pocket. "But I do have one question." He paused for dramatic effect. Then he dropped his bomb. "Why did you change your name?"

The smile on Thomas Bevin's face disappeared. "My . . . what?" he stammered.

"Your name. Why did you change it?" he repeated, his pen poised over his paper, waiting for the answer. "You see, I ran a background check on you. I know you legally changed your name and I was just wondering why? You have no criminal record on either name so what's the point in changing it?"

Bevin flinched for the first time. It was subtle. His eyes darted to one side then back again as he tried to think of something to say. And Alan saw it. He knew now that his instincts had been right. This guy was up to something and his name change was involved.

"I simply wanted a new start," he said innocently.

Alan nodded. "I had to ask." He scribbled on his paper, not really writing anything but hoping to make Bevin more nervous by pretending to.

"I wish I could help you more." Bevin stood and walked to the door.

Alan realized the interview was over. "Well," he said, recapping his pen. "I appreciate the time you gave me."

They shook hands again before Alan left.

Diane sat at her desk. The file from Chicago had arrived less than an hour earlier. The contents were spread in front of her, but she had looked at only one item since opening the package. She held the newspaper clipping dated five years earlier close to her face, staring at the photo of the man it displayed. Nicholas Cross. He was coming out of the police station, his face just beginning to turn away from the camera, his body shielding the small boy whose hand he held.

But even in the grainy newspaper photo, Diane could see his eyes, hollow and distant. He did not look like the same man she had met yesterday. The picture showed a too thin, very pale man who seemed older than the one she knew.

Setting the article aside, she began sorting through the rest of the information. If something was going on, she planned on stopping it before Nick ended up resembling the man in that old photograph.

Some of the information matched the faxes she had received the night before. She scanned the new pages looking for anything that might connect the two cases. It surprised her to read that Linda Cross had not been raped, just brutally, sadistically murdered.

A manila envelope sat on the bottom of the pile. CRIME SCENE PHOTOS—DO NOT FOLD was printed in bold black letters across the front. Silently, she thanked Rick.

Opening the flap, she pulled out the photos of Linda Cross. She had told Rick about their current case and how Nick had claimed that the position of Daniel's body matched that of his wife's. The photos would now confirm that for Diane.

"Christ," she breathed, staring at the woman in the chair, wondering if Nick had seen her that way, remembering in the same instant that Jeff had. Her shoulder-length blond hair, matted with blood, covered most of her bruised face. The skin on her bare arms showed deep slashes, bone showing through in some places. Diane flipped through the photos, each taken from a different angle. Nick was right. Linda Cross sat in a chair, before a computer, the knife on the floor at her feet.

Diane's brow furrowed. She held the picture closer, trying to see the weapon on the floor. Sorting quickly through the other pictures, she found one that clearly showed the murder weapon.

"Damn," she muttered, studying the photo. She couldn't

be sure but she would bet that the knife was a perfect match to the one they'd taken from the Cross house yesterday.

Two theories came to mind. One: Daniel knew about the murder weapon and purposely used the same knife to impress his favorite author. Or two: The murderer was back, as Nick suggested.

Sorting through the papers on her desk, she found the results of the fingerprinting taken from Nick's house in Chicago five years earlier. Getting up from her desk, she headed toward the lab, paper in hand. Suddenly she wanted the results from yesterday's fingerprinting now.

CHAPTER NINE

ξ

Nick sat in the darkened kitchen, the evening sky casting deep shadows throughout the room. The day had gone by in a blur, the hours passing without him realizing it, until it was once again night.

Lightning crackled in the distance, flashing a bright, eerie light every few minutes. Nick could hear the rain on the house as it began its slow, steady pattern. He smiled bitterly. Maybe the rain would get rid of the reporters that still milled about on his lawn. They were having their dinner. He had heard them earlier as they all called out their orders to each other. Now the smell of the food drifted inside. He supposed he should think about making dinner. He stared ahead, not moving. What was the point? Jeff would not come down to eat it.

Nick rubbed his temples, wishing he could erase the harsh memories of Linda's death that still burned so vividly in his mind.

Jeff had looked so small and weak to him then, his eyes blank and staring. He would not speak to anyone at first. Not to the police, not to the doctors, not even to Nick. For almost a week, he had just sat staring ahead, rocking back and forth and making strange mewling sounds. Nick had been worried he'd stay that way forever. But one morning, he had begun screaming and Nick thought it was even worse than the silence.

Why is this happening again?

Three times today, Nick had gone upstairs, knocking lightly on Jeff's door. Each time, he was greeted by silence. On the second trip up, Nick tried talking through the door, trying to explain himself. But the words sounded feeble even to himself. It was too late. He had destroyed whatever hope he had of becoming close to his son. Once this was all over, Nick knew Jeff would leave him. Not right away. They would still go through the motions of father and son. Small chitchat over dinners, television in the evenings, but there would always be a wall between them. And when it came time for Jeff to go to school, Nick would not hear from him. He would visit only when it was mandatory and then eventually move out of state, Nick getting a phone call on Christmas and his birthday.

Why is this happening?

He did not want to stay in the house tonight, had planned on taking Jeff to a hotel for the next couple of days. But now he knew Jeff would not agree to that. Besides, when it came right down to it, Nick did not want to walk through the mob of reporters that still lingered outside.

I'm a prisoner. A prisoner in my own home.

Standing, he paced to the sliding glass door and stared out. At least the privacy fence that surrounded the house had kept the reporters out of the yard. So far.

The phone rang again, as it had been doing all day, and Nick glanced at it. As the machine beeped, signaling for the caller to leave a message, a woman's voice rang out.

"Mr. Cross, it's Detective Nolan. Are you there?" She paused for a moment. "Please, I need to talk to you. If you're there, pick up." She paused again.

Nick stared at the phone, debating with himself, not wanting to pick it up but unable to ignore the urgency in her voice.

He reached out toward the line but before he could lift the receiver, the doorbell rang, jarring him. "Shit," he muttered, his hand shaking slightly from the momentary scare. He was more than a little jumpy.

Nick looked at the machine again but it was already clicking, rewinding and resetting itself. She had hung up.

"Terrific."

The bell rang again.

"I'm coming!" he yelled, making his way through the house, not bothering to turn on any lights as he moved.

They can see me in here when the lights are on.

Someone pounded heavily on the other side of the door as he drew closer.

Reaching the door, he yanked it wide. "What!"

Detective Alan Howarth stood on the porch. "I need to talk to you." A light rain fell, pasting Alan's hair to his head.

"About what?" Nick was not exactly thrilled to see the man.

Alan glanced over his shoulder as the surge of reporters who had taken temporary cover in their news vans now moved forward, noticing the open front door. "Can we go inside?"

Nick stepped aside to allow the detective in, slamming the door shut as soon as the man cleared the frame.

"Nice." Alan hooked a thumb over his shoulder toward the door, indicating the reporters on the other side. "But

I think they'll give up soon, especially with the storm coming."

Nick said nothing. They stood in the foyer, Alan dripping on the floor, wiping at the occasional drop of water that slid from his rain-wet hair down the side of his face.

"Why did you come back?" Nick asked. His voice held no emotion.

"Can we go inside, please?" Alan took his coat off, draping it over the ledge beside the door.

Nick did not move. "If you're here to apologize, well to hell with you."

"I'm here to talk."

"Then talk." Nick had decided hours earlier that he would not cooperate with these people anymore. They had done nothing to help him. He had to help himself.

Alan wiped at his face again as the water continued to drip from his hair. "I've been trying to call but you haven't been answering your phone."

"I didn't want to be disturbed." Nick smiled bitterly. "What do you want, Detective?"

Alan shifted where he stood, his shoes making a soft, squishy sound. His eyes narrowed slightly. "We didn't talk to the press, if that's what you think. They have their own sources."

Nick stared at him, unconvinced.

"I just thought you should know that." He paused. "I also came back because I have a few more questions about Thomas Bevin, questions I didn't ask yesterday."

"You came back here tonight for that?"

Alan nodded, flicking drops of water from his damp hair. "There are just a few things that need clarification."

Nick crossed his arms over his chest, leaning back against the wall.

"It's no big deal," Alan said casually.

Nick's expression did not change.

"Please, Mr. Cross, this is very awkward."

"Yes, I know." He continued to stare at the man, a small puddle now forming around his shoes. "You're here for a reason. Something to do with Daniel. Something wrong."

For a moment, Alan's face showed his surprise at being discovered. But he recovered quickly, putting his stone detective face back in place without much effort.

But it was too late. The mask had slipped, if only for a moment, but long enough for Nick. He knew now that he was right and he'd be damned if he was going to let them push him around any more. "You want to really talk with me, fine, we'll go inside and really talk. You want to keep bullshitting me and you can stand there and melt for all I care."

"I don't know why—"

"You didn't give a damn about Bevin yesterday," Nick said, his voice overriding the detective's question. "Now you make a special trip back to question me about him. Come on, Detective, I'm not a fool."

For a moment, Alan looked as if he were going to keep up the false front. But then as a clap of thunder rattled the windows, he seemed to change his mind. "All right. Okay. Let's go inside and we can talk."

Thomas Bevin locked the door to his office. He had given Sandy specific instructions not to disturb him for any reason. Now as he lay back on the couch and closed his eyes, his breathing became calm, almost undetectable. Within seconds, he was floating above himself, easily separating body and soul.

He thought of Nicholas Cross, and immediately, the

essence that was Thomas Bevin sped toward the author's home. A visit was long overdue.

Nick led the way into the living room. He couldn't help but feel slightly vindicated. They had been so sure he had been simply overreacting earlier. Now something had happened to change that opinion of the situation.

Nick dropped into a chair.

"Mind?" Alan asked, indicating the lamp beside him.

Nick waved his hand absently. "Whatever." A moment later, the room came alive with light.

Alan took the seat across from Nick. "I'm sorry. I think I'm still a little wet."

Nick almost laughed.

I have blood staining the carpet in the study and this guy thinks I'm going to get worried about a few water spots?

"Don't worry about it," he said dryly. "Just tell me what's happened."

Alan sat perched on the edge of the chair. "After looking at some of the prelim work," he began, "Daniel's death looks . . ." He paused for a moment, as if searching for the right words. "A little odd at best."

Nick leaned forward in his chair. "What is it?"

"Fingerprints," he said simply. "The ones on the knife are not Daniel's."

"Which means Daniel was not alone in that room," Nick added.

"Exactly." The detective began feeling his pockets, obviously looking for something. "The prints we found are real clear samples, but we haven't gotten a match yet."

"I'm surprised you didn't check them against mine."

Alan pulled some papers out of his shirt pocket. "I did.

Lifted 'em when I was here. Checked you and your son. No match." He began sorting through the papers he held, reading each one briefly.

"Thanks for your vote of confidence."

Alan looked at him. "I'm just doing my job, Mr. Cross. I don't know you from Adam. You seem like an upstanding citizen but so do a lot of the people I arrest."

There was another bright flash of lightning, followed almost immediately by a clap of thunder. The house shook with its force.

"But there was something else." Alan continued to sort through his papers. He stopped several times, reading one page, then another.

"Detective?" Nick said when he continued to sit quietly and read.

Alan looked up. "I'm sorry." Then, holding up the mismatched papers, he said, "My notes."

Nick wanted to jump up and grab this guy by the collar and shake the information out of him. But he did not. Instead, he said in a calm, rational voice, "You said there was something else?"

Alan looked confused for a moment and then nodded. "Yeah, there was something else. The knife wound wasn't consistent with suicide. The kid's wrists . . . there were no hesitation marks."

"Hesitation marks?"

"Yeah." Alan held up a wrist and laying a finger across it like a knife, continued, "Usually with this type of suicide, people tend to make a few tries, you know working up their nerve, like this." He moved his finger back and forth across his wrist to demonstrate. "But this kid," he shook his head, "the cut is clean and straight. No sign of hesitation at all."

Nick cringed as he pictured Daniel sitting in his study all night, slowly dying.

Alan began sorting through the scraps of paper again. "We ran Bevin's name through the computer but it came up empty. No priors. But Thomas Bevin did not exist until ten years ago."

In his office, Thomas Bevin tensed. He lost control and slammed painfully back into his body. The force of the return was so strong that it sent him to the floor gasping for air.

What was the detective doing? Did he suspect? Thomas had not thought so that morning. But his presence changed things dramatically. He could ruin everything.

Crawling back on the couch, he tried to calm himself, tried to bring himself back to the relaxed state he had been in only moments before. Everything would be fine— he was still in control. Things would just have to be sped up slightly. But no real damage had been done.

Lying back on the couch, he focused on Ginny Lambert.

Alan wiped at his dripping face again. "Thomas Bevin changed his name." He scanned each piece of paper. "Dammit, I can't find it. I must have left it on my desk."

"Did you find something on the old name?" Nick asked as he watched the detective search.

"No. Nothing on either name, which puzzles the hell out of me. Usually people change their name because they're hiding from something. This guy ... I don't know."

Alan started reading from one small sheet of paper. "He inherited a bunch of money from his late wife. She fell for the guy and his routine hook, line, and sinker. She was loaded. Died less than a year after they were married and he got it all." He stuffed the papers back in his shirt pocket. "Now he runs that institute for psychic learning. It's a pretty big operation actually. But Bevin's never gone out of his way to draw attention to himself until now."

"Maybe he's trying to drum up some free publicity," Nick said, wondering aloud about the man's motives.

"That's a good possibility," Alan agreed. "The other guy."

"Carl Neff?"

"Yeah," Alan fished in his back pants pocket pulling out yet another set of wrinkled pieces of paper. "He's Bevin's bodyguard. He has a record. Aggravated assault. Assault with the intent to do bodily harm." He looked up at Nick. "It goes on and on."

"Has he done any jail time?"

"Plenty." Alan handed Nick the pieces of paper listing out the charges Carl Neff had managed to accumulate over the years. "It seems he heard our Mr. Bevin speak at a prison program and was suddenly reformed."

Nick looked at the detective. "You've got to be kidding."

"Guess he saw the light," Alan smirked. "Now it's your turn. I want to know exactly what Bevin did and said at that conference on Saturday. Did he threaten you in any distinctive way? Something we could use to maybe get a search warrant?"

Nick shook his head. "It was all very vague. He told us he was an occultist . . ." His sentence dropped off as he heard a door upstairs open. He glanced up expecting to see Jeff. When he didn't materialize, Nick frowned.

Alan followed his line of vision, also looking up the stairs. "What's up?"

"Jeff, I thought." Nick rose from his seat, handing the

papers back to the detective. Another clap of thunder rattled the house, accompanied by the bright lightning, the two now simultaneous as the storm grew in intensity. "Jeff," he called, and a sudden chill passed through him, making him shake lightly. In that moment, he was sure the room felt somehow . . . colder.

"I didn't hear anything," Alan said from his seat.

"I did." Nick began up the stairs. "I'll be right back," he called over his shoulder. But as he glanced down into the living room, he thought he saw something move behind the detective.

Just a shadow? The lightning making the darkness dance and weave on the walls?

"What now?" Alan asked when Nick stopped his upward climb, and instead, continued to squint into the room.

"I thought . . ." Nick began, but a loud boom of thunder accompanied by a brilliant flash of lightning drowned out the rest of Nick's sentence. A moment later, the single light that had been burning in the living room blinked out.

"Great." Alan's voice drifted toward Nick in the darkness, but he could no longer see the detective. "This has not been my day."

"Detective." Nick's voice was strained. He did not like the sudden blackness that now surrounded him, feeling as if it were smothering him.

"Nickie." The quiet whisper drifted through the room.

"What the hell," Alan's voice rang out sharply. "Who was that?"

Thunder boomed. Lightning lit up the room. But to Nick, the brightness seemed to last an eternity. In that moment, he could see the scene in the living room below clearly as it played out.

Detective Alan Howarth stood, his face flushed with alarm. He apparently had heard the man behind him, the man with the tattoo of a snake on his arm, because he began to pull his gun from its holster. But the man was quicker. Stepping forward, he jammed the knife he held into Alan's stomach and pulled upward with great force.

"No!" Nick screamed, his own voice sounding feeble and ineffectual.

But then the lightning was gone and the room was once again washed in blackness. Nick sank down on the stairs, frozen with shock.

It's not possible. This isn't happening.

The sound of the rain pounding against the house filled his ears and echoed through his mind. He closed his eyes, squeezing them tightly shut.

Think, goddammit. Think!

He had to clear his mind, had to get a hold of himself.

"Nickie." The whisper again.

Nick's eyes snapped open; the voice was so close.

"He's not dead, Nickie."

Nick could hear the gurgling sound as the detective's life drained slowly away, spilling out onto Nick's living room carpet.

"Not yet." The laughter that followed sent Nick up the stairs in a panic. He scrambled over the steps. His breath heaved in and out. His mind raced.

I've got to get Jeff out. I've got to get Jeff out. That was the only thought in his mind running over and over.

Nick reached his son's door and threw it wide. The room was empty and his heart sank. Another loud clap of thunder shook the house and a brief flash of lightning lit the room. Jeff lay in his bed asleep, almost completely covered by the tangle of blankets.

A wave of dizzy relief flooded through Nick at the

sight. He closed the door and crossed the room in two long strides.

"Jeff." He shook him roughly. "Jeff, get up!" He had to hurry. The man could come bursting through the door at any moment.

"What?" Jeff's eyes fluttered open slowly.

Nick threw back the blankets. "Get up!" He pulled Jeff into a sitting position. He wore only a sweatshirt and underwear. Nick tossed him a pair of jeans. "Get dressed."

He went back to the door. Reaching out, he took a trophy from atop Jeff's dresser. He liked the feel of the weight in his hand. Slowly, carefully, he opened the door a crack and peered out. The hallway was empty. He heard no sound from below.

Where are you, you bastard?

He thought about going to the window and trying to call out to the many people gathered outside. But Jeff's bedroom overlooked the back of the house and Nick did not think anyone would hear him. And with the rain that was now pounding the house, he was sure they had all taken cover out of the storm.

"What is it?" Jeff asked, struggling to get into his pants before pulling on his sneakers.

Nick remained at the door, keeping watch. "Hurry." He glanced back at Jeff. "We have to get—" But the rest of his sentence was cut off as the door slammed open. Nick sprawled backward. The trophy tumbled from his grip. He fell against his son's desk, pulling papers down on top of himself.

"Dad!" Jeff's voice, so filled with desperation, seemed to echo off the walls all around them, reverberating over and over in the darkened room.

Nick struggled to his feet, straining to see through the blackness. Lightning flashed. The room was washed in white. Nick could see the man. He loomed toward Jeff, the knife held high.

"No!" Nick screamed, as the glint of steel caught his eye. The thunder boomed, drowning out his cry.

The knife drew downward. Jeff darted away from the blade. He threw himself sideways, knocking into his dresser.

A moment later the room grew black again.

Nick rushed forward, through the shadows that surrounded him, toward the spot where he had last seen his son.

Somehow, he managed to find Jeff in the darkness and grabbing hold of his shirt, literally pulled him from the room, slamming the door shut behind him.

"Outside!" Nick yelled as they stumbled through the darkened hallway, heading toward the stairs.

Halfway down, another flash of lightning lit up the room below. And the body of Alan Howarth. The detective lay on the floor, in a puddle of his own blood, his lifeless eyes staring out blankly.

Jeff froze on the stairs, his gaze locked on the body.

"Keep moving!" Nick yelled, turning toward Jeff. But as he looked back at his son, he lost his footing and tumbled head over heels the rest of the way down the steps.

Jeff watched his father as he toppled away in the darkness. "Dad!" he yelled, starting down the stairs after him. His heart raced. His pulse pounded against his temples. Even in the blackness of the room, he could see the dark form of the corpse that lay only a few feet away.

He's back. He wants to finish the job.

Jeff gritted his teeth, ignoring the fear that threatened

to paralyze him. He had no time for it. He had to get his father and get out of the house.

Nick was already attempting to sit up when Jeff reached him. "Are you okay? Can you stand?" Jeff knelt down beside him. Grabbing his father's arm, he pulled it around his shoulder and managed to get him to his feet.

But before they could take even one step, lightning flashed, revealing the man with the tattoo. He loomed over them. An instant later, the man reached out, gripped Nick by the front of his shirt, and wrenched him from Jeff's grip. Then, twisting around, he shoved Nick away, sending him stumbling back into the living room. Another clap of thunder shook the house.

The man turned back to Jeff. "Your turn." The knife flashed as it arced high above his head.

Jeff fell back against the stairs. The knife sliced within inches of his face. Panting, he scrambled up the steps on all fours.

"We're having fun now, Jeffrey!"

And as the voice rang out, Jeff thought he might go insane. For he recognized the voice. He had heard it five years earlier as it taunted and then murdered his mother.

"No! No! No!"

Jeff heard the word repeating over and over, echoing off the walls. It was a minute before he realized it was his own voice speaking.

As he reached the top of the stairs, he rushed forward toward the bedrooms.

"What now, Jeffrey?"

Jeff turned as he felt the hot breath against his neck. *How can he be that close?*

The knife flashed again, this time catching Jeff on the side of his arm, slicing into it neatly. He fell back against the wall, stunned. But as the knife raised high again, ready to strike once more, Jeff pushed away and sprinted toward his father's bedroom. A plan formed in his mind.

Nick slammed into the coffee table, his left side taking the impact of the blow, his temple cracking against the wood. He landed on his back, staring up at nothing, dazed. Moisture wet his shirt. Had he been cut? He didn't think so. Turning sideways, he found himself looking directly into the dead eyes of Alan Howarth.

Nick rolled away, repulsed as the detective's blood continued to soak his clothes. A wave of dizziness washed over him as he moved. He closed his eyes, willing it to pass. A bolt of pain shot through his head as he got to his knees.

He pushed it aside, ignoring it, and crawled toward the couch. Using the couch as support, he managed to stand.

Jeff. I've got to help Jeff.

He wiped a hand across his mouth. It came away bloody, but he did not know if the blood was his own or Detective Howarth's. Nick staggered toward the stairs. But before he could take two steps, a new thought filled his mind. Turning, he looked back at the body on the floor.

He knelt beside Alan and turning him over roughly, grunting with the effort, he searched the body, knowing the man had to be carrying a gun.

Slamming the bedroom door shut, Jeff turned the lock, keeping his assailant on the other side, even if only for a few minutes. With luck, it would be all the time he needed. He rushed toward the walk-in closet. He could hear the man as he pounded on the door behind him, trying to force it open.

Jeff did not hesitate. Opening the closet door, he stepped inside the darkened cavern and closed the door behind him. A moment later he lifted his hands over his head and began searching the air for the rope he knew hung there. As his fingers came in contact with the rough twine, he pulled hard. A set of stairs unfolded from the ceiling.

Climbing quickly into the attic, Jeff pulled the stairs up behind him. The attic had no windows; its blackness was complete. But as Jeff moved backward, away from the stairs, clumsily feeling his way with his hands, he did not care about the darkness, did not even notice it. He was safe. For the moment, he was safe. Reaching the wall, he pressed his back against it and fought to regain control of his heaving breath.

Nick stumbled toward the stairs, the dizziness still threatening. He could hear pounding from above. It spurred him on. Grabbing the railing for support, he began his ascent, dragging himself up one step at a time.

Lightning flashed as Nick reached the second floor. For an instant, he could see the man at the end of the hall. Nick raised the gun he held and aimed. His vision blurred. His hands shook.

But the man popped the door open before Nick could fire. He disappeared into the bedroom as the hallway grew black again. Nick lowered the gun. He could not take the chance of hitting Jeff by mistake. Moving more quickly now, he staggered down the hallway. His heart pounded against his chest, his fear high. But not for himself. For his son. He would not lose Jeff the way he had lost Linda.

Jeff heard the door slam against the inside wall as the man forced his way into the room below. He froze, staring into the unbroken blackness around him. He did not move, did not breathe, did not make a sound. He was safe as long as the man did not know where he was. But a moment later, when the stairs were pulled down from the ceiling and the low chuckle drifted up, Jeff panicked.

He did not wait to see the man who was now climbing the stairs. Pushing away from the wall, he scrambled across the floor, keeping his head down, knowing there were low-hanging beams crisscrossing the ceiling.

The rain on the roof grew in intensity, and the sound of it hitting the house was almost deafening. Jeff could see nothing in the blackness of the attic. He banged into boxes. Knocked over stacks of paper. Stumbled on the beams in the flooring. He fell and got right back up. Kept moving.

He tried to listen for the man he knew must be behind him in the blackness. But as the rain and thunder continued to pound the house, he heard nothing else.

He stumbled forward, his mind on autopilot. Suddenly, he realized he was lost in the darkness, unsure if he was still moving away from the stairs or if he had somehow turned himself around and was now stumbling back toward them. He slowed his pace, needing to get a bearing somehow. His foot caught in the spokes of an old bike. He fell hard, the bike falling on top of him. The handlebars hit him high in the right shoulder before smacking his cheek.

Reaching out, Jeff pulled on the bike, trying to untangle

himself from its embrace. "Come on!" he screamed when it did not budge.

A moment later his foot twisted painfully as the bike was suddenly ripped away and flung across the attic. It struck the ceiling once before falling with a loud crash, loud enough to be heard even over the storm outside.

Jeff lay on his back panting, staring up into the blackness above him. Terror stabbed at his heart. He could see nothing but knew with a certainty he had never felt before in his life that the man now towered over him.

Nick moved through the bedroom, his back pressed against the wall, the gun held out before him. But the room was empty. The closet door stood wide. Nick stepped cautiously toward it, his breathing shallow.

As he drew near the door, his finger tensed ever so slightly on the trigger of the gun. But the closet, too, was empty.

"Shit," he breathed, as the attic stairs came into view. His gaze shifted upward. Why the hell had he gone up there?

Reaching inside the closet, he removed the flashlight he always kept on the shelf. A moment later he climbed the steps. He held the gun in one hand, the powerful flashlight in the other. He did not turn the light on as he climbed, not wanting to reveal his presence too soon. But as his head came level with the floor above him, he clicked it on, sweeping the room with the light, the barrel of the gun following the white trail.

"Jeff!" he yelled, as the light crawled over the piles of boxes and stacks of junk that filled the attic. "Jeff!"

He swept the room again, back and forth, back and forth. Nothing. Only the piles of junk. He moved up a few more steps, trailing the light across the floor. Cold air wrapped itself around him, making him shiver. His breath plumed out before him. The rain began to subside. Nick cocked his head sideways listening. Nothing.

The attic was empty.

CHAPTER TEN

ξ

Thomas gasped; sitting upright on the couch. His chest burned, on fire with pain. He tried to catch his breath, gulping in air. He wiped a shaking hand over his face, clearing the sweat from his brow. His heart raced, and his stomach felt queasy. Standing, he made his way to the bathroom as quickly as possible and threw up his dinner. He flushed the brown-yellow liquid. As it swirled down the toilet bowl, he felt his bile rise. Leaning over the bowl, he heaved again. His body was racked with chills, but the nausea was slowly subsiding.

It had been more difficult than he had imagined but it was done.

He waited until his breathing became normal and the pain in his chest was a dull ache before standing and crossing to the window. The wind was still blowing, but the storm seemed to be dying down. He rubbed his chest where the pain had been.

Unlocking the window, he pushed it open. He breathed deeply, taking the crisp fall air into his lungs. It helped clear his head.

He looked to the east, toward the direction of Nick's house.

"Now we'll see how afraid you are," he whispered, smiling.

Would it be on the news tonight?

Turning, he moved to the VCR and slipped a blank tape inside. He whistled as he set the timer to tape the news. Later, he would watch the tape, maybe catch a glimpse of Nick's worried face on the small screen.

Just as he had done five years earlier.

It was only a matter of time now. All he had to do was wait. Sooner or later Nick would come to him . . . begging.

Evelyn Lambert opened the door to her granddaughter's bedroom. "Ginny, it's late," she said, stepping inside. "You should be asleep by now."

The room was lit by a single lamp that sat atop a small bedside table. It cast a soft glow, gently illuminating the figure on the bed. The girl lay motionless, her breathing slow and even.

"Honey?" Evelyn whispered. Leaning over her grand-daughter's still form, she thought Ginny must already be asleep. A book lay open beside her, Ginny's hand resting atop it. Evelyn slid the book off the bed. She slipped a small puppy love bookmark inside and closed the cover, setting it aside.

Still, Ginny did not move.

"Time for lights out," Evelyn said, shaking her gently. "Brush your teeth and then get into your pj's."

Again, Ginny did not stir. And for the first time since stepping into her granddaughter's room, Evelyn Lambert realized that something was wrong.

"Ginny," she said, this time louder. Grabbing her shoulders, Evelyn began shaking her, gently at first, but when Ginny did not respond, she became more insistent. "Wake up!" she shouted.

Evelyn was crying as she snatched up the phone and dialed 911.

As Detective Diane Nolan steered her car onto West Haven, nearing the Cross home, she couldn't help but glance at the detective beside her.

"Okay, Roger." She eyed him suspiciously. "What gives? Why did you want to come on this call with me?"

He shrugged, his large shoulders moving up and down. At twenty seven, he was the youngest detective in the department. "I don't have any pressing cases and I thought you could use my opinion."

"Give it up, Roger," Diane said, nearly laughing. "You think I'm buying this?"

The storm which had raged so fiercely only moments earlier now seemed to be ending, a light rain the only remaining evidence of its existence.

She parked her car across the street from the Cross house, unable to get any closer because of the news vans that now covered the area. Shutting off the car, she turned to face him. "Well?"

"I'm a fan. I just want to meet the guy." His smile was playful.

"I should have known." She glanced out her window and frowned. The reporters swarmed around the house, trying to see inside, trading stories and news clips. Vultures, she thought, all of them so hungry for this story without any thought to the people involved.

But as she stared at them, her gaze was drawn to something else. *Stella.* Alan's car was parked in front of the Cross home. Her brow furrowed. Why would he be here? But she thought she knew. Alan had a hunch that he wasn't ready to share yet. Standard operating procedure for him. He wouldn't bring her in until he was sure he was on the right track.

Not this time, Alan. This time you're going to tell me what you think whether you like it or not.

"Looks like the electricity is out," Roger said, regaining her attention.

Diane shifted her gaze to the houses that lined the street. "You're right. Must be the storm."

He pushed the button on the small glove compartment door and reaching inside, pulled out a flashlight. "I'm ready," he said, clicking it on and off, checking the battery.

Diane smiled as she looked at him. He was almost giddy, he was so excited about meeting Nicholas Cross. "You can come up. But Roger, this has been difficult for him. Don't slobber too much." Looking at the large detective beside her, she could not imagine him ever gushing over anyone.

She grabbed the flashlight from him, pushed her door open, and stepped out into the cool night. She walked slowly toward the house, weaving between the equipment and people that crowded the front lawn, ignoring the questions called out to her.

Stepping up on the front porch, she rapped loudly on the door before her. "I can't believe this has gotten so out of control," she muttered, glancing back at the crowd behind her. A media circus camped out on the man's front lawn. What a nightmare.

She turned her attention back to the door. No one had answered. She knocked again.

"I wonder if maybe they're trying to find lamps or something for light," Roger suggested.

She tried the door. It opened easily. "Mr. Cross?" she called, leaning inside. No answer. Clicking on the flashlight, she stepped over the threshold and into the house.

"This is Alan's," she said, touching the still damp coat that hung over the ledge. "Alan!" she yelled, skimming the light over the room, searching for any sign of the people she knew were inside.

Something's wrong.

She could feel it in the pit of her stomach, a queasy, nervous sensation. She had been a cop too long to ignore the feeling. Resting her hand on the butt of her gun, the feel of the cool metal calming her slightly, she continued to search the room with her light, moving slowly forward.

"What was that over there?" Roger said, directing her attention back toward the couch.

Diane shifted the light. As it came to rest on Alan's bloodsoaked body, she stiffened. "Get backup." she said, pulling the pistol out of the holster under her arm.

Roger did not hesitate. He moved back toward the door and the radio inside the car.

She advanced toward the body. Her legs trembled. Her pulse pounded an irregular beat in her ears. As she walked, she swept the room with the light, making sure she was alone. Reaching Alan, standing over his corpse, she focused the beam downward, illuminating the mutilation. There was no doubt he was dead. Her stomach tightened as a dark anger passed through her.

Why did this happen? Why did he come here alone?

She bent down toward Alan to feel for the pulse she knew would not be there. Before she could touch him, the electricity hummed to life, washing the room with light.

She blinked hard as the sudden brightness temporarily blinded her. But as she looked down at Alan, her sight clearing, she wished once more for the darkness. In the dull beam of the flashlight, she had not been able to see the extent of the damage done to him. Now, as she stared down at him, his intestines spilling out on the living room carpet, her stomach heaved. She breathed through her mouth until the sensation passed.

"Alan." She knelt down, her shoes making a squishing sound on the bloodsoaked carpet. His eyes were still open, the look of shock he must have felt upon dying forever frozen within them.

She looked toward the door as Roger reentered.

"Backup's on the way," he said.

She nodded, not trusting herself to speak, afraid he would hear the grief in her voice.

A loud crash boomed through the house. She jerked toward the darkened hallway above.

"Second floor," Roger whispered.

She nodded, already moving toward the stairs. Roger fell in step beside her. They could not wait for backup. The butcher who had slaughtered Alan so brutally would not hesitate to kill Nicholas Cross and his son. They climbed the stairs to the second floor together.

Quickly, they moved through the upstairs, making a cursory scan of each room. But as the master bedroom came into view, Diane's heartbeat doubled. The door hung off its hinges, the wood splintered on the left side.

Moving carefully, she made her way to the bedroom, Roger two steps behind. She stopped beside the door, her breathing shallow, tense. Leaning forward, she glanced into the room, making a quick scan of it.

"Empty," she whispered, pulling back into the hallway. A moment later something banged overhead.

They both looked up.

"Attic." Diane glanced in the room again. The closet door stood open. She hesitated, weighing the choices she did not have. "I'm going." She darted into the room before he could protest. Sliding on the floor, she took cover behind the bed. No shots rang out. Nothing moved.

She glanced back at the bedroom door. A moment later, Roger slipped into the room, throwing himself against the side of the dresser.

Diane nodded toward the closet door, telling Roger her intentions with a small motion of her head. He licked his lips, nodding his acceptance.

Diane stood and rolling over the bed, landed on the other side, now able to approach the closet from the back, the opening facing away from her.

Reaching the door, she peered through the crack at the back. She saw no one standing in the dark cavern. But the clothes lining each side could easily be hiding some-one. The stairs inside were pulled down.

A moment later, there was another crash as something toppled over above them.

Roger crept cautiously toward her.

But before either one of them could make a decision as to their next move, they heard the sound of footsteps pounding across the floor above them. Theirs eyes turned upward, following the journey with their gaze. Someone was hurrying toward the exit.

Diane stepped backward, away from the door, her gun aimed at the opening. Roger moved to the side, mirroring her shooter's stance.

"Police!" she yelled as the footsteps began down the stairs. "Stop where you are!" There was no hesitation. The man kept right on coming despite her order.

Both officers tensed to fire. An instant later, Nicholas Cross burst through the closet doorway into the bedroom.

"Mr. Cross." Diane lowered her weapon, her hands shaking. "Are you all right?" she asked, taking in the sight of his blood-covered shirt.

"Where's Jeff? Is he with you?" he asked, ignoring her question. He rushed toward the bedroom door before she could answer. "Jeff? Jeff!"

"Mr. Cross." Diane followed him into the hallway. He held a gun down at his side. It was only a moment before she realized it was Alan's. "Mr. Cross, wait," she said, when he did not respond. He was looking in each room, calling out to his son. She grabbed him by the shoulder, stopping him just as he reached the stairs.

As he turned to face her, she could see a line of blood running from his left temple down the side of his face. But the blood on his shirt did not appear to be his own. "Mr. Cross." Reaching out, she took the gun from his hand without protest. "I want to help you. But you have to tell me what happened."

He stared at her. Shock, fear, and remorse flashed behind his eyes. "I need to find my son."

She could hear sirens approaching as their backup arrived. "Roger?" She looked around for the big detective. "Go down and let the others in," she told him as he stepped out into the hall. "Mr. Cross," she said staring intently into his eyes. They did not seem to focus on her. "I need you to tell me what happened."

"A man . . ." His eyes darted from side to side. "He killed Howarth and then he chased us . . ." He closed his eyes, covering them with a shaking hand. "How could I let this happen?" He leaned back against the wall behind him and slowly slid down until he was sitting on the floor, his knees pulled in tight. "God, where's my son?"

"Mr. Cross? Mr. Cross!"

Nick blinked, the haze in his mind dissipated by the voice that spoke close to his ear.

"Can you stand?"

He nodded and a moment later, he felt an arm on his, pulling him to his feet.

"Mr. Cross?"

He turned and found himself staring at Detective Diane Nolan. *When had she arrived?*

She led him away from the bedroom, toward the stairs and the living room below.

"What can you tell me about the man that was in your house tonight?" she asked. Her strong, confident voice helped give him strength.

He took a deep breath, concentrating, trying to remember. "I saw a tattoo on his arm." He tried to recall the details, knowing how important they could be later. But his mind was blank. "It was dark."

He could see uniformed officers below, staring up at him as they started down the stairs. Two of the officers stood over Detective Howarth's body, seemingly mesmerized by the corpse.

"Hudson. Carlyle," Diane yelled at the men who leaned down toward Alan's body. "Get away from there. I want this scene preserved."

They reached the first level.

"You two check the attic," Diane ordered a pair of uniformed officers. She turned to Hudson and Carlyle. "You two check the second floor. We're looking for a seventeen-year-old boy. Check closets, under beds, everywhere." Her voice was curt, her words clipped. "Avoid touching or moving anything. This entire house could be our crime scene. I want it treated as such. Preserve everything. I just need to establish that he's no longer in the house."

"What?" Nick gaped at her. Had he heard her correctly? Did she really think Jeff was gone?

"Roger," she snapped. "Where the hell are the techs?"

Roger said, "Should be here soon."

And as if on cue, the crime lab unit arrived on the scene, followed closely by the EMT van.

Diane turned back to Nick. "Mr. Cross, do you need medical assistance?" She leaned toward him, staring at the wound on his head.

Reaching up, he touched it gingerly. "I don't think so." He was having difficulty thinking, unsure of what he should do.

Moments later the lab techs spilled into the room, carrying bags and equipment. After promising she'd be right back, Diane crossed over to the other officers. She talked with several, directing their movements, clearly in charge. They strung up tape, took out small plastic bags, and dumped microscopic evidence into each one. The scene was all too familiar to Nick. It was exactly as it had been with Linda. First, they crawled all over your house taking anything and everything they needed to catch the criminal. Then they left, never looking back, never giving answers. And he was left behind to clean up and try to move on.

Nick watched the commotion around him without much interest. Instead, he found his attention drawn to the stairs. In his mind, he could still see Jeff racing upward, disappearing into the darkness, swallowed by the shadowy hall above.

A brilliant flash lit up the room, catching Nick's attention. He glanced toward the large front window, wondering if the storm had started again. It was a moment before he realized it was just another police officer taking pictures of the crime scene.

Flash.

Alan Howarth's mutilated body.

Flash.

An overturned coffee table.

Flash.

A bloody hand print on the wall.

And Nick looked down at his own hands. They were stained with dried blood.

Did I do that?

He held them out in front of him as if waiting for inspection. He tried not to think about the blood that covered his clothes, slowly stiffening the shirt he wore. His stomach suddenly felt queasy and he thought he might throw up.

Flash.

Nick wiped his hands on his pants, trying to clean off the blood. It did not work. He felt flushed, heat rising through his body. He swayed where he stood.

"Mr. Cross?" A hand gripped his arm, supporting him. He turned toward Detective Nolan. The photographer who had been snapping pictures since his arrival stood beside her, looking at him quizzically. "Are you okay?" Diane asked. "Maybe you should sit down."

"No, I'm fine," he said. "Did you find Jeff?" But he knew they had not. Jeff would be here now if they had, standing by his side.

"We're still looking." She glanced at the photographer. "But it would help if you would let us take a few pictures of you for our files. Then you can wash up and change your shirt. Is that okay?"

He still felt ill but he did not protest.

The photographer, Jerry, moved into position, his jaw moving aggressively as he chewed on a large wad of gum.

"Okay, Mr. Cross, now just stand there with your arms at your side. That's right."

Flash.

Nick blinked as the light blinded him. Where was Jeff? Why hadn't they found him? How could he be gone?

"Now, hold your arms out in front, palms up first. Okay."

Flash.

"Palms down."

Flash.

Nick felt helpless standing in his home, watching the police search for clues to what had happened. *Flash.* He closed his eyes, trying to clear his head. Jeff will be found. Everything will be fine, he told himself.

Flash.

"Mr. Cross?"

Nick opened his eyes.

The photographer was staring at him, his jaw going into overtime. "Just one more and we're done, okay?"

Nick nodded. He wanted them to leave. Maybe this was all a bad dream and when they left, he would wake up and find Jeff asleep in his bed.

Flash.

His gaze drifted to the area where Alan's body still lay. The detective's left hand was sealed inside a small plastic bag. As Nick watched, another bag was slipped over his right hand. He did not want to see the damage done to the body. But before he could turn away, he noticed the man's eyes. They were open. No one had bothered to close them to the world around him. Nick stared into them, unable to look away, his eyes locked with the dead man's. He could see the fear and pain Alan had felt upon his death still so clear within them. But that was not what was holding Nick now, like two strong hands on the side of his head, forcing him to look when he did not want to.

Condemnation. It held him tightly in its grip. This was

Nick's fault. This man was dead because he had come to Nick's house tonight, trying to help him. And Nick was trapped by that blame.

A technician leaned over Alan, blocking his eyes for a moment. Nick looked away quickly.

"Mr. Cross?" Diane said, stepping in front of him, further blocking the grisly view of Alan's corpse. Jerry was gone. "Are you all right?"

Nick blinked several times, trying to clear the morbid images from his mind. "Why did this happen?" he whispered.

She took his arm again. "Maybe you'd be more comfortable in the kitchen." She steered him toward the doorway. "We can talk in private there."

"Diane," Detective Roger Clemens stopped them before they could escape the commotion of the room around them. "Lieutenant Parks just got here. He's looking for you."

"Great," she muttered, glancing around the crowded room. "Mr. Cross," she said, turning back to him. "Why don't you go into the kitchen with Detective Clemens. He can get you a clean change of clothes and you can wash up. I'll be in in just a couple of minutes to talk."

Nick nodded, overwhelmed by all that was going on around him. He watched as she disappeared into the crowd before turning and heading into the kitchen.

"Lieutenant Parks," Diane said, approaching her supervisor. He turned toward her stiffly. His styled hair and expensive suit were out of place with the rest of the department people on the scene. "I heard you were looking for me."

He nodded curtly, his eyes narrowing. "What happened here?"

Diane wasn't sure, but she thought she detected a note of accusation in his voice. "We're trying to determine that right now, sir. I have—"

"Stop." He held up a hand, cutting her off mid-sentence. "You don't know?"

"No sir, not yet. The techs just arrived. We're still gathering evidence."

"You weren't here when Detective Howarth was killed?" He stood, his hands on his hips, his feet shoulder-width apart, daring her to lie.

"No, sir, I wasn't. Detective Howarth was work—"

"Stop," he said again, once more holding a hand up. She hated that about him. "Who is the primary on this case?"

"I didn't know Detective Howarth had come here. He must have—"

"Who is the primary on this case, Detective?" His voice was loud, carrying through the room. Several heads turned.

"I am, sir." She felt her face grow hot and hated herself for not being able to stop it.

"But you weren't here when Detective Howarth was here?"

"No, sir, I was not."

"So you have no idea what transpired before you arrived?"

"That's correct, sir." Diane spoke quickly, her words coming out in short, choppy phrases.

Parks stared down at the floor, seeming to study the pattern of the carpeting under his expensive shoes. "This is not the first time you were not on the scene with a second officer, and now Detective Howarth has paid for those tactics."

"Sir, you cannot blame me for Detective Howarth's

death," she said, her voice rising above the commotion of the room. Again several sets of eyes turned toward the twosome in the corner.

Lieutenant Parks's gaze swept the room, stopping on several officers. "There will be an internal investigation into your skills and judgment as a detective. We will decide the actual charges later. For now, I want to talk with Mr. Cross."

Diane's mouth clamped shut. She could say nothing more here. Not now. She had already shot her mouth off too much. She probably could have gotten off with a verbal warning if she had just nodded and said "yes, sir." Normally, Alan was there keeping her in line, keeping her under control. She felt warm tears build up behind her eyes. *Alan.* She closed her eyes and swallowed her emotions. She could not lose control, not now. She would lose every shred of credibility she had. Instead, she turned and led the way into the kitchen.

They sat at the table. Nick had changed into a clean, white shirt, his old one stuffed into a large paper evidence bag. He had also finally been allowed to wash. But he had done it hastily and his hands and the lower part of his arms still showed some of the reddish-brown of Detective Howarth's blood. No one noticed.

"You said that Detective Howarth came here tonight to talk to you about Bevin. Is that right?" Diane asked, looking over the notes she had taken so far.

"Yes. He said something about Bevin changing his name, but he didn't have all the information with him." He leaned back in his chair, trying to see into the living room.

"Mr. Cross," Lieutenant Parks said, bringing Nick's

attention back to the kitchen. "Try and forget about what's going on in there. We need you here right now."

Nick nodded, turning his gaze back to Diane.

"I came here tonight because I had some very specific information for you." She pulled out her notes. "I got the file on your wife's murder in Chicago and found some. . . ." She paused, trying to find the right words. "Some of the evidence clearly matches your case now."

His eyes widened. "What?"

Diane took a deep breath. "The prints on the knife left at your wife's murder match those found on the knife left by Daniel."

She continued talking, but her voice sounded very distant to Nick, as if coming though a large hollow tube. He had been right. The man who had murdered Linda so long ago had come back and had been in their house tonight. "Jeff," he murmured. Where was he? What had happened to him?

Diane reached out and gripped his arm. "Mr. Cross?"

His eyes found hers. "Are you sure," he said, his voice a whisper. "Absolutely sure?"

She nodded. "The knives he used each time are the same. I'm sorry."

"My son . . ." He stared ahead, focusing on nothing. "This man has my son." He turned to Diane, his voice pleading. "Why? I don't understand."

"Mr. Cross, I know you're upset," Lieutenant Parks said, his voice devoid of any actual emotion. "But you won't do your son any good if you get hysterical."

"What good are you doing him?" Nick yelled.

"You don't understand," Parks began.

"No, I don't. This is a waste of time."

"Mr. Cross, please—"

"I have to get out of here." He stood.

Diane stood with him. "I feel as frustrated as you do," she said, her voice low. "I don't want to sit here doing this any more than you do. But we have to. We need some answers or we won't catch this bastard."

"I don't have any answers!" he shouted. "This is a waste of time. You should be out looking for Jeff."

Lieutenant Parks said, "That's what we're trying to do."

"No you're not. You're just sitting around talking."

"We have canine out right now checking the area around your house for any kind of fresh scent," Diane explained. "We have helicopters searching the nearby woods with heat-seeking devices. We have a special alert bulletin out to all neighboring police. We're in the process of trying to get a phone tap—"

"I'm sorry." Nick raised his hand, stopping her. "I just feel like I should be doing something.

"You are doing something," she said. "You're trying to help us piece together this puzzle. Please." She gestured toward his chair. Sighing, he sat down. "You describe this man as muscular," Diane continued, "with a very distinct tattoo on his arm. What about his face?"

"I couldn't see it, but something . . ." he paused. "Something about him was familiar. I just . . ."

There was a sudden flash of light. Diane turned toward the sliding glass door as a second flash lit up the room. A reporter stood in the yard, peering through the glass.

"Goddammit!" Going to the window, she pulled the shades closed. She stormed out of the room, shouting at someone to get the goddamn press out of the backyard.

Lieutenant Parks turned to Nick. "Maybe we should move this down to the station. We can get a formal statement and you could look through some books. You said something was familiar. Maybe you'd recognize someone."

"I don't want to leave the house."

"You can't do any more good here," he said, straightening his tie and smoothing his hair into place. "We'll have officers inside until you get back. It'll take them all night as it is."

Diane came back into the kitchen. "I've got a few uniforms posted next to the side gates. Won't happen again." She sat down again. "Where were we?"

"Mr. Cross has decided to finish this downtown," Parks said, rising from his seat and buttoning his jacket closed.

Diane's brow furrowed. "Have you seen the pack of reporters outside?" Looking at Nick, she said, "Do you really want to walk through them?"

Nick opened his mouth but before he could speak, Lieutenant Parks said, "We'll be with him. It'll be fine." Reaching down, he pulled Nick to his feet. "Don't worry, I'll handle the reporters." He glanced at his reflection in the window over the sink, putting a stray piece of hair back in place.

Diane didn't like it. There was no reason to pull Nick through that crowd outside. She glanced at Parks. He wanted the publicity. That was obvious. But she couldn't believe he was willing to put Nick through this just to get a few minutes of airtime on the local news.

She glanced at Nick. He looked dead on his feet, his skin a pale white. She knew he was not up for this. "You don't have to do this," she said when they reached the front door.

"He's fine, Detective." Parks glared at her.

The plan was simple enough. Roger would go first,

clear a path through the reporters, and then make sure the street was clear for their car to get through.

Lieutenant Parks and Diane would lead Nick, one on each side, answering as few questions as possible.

They stood at the front door.

Diane turned to Nick. "Ready?"

"I guess," he said, but he did not sound ready at all.

She took his arm. It shook slightly in her grip.

This isn't right. He can't do this.

"Lieutenant," she said, finally finding the courage to say what she had been feeling all along. Parks seemed not to hear her. Without hesitating, he reached out and pulled the door wide. Immediately powerful lights snapped on and the reporters swarmed forward.

"Mr. Cross, who was that . . ."

". . . reports of a second body . . ."

". . . any response you can . . ."

Diane did her best to try and steer Nick through the crowd of persistent reporters who were shoving, shouldering, and jockeying for the best position. But as she emerged from the crowd, she realized Nick and Parks were no longer with her.

Turning, she saw them both drowning in a sea of microphones and cameras, each question from one reporter spurring on another. Even the light drizzle of rain that still fell did not discourage them.

She glanced in Roger's direction but he was busy trying to get the street cleared. She had no choice. Shoving hard, she waded back into the crowd.

"Mr. Cross will give a statement tomorrow," Lieutenant Parks shouted, trying to be heard above the noise. "This has been a difficult experience for him." He was no longer trying to move through the crowd. Instead, he stood beside Nick, turning in each direction, making sure his face was captured by every camera at every angle. As Diane drew up next to Nick, she could see relief register on his face at her reappearance.

"Let's go," she said, trying to pull him forward. But the crowd pressed against them, blocking their way. One woman stood out from the others. Early thirties, small, feminine-looking. She was out of place with the rest of them. Diane was sure she was not a reporter. She kept reaching toward Nick, grabbing at him. Diane shifted closer to her, placing herself between Nick and the woman.

"We have no comment," Diane said, cutting off the lieutenant's words, her voice booming over the crowd. The reporters turned their mikes away from Parks and toward her, ready for any tidbit.

Diane pulled Nick forward again but when she looked at his face, she did not see the relief that had been there only moments earlier. Instead, his face was frozen in a look that could only be described as panic.

"That's him." He spoke so quietly she did not hear him the first time.

"What?" She turned and looked in the direction he was now pointing.

"That's the guy!" he shouted, shoving at the reporters all around him. "That's him!"

Diane heard him clearly that time.

"Roger!" she cried, spotting the large detective. He did not respond, but simply continued to direct the cars off the street, completely oblivious to the man who stood less than twenty feet away from him, the man with the snake tattoo on his arm.

She looked around for Parks, hoping to get help from him. But he had been swallowed up by the crowd, left behind somewhere.

"Roger!" Diane tried again, looking around wildly. What could she do? "Roger!"

"Diane!" he yelled, turning and heading for her, ready to help with the crowd.

"No!" she yelled. "Go back!" How could he have misinterpreted her so completely? She pointed over his shoulder. "Get him. Grab that guy!" But it was already too late.

A moment later, Diane heard Nick yell "No!" as the man walked up to one of the many news vans parked in the street and slipped inside.

Nick became frenzied. He knocked people aside, desperate to reach the van, panicking at the sight of Jeff's captor simply driving away. Reporters fell over their equipment, pulling down others, the microphone cords tripping them even more.

"Stop him!" Nick yelled.

Dave Belmore from Channel Six tripped over his cord, taking down Donna Provost from Channel Eleven. It was chaos and Diane was in the middle of it.

"Mr. Cross!" She moved forward, her sneakers sliding on the slick grass. "Wait!" she shouted, but in the next instant, something heavy banged against her left shoulder from behind, sending her sprawling on the ground. She pushed herself up, but before she could get her legs beneath her, someone tripped over her, falling heavily across her back, pinning her down and sending mud splattering out from beneath her.

She struggled to find a footing but before she could move, a sharp pain shot through her hand. She cried out as a high heel dug deeply into her flesh.

"Diane!"

She felt strong hands grip her beneath her arms and pull upward. A moment later, she was being led away from the crowd, Roger's arm around her waist, supporting her.

"Where's Cross? What happened to Cross?" she asked, still not able to put one foot in front of the other and walk on her own.

Roger glanced around. "He's gone."

She scanned the street, a sinking feeling beginning in the pit of her stomach. "There!" she yelled as she spotted him, running down the street, chasing the retreating tail-lights of the van he believed contained the kidnapper of his son.

Diane began feeling in her pockets for the keys she knew they held. "I can catch them." She pulled away from Roger.

"You're in no shape," he protested, "You can't—"

"I can catch them!" she said again, moving around the Chrysler, using the hood for support. As her hands moved over the car, she noticed for the first time the small hole in her throbbing hand and the blood that was slowly staining the sleeve of her jacket.

She reached her door but before she could get inside, a hand fell on her still-aching shoulder, stopping her. Diane turned.

"Detective, I must speak with you. It's urgent." It was the persistent woman from the crowd, the grabber.

Diane pulled away roughly. "Talk to someone else." She slid into her car and slipped the key into the ignition.

Leaning down, the woman looked in the window. "I have something to show you." She reached inside her coat pocket.

Instinct took over. "Hold it!" Diane yelled. Using her wounded hand, grunting with the pain, she pulled out her pistol and aimed it at the woman outside the car. "Don't move your hand," she ordered, the muscles in her own hand throbbing anew with each movement. She could feel blood dribbling slowly toward her wrist. "Roger!" Her voice cracked slightly and she felt the sting of tears behind her eyes.

I will not cry.

She swallowed the lump in her throat. "Take care of this for me."

He also had his weapon pointed toward this new threat. "I got it."

Diane slid her gun back into its holster with some effort, wincing in pain as the strap pulled against her shoulder. A moment later, she started down the street, her headlights washing over Nick as he continued his chase.

She drove past him, pulling the car to the curb. Then reaching over, she pushed the passenger door open. "Get in!" she yelled as he approached.

In one fluid motion, Nick slid into the car, pulled his door shut and said, "Go!" his voice winded from the long run.

"What the hell does she think she's doing?" Parks demanded, trying to brush some of the mud from his suit. He stood in the middle of the street, watching Diane's car disappear around the corner at the end of the block. He spun around, searching for someone to give him the answers he wanted.

Roger stood a few feet away, talking quietly with a woman and looking at papers she handed to him. Parks strode over. "Detective," he said, trying to hold onto any dignity he could. "What is going on?" He looked at the small woman that stood with Roger.

"Sir?" he asked, unsure of what the lieutenant wanted to hear.

"What are you doing?" He eyed the young woman.

"This woman claims she can help with the case, sir." He handed over the drawings.

"My name is Miriam Cramer," she said. "I must talk to Nicholas Cross."

"He spotted us. Damn!" Diane accelerated, matching the van's speed.

"So what?" Nick said from beside her. "I just want to get Jeff back."

"Yeah, but now he'll take chances to get away. Before he had no reason to drive unsafely. Now he does and with this slick pavement . . ." She let the sentence drop off.

Nick's eyes widened with realization as her words sunk in. "Maybe we should—" But the sentence was cut short as Diane swerved around a corner and Nick was thrown painfully against his door, his already aching head knocking against the window.

"Shit," she cursed, struggling with the wheel, trying to regain control of the situation. But as the back tires of the car continued to skid sideways, Nick was sure they would slam into the Chevy pickup parked on the side of the road less than ten feet away. Just before they should have collided with the parked vehicle, Diane managed to get the car under control and only clipped the front fender of the truck with the back fender of their own car. With little effort, she was once more on the trail of the van ahead.

Nick was grateful for the absence of traffic on the road. The few cars they did pass were moving slowly, the slick pavement giving them cause for concern. Twice angry drivers flipped them off, honking and yelling obscenities as first the van and then the car following it sped past.

She wove through the traffic with practiced ease, the wet pavement no longer seeming to be a problem for her. Reaching out suddenly, Diane plucked the radio mike from her dash. "724 to 50DB," she said.

Nick watched as she drove the car and talked into the small instrument. He couldn't help but wish she had asked him to do the talking.

"Go ahead, 724," came the short reply.

She released the mike, letting it fall to the floor as the car threatened to skid again. "Goddamn," she uttered, and corrected the problem easily.

Nick scooped up the mike before she could. "What do you want me to say?"

"Tell them we are in pursuit of a late model white Ford van, license number Sierra Victor Kilo 943."

Nick repeated the information just as she had relayed it.

"We have your position, 724," came the clipped response.

"Tell them to get someone out at the freeway ramps—75 and 94." Diane spoke quickly. "Tell them that I think that is where the guy is headed."

Nick nodded, "Okay," he said, taking in the information. He pushed the button on the side of the mike, "Dispatch . . ."

"Tell him to have them blocked off," Diane continued, never giving Nick a chance to speak. "I—Shit!" An instant later, an oil patch in the road sent them into a 360-degree spin. She jerked the wheel into the spin, trying to stop the car. "Hold on!"

Nick did, realizing for the first time that neither of them had bothered to put on their seat belts. He braced his feet against the floor, his arms locked against the dash. He strained to hold on as he was pulled first toward

Diane and then back against his own door. When finally the car did stop, suddenly and without any loud crunch of metal or shattering of glass, he was shocked. They were fine, the car stalled less than ten feet from a ditch, twenty feet off the road itself.

Diane's knuckles were white where she gripped the steering wheel. She blew out a breath of relief. "You okay?"

Nick nodded. "Yeah." He released his grip on the panel before him, almost expecting to see indentations where his fingers had been. "Let's get going."

Diane hesitated for only a moment before starting the car and steering slowly, carefully back to the road. "We may have lost—"

"Don't say it. We'll find him." Nick's eyes darted back and forth, searching continuously. "We'll find him," he repeated.

CHAPTER ELEVEN

ξ

watched the late news. They were replay-
d made earlier that night.

s house, flanked by two police officers.
obbed him, calling out questions, shoving
m his face. Thomas leaned forward in antici-
had already seen the tape two other times but
it didn't matter. Each time he viewed it, he felt himself
grow more and more excited. He smiled as he watched
Nick suddenly lash out, shoving through the crowd. He
laughed as the chaos worsened and people began tripping
over each other, falling to the ground.

"We still have no idea what set Mr. Cross off," the
reporter on the scene said as the tape ended. "We're
checking into—"

Thomas muted the volume. He had seen more than
enough. Leaning back in his chair, he felt satisfied with
the day's events.

The detective was out of the way. The boy was his.
And soon Nick would be knocking on his door.

Nick stared out the window, searching for the van. Twice
in the last two hours he had asked Diane to stop the

car, both times sure he'd spotted the van, first parked in someone's driveway, then tucked in the corner of a parking lot. But each time the sighting turned out to be a false alarm.

Now they were simply driving in circles, searching roads they had already been down before.

It had been forty minutes since their last contact with Lieutenant Parks. He had called them steadily for the first hour, trying to convince Nick to come back. He wanted them to come to the station, said he had someone down there who could help with the case. But Nick refused. He needed to be on the streets. Needed to keep looking. Needed—

"This is pointless."

He turned, Diane's voice cutting off his thoughts. "   to me."

"You must realize that he won't keep the van   ditched it by now."

His back stiffened. This was her third attempt at trying to talk him into giving up the search. He wished she would just keep quiet and drive.

"Maybe you're right. But I want to know for sure."

She sighed. "We can't stay out here all night." Signalling left, she steered the car down yet another road. "We should go to the station. You heard Lieutenant Parks—"

"I don't want to give up," he said tersely.

Without him asking, she slowed down as a half empty parking lot came up on their right. He scanned the cars. Nothing. No white van. No van at all.

"We're not giving up," she said, resuming their regular speed as the lot dropped off behind them.

"Take a left up here and we'll backtrack to the freeway," he said, as if she had not spoken at all.

With some reluctance, she did as he asked. "We have cars out looking for the van. We don't have to be out here."

"I do," he muttered.

"But you heard the lieutenant. He has someone at the station he thinks could help. This could be what we're looking for. Give me an hour—"

"I can't—"

"One hour," she persisted. "If you still want to go back out, I'll be more than happy—"

"I can't give up!" Nick's voice boomed through the car. He glanced toward her then quickly away, running a hand through his hair. "I'm sorry. I didn't mean to shout."

"It's okay."

"I just . . . I feel like I'm going crazy."

"I understand."

"No, you don't." He glanced out at the empty streets. The rain had stopped but he still felt its chill deep in his bones. "I wasn't there. Someone came into my house in the middle of the day and . . . he . . . my . . ." He could not finish the sentence, the words choking him, making his breathing difficult. For a moment, he found himself staring into his own eyes reflected back in the glass. He turned away quickly, unable to face the accusation he saw within them. "I wasn't there for my wife when she needed me the most," he said finally. "But I promised myself then that I would protect my son. Now, I've let him down too."

Diane glanced at him. "None of this is your fault. You did everything right."

"No," he said, shaking his head slowly back and forth. "If I had done everything right, Jeff would be here right now." He closed his eyes, leaning his head back against the seat. "He's always blamed me for what happened." In that moment, the last five years seemed to flash through his mind. The anger. The hurt. So much bitterness between them. So much unsaid. "I think if it were possible, he'd exchange me for his mother and you know what?" He glanced at Diane, his voice a hoarse whisper when he spoke again. "I wouldn't blame him one bit."

"You can't be serious? Your son may want his mother back but I don't think he'd be willing to give you up to get her."

"Jeff and I were not close before my wife died." And for the first time, Nick found himself admitting the truth behind his own guilt. "I was too busy for him. I kept telling myself that once I was really established as a writer, I'd get to know my son." He took a deep breath. "I never reached that point, never would have."

"You're not that different from a hundred other fathers I've talked to," she said.

"That doesn't make it right." He glanced out the window, the memories of his past suddenly so vivid in his mind. "Nothing was ever enough for me then." He paused. "Sold my first three books right in a row . . . didn't satisfy me. Made the best-seller lists . . . still not happy." He ticked each one off on a finger, counting up his past errors one by one. "Got a six-figure book contract . . . didn't matter." He stopped then, no longer wanting to remember his selfishness.

"You were just trying to do what you thought was best," Diane said, offering him an excuse to rid himself of the guilt.

Nick did not take it. "After Linda was gone, I was left with this stranger who blamed me for the loss of his mother and hated me for it."

Diane said nothing, offered no more advice.

"I should have never left that night," he muttered. "I went on a last minute trip to New York. Linda was furious. We had planned to take Jeff to the zoo the next day. Like I had a million other times, I told her to just take him herself or wait until I got back. As soon as I got to New York, I called her. I was always a great one for apologizing from a couple of states away." He shook his head as the memories of that night flooded through him. "She didn't answer the phone when I called. I thought it was because she was still angry. I thought she was avoiding me." He paused. "Later, when I found out the time of death, I realized that she was already dead when I called."

"This isn't helping."

"I think about Jeff in that house all night with her."

"Mr. Cross . . ."

"Our neighbor found him the next morning brushing her hair, standing behind her, brushing her hair."

"Stop this."

"It took nearly three hours to pry that brush from his hands. Three hours."

"Stop!" she shouted.

He looked at her sharply, pulled away from the past.

"This isn't helping," she said. "It wasn't your fault."

They drove in silence for the next few minutes.

"I always tell people that it takes a lot to scare me," he said finally. "But that's not true. You know what really scares me?"

"No," she whispered.

"The thought of losing my son."

"We'll find him," Diane said quietly, her voice determined.

Nick looked at her. She had tissue paper wrapped around her bleeding hand, the best bandage they could make inside the car. The front of her clothes were covered in slowly drying mud and her cheek was just beginning to show signs of bruising, yet she did not seem at all discouraged. In fact, she seemed more determined than ever. "How's your hand feel?"

She glanced down at it, flexing the fingers slightly. "It's fine."

"It was my fault you got hurt back there," he said, remembering the chaos he had created. "I'm sorry."

Diane glanced at him. "It's okay."

"What are the odds," he began, not sure if he could finish the question, but needing to know the answer. "What are the odds of getting Jeff back . . ." He paused. "Unharmed."

"Mr. Cross," Diane began, "I don't think—"

"I want the truth," he said, his voice holding a new edge. "Every minute that ticks by, I assume the worst. Linda's death gave me a new lesson in imagination. In my mind, I have imagined every possible thing that could happen to my son. Whatever you tell me can't be any worse, Detective."

"This is pointless," she said, not answering any of his questions. "I'm not going to sit here and theorize about what may or may not have happened to Jeff." Glancing in her rearview mirror, she did a quick U-turn. "This just isn't getting us anywhere. We're only a couple of blocks from the station and I'm going there whether you want to or not."

Nick did not protest but said instead, "If whoever has Jeff were going to contact us, he would have done it by now." He looked at her but Diane kept her eyes locked forward. "You know that as well as I do. He has no intention of contacting us because he has no intention of returning Jeff to me."

"We need to get more information," Diane said, passing

the car ahead of them on the road, her speed faster than the legal limit. "Then maybe we can begin to theorize, begin a real search. The man's not invisible. We'll catch up to him sooner or later."

"But he has been invisible for the last five years."

"You can't lose hope," Diane said.

Nick almost laughed. "Lose hope? The man butchered my wife five years ago. That almost killed me. I wouldn't have gotten through it if I didn't have Jeff." He covered his face with his hand, trying to wipe everything clean from his mind. "He waited until I felt safe again. Waited until Jeff felt safe."

"We'll find him."

But Nick didn't want reassurances. He wanted his son. And suddenly, he felt as if all of his energy was gone, drained from him in one split second. "I can't do this again. I can't look into every stranger's face I see and wonder if it's him. I can't go to bed at night afraid to close my eyes. I can't."

"I know how you must be feeling."

"No, you can only guess what it's like. You have no real concept. For months, I didn't sleep through the night. I got up every few hours just to make sure my son was still in his bed and that he was still alive. Even now, when I wake up in the middle of the night, I have to resist the urge to go into my grown son's bedroom to check on him."

"But it's not the same. Don't you see that?"

Nick turned wearily toward her. "What are you talking about?"

"Why the show?" Diane said, her brow furrowed. "Five years ago, this guy was completely anonymous. Never a clue that would help the police. Now, he comes right to your front door and announces himself. Why?"

Nick thought for a minute. "You're right. There would have been a million opportunities to get at Jeff without ever telling me who he was."

"So something's different now. For some reason, he wants you to know," Diane said, turning into the parking lot of the police station.

"Maybe," he said, slowly. "But I'm not so sure."

Diane pulled the car into a parking space and shut off the engine. She turned and looked at him, one eyebrow going up curiously. "Mr. Cross, I think he has planned this whole thing out very carefully. He wanted you to know because he wants you to chase him. And if I'm right then I don't think he'll do anything to Jeff. He's playing a game now. We figure out his game and we'll find Jeff."

Diane and Nick entered the station together and were immediately directed to interrogation room one. But instead of going into the room itself, they entered the observation area. Roger Clemens and Lieutenant Parks waited inside. Parks sat at the table and offered Nick the only other chair in the small room.

As Diane stepped inside, she glanced at the two-way mirror that separated this room from the interrogation area beyond the glass. A woman was seated at a table on the other side of the two way mirror. The grabber, she thought, immediately recognizing her from the crowd outside Nick's house.

"Is she under arrest?" Nick asked.

"No," Lieutenant Parks said immediately. He had changed his suit and once again looked immaculate. "I told her she could go. But she insisted on waiting for you." He looked at Nick. "Do you recognize her?"

He shook his head. "Who is she?"

Diane stood behind the others, leaning casually against the wall. This was Parks's show and she was giving him the room he wanted to work.

Parks glanced toward Roger, who was already flipping through his notes, lifting up the first page and reading from the second. "Uh, Miriam Cramer."

Diane rubbed her sore hand. It had been a long night. "What does she want?"

"That's the weird part."

Diane looked at the young detective. He shifted uncomfortably where he stood, his uneasy gaze sweeping over Parks. The lieutenant simply continued to stare ahead, his gaze locked on the woman in the room before him.

"Come on, Roger," Diane said, seeing the look and wondering why he was hesitating. "Tell us. We're all tired."

He took a deep breath. "She says she's a psychic artist and thinks Mr. Cross is in danger from a spirit or something." He looked directly at Nick. "She has some pictures she wants you to see."

"She's a what?" Diane wasn't sure she had heard him correctly. This was the reason Parks wanted her to bring Nick in? He couldn't be serious.

"A psychic artist," Roger repeated.

"What's a psychic artist?" Nick asked.

"She draws pictures of dead people. Says they just come to her." Roger glanced at his notes again. "I ran a check on her. She's legit. Been doing this professionally for nearly fifteen years."

"Now, Mr. Cross," Parks began. "I know the idea of a psychic is wild but we have worked with others in the past on certain cases. Not this woman." He indicated Miriam Cramer with a jerk of his head. "Or her type. But I think we should give her a chance."

Diane sat on the edge of the table, arms crossed. She studied the woman in the next room. Miriam Cramer sat quietly, her hands folded neatly in front of her. She stared at her own reflection in the mirror. Something about her unwavering gaze gave Diane the creeps.

There's something in the air. I can feel something in the air.

And she was sure she did. Like static electricity. It was making the hairs on the back of her neck stand on end.

"She knows we're here," Nick said, the tone of his voice seeming to mirror Diane's own eerie feelings.

Roger, who was still digging around in his file, looked up. "Yeah. It's rare nowadays when they don't know."

"But she can't hear us," Parks added.

"These are the drawings she had with her. She wanted you to see them." Roger slid three white lined sheets of paper in front of Nick.

"She drew these pictures?" Diane asked, glancing over Nick's shoulder at the face on the page. She could not believe Parks was wasting their time with this. "Who is it supposed to be?"

Nick held one of the pictures, the paper rattling loudly as his hands shook.

"Mr. Cross?" Diane knelt down beside him. The color had drained from his face and sweat stood out on his brow. "What's wrong?"

He looked up from the drawing and stared at the woman in the next room. "Who is she? Why did she draw this?" His voice rose in volume as he spoke. "What the hell is this?" He turned toward Roger for answers.

"She claims that the drawings are just coming to her and that when she saw you on the news, she knew they were connected to you," he blurted out, nervous under Nick's angry gaze.

"I need to talk to her." Nick rose from his seat so quickly it fell over behind him. Still clutching the drawing that was the most defined, he moved toward the door.

"I don't know if that's really such a good idea," Diane said, blocking his way. She did not think he was in any shape to talk to this woman. "We don't really know who she is, much less what her motives are."

"I don't give a damn about any of that," he said quickly, his gaze hard. He turned the drawing toward her, showing her the picture. "This is my wife," he whispered.

Diane was dumbfounded. "What?" She turned toward Parks. "Did you know this?"

"Mr. Cross," Parks said, ignoring Diane. "I know this is a shock but I've talked to this woman at length. I believe she will be able to help you." He opened the door. "I'd be happy to accompany you."

Nick nodded, taking a step toward him.

"I don't think this is a good idea," Diane said, once again trying to stop him. "Let me look into this a little more first." She shifted her gaze to Parks. "I just can't authorize this."

Nick spoke quietly. "I have to talk to her. I have to know."

Parks's gaze was on Diane when he said, "You don't have to be there."

Diane's eyes narrowed as she looked at him. That's what he's hoping for, she thought. He wants this case for himself. "Let's go," she said. She then added, "It's still my case."

Nick sat down across from Miriam, his back to the mirror they had been watching her through only moments before.

"I'm Nicholas Cross." He extended a hand across the table toward her.

"Yes, I know." She took his hand but did not shake it. Instead, she simply gripped it tightly in her own and held on.

Nick tried to pull his hand back but her other hand snaked out and fell on his wrist, ensuring her hold on him. Her eyes never left his.

"What is this?" Diane stepped toward the table, her voice tense. But before she could do anything, Miriam released Nick and dropped her hands on the tabletop. Nick pulled away from her, shocked by her behavior.

"I think this was a mistake." Diane gripped Nick's arm and began to pull him up from his seat.

"No," he protested.

"I need some paper and a pencil," Miriam said quietly. Nick noticed that her hand, the one that had gripped his so tightly, now twitched where it lay on the table. "Please, quickly."

It was only a moment before Roger slid the necessary tools in front of her. She immediately plucked up the pencil. Her hand began to skid and jump across the page.

Nick sat back down, his eyes locked on the paper as the picture quickly took shape.

Diane stood behind him, staring over his shoulder. "It's the same woman," she said, the face becoming somewhat familiar now.

"Yes." His shoulders slumped forward as if a large weight had just settled on him. "Yes, it's my wife."

Miriam's hand slowed down slightly, working on the small details of shadow around her eyes and mouth. "She's afraid for you." Miriam voice, eerily quiet, seemed to penetrate to Nick's body and vibrate off his bones. "Afraid for your son."

Nick looked up sharply from the drawing. "Jeff," he whispered. "Can you tell me where he is?"

Miriam's eyebrows knit together. Her hand stopped suddenly, the pencil hovering over the paper as if not quite sure if it was done or not. "She's afraid it's happening again."

Nick's mouth went dry. He swallowed several times. "What?" he asked, his lips having trouble forming the question.

Miriam set the pencil down, finished with her drawing. "She just keeps telling me to warn you, that she's afraid it will happen again," she said, choosing each word carefully.

Reaching across the table, he touched the drawing before slowly sliding it toward himself. He stared at the familiar face on the page. Her eyes bore into his.

Jeff's eyes.

Nick blinked. For a moment, it seemed the drawing had changed and that his son was looking up at him from the paper. But when he looked again, it was Linda, just as Miriam had drawn her. He shivered as a sudden cold stole over him. He was freezing, yet he could feel the sweat that rolled slowly down his back. He could not breathe, could not think. Looking up, he said, "Can you help me?"

"Mr. Cross." Diane squatted down beside him, her voice soft. "Let's not get carried away here. I—"

"Detective Nolan," Parks said, cutting her off before she could finish. "Why don't we just wait and see what the lady has to say."

She did not turn to face him. "Because I think this is all—"

"Detective," Parks's curt voice stopped her again. "I'd

like to talk to you in private." He stood and headed for the door. Pulling it open he turned toward her, waiting. A moment later Diane rose and left the room, her fists clenched at her sides.

CHAPTER TWELVE

ξ

Diane glanced down the hall, making sure they were alone. "Yes, Lieutenant?"

"I don't want you discouraging Mr. Cross in regards to this new lead," he said, straightening his already straight tie.

"Lead?" she repeated. "Lead?" she said again, a little louder. "You call a psychic a lead? I thought when you called on the radio, you really had something . . . something legitimate."

"This is legitimate." Parks's eyes locked with hers, his stare daring her to challenge him. "You heard Clemens, she does this profess—"

"I gave that man real hope." She ground the words out between gritted teeth, barely able to release them without shouting. "Do you have a clue what he's going through right now?"

Parks's lips curled into a half smile. "I don't appreciate you questioning my judgment. I am your super—"

"His son is missing!" Diane shouted. She had heard his "I am your superior officer. I expect to be treated as such" speech a dozen times before. She was not in the mood to hear it again. "Odds are, that kid is already dead. You know that. How—"

"Stop." Parks held up a hand.

"I won't stop!" Diane yelled. "You had no right to do this. It was irresponsible."

"That's not your call."

"Maybe not. But I don't have to sit by and keep my mouth shut if I don't agree with what's happening."

"What leads have you come up with?"

And then it dawned on her. Diane's eyes narrowed slightly as she looked at him. "You think this will play well in the press."

"That's ridiculous," Parks said, trying to cover. But Diane knew she was right. She could see him squirming just below the surface.

"Cross writes books about the supernatural," she continued. "So you want to use supernatural means to catch the bad guys. It'd make a great story."

There was a long pause before Parks spoke again. "Detective, I think you're a little overworked. I want you to go home and get some sleep."

Diane blinked several times. "What?"

"You heard me. Go home, get some sleep and come back tomorrow morning when you're fresh." Turning, he reached for the door.

Diane grabbed his arm and pulled him roughly around to face her again. "What are you talking about?" She was stunned, completely taken off guard. "This is my case. I'm not going—"

"Go home!" he shouted. Then, leaning in close, his voice low, he whispered, "I could have suspended you when I got the call about Howarth. I didn't. But I will if you push me."

Diane clenched her jaw but said nothing. He was her

superior officer. If he wanted to, he could pull her off the case. And that was the last thing she wanted.

"Go home," he said again. And turning, he walked back into the room, the door clicking quietly shut behind him.

Nick looked up as the door to the room opened. Lieutenant Parks strode in. "Where's Detective Nolan?"

Parks smiled, smoothing his hair back with his hands. "I sent her home." He walked to the table and sat on its edge, his arms crossed in front of him.

"But this is her case," Roger said, his voice clearly displaying his confusion.

"She was tired." Parks's gaze locked on the big detective. "She'll get some rest and be fresh tomorrow."

"So she will be back?" Nick asked.

Parks nodded. "As Detective Clemens just said, this is her case. However, I think she's taking Detective Howarth's death hard. I felt she needed some down time."

Nick heard his words and they made sense, yet for some reason he did not believe him. But it was more than just that, he wanted Diane there. She had taken charge at his house when Detective Howarth died, she had followed him in her car, and she had tried to catch the van as it sped away. She had helped him when everyone else seemed lost and unsure.

"Mr. Cross," Parks began, "I think Mrs. Cramer could potentially be a very big help to this case," he said, effectively changing the subject away from Diane's sudden departure. "If she is in communication with your late wife," he picked up the latest drawing, "then who knows what other possibilities she can open up to us."

Nick looked at the woman who sat across from him.

He wanted to believe her, wanted to believe Linda could speak to him again. "Do you think you could help me?"

"I don't know," she said, her voice low. "I can only tell you what I feel." She touched the drawing. "This woman, your wife, has been coming to me for days. Until today, I didn't know who she was."

"What does she want?"

She hesitated briefly. "She keeps telling me not to let it happen again. She was frantic to warn you. But when I touched you," she hesitated again. "I think I may already be too late."

"Too late," Nick repeated the words numbly. "What does that mean?" He thought of Jeff, running up the stairs and away in the darkness, the man behind him. "My son . . ." But he could not finish the thought.

"When I touched you," Miriam explained. "I felt a great sense of hopelessness and loss. I had never felt that before from her."

Diane sat in the room watching the people on the other side of the mirror. She had turned on the intercom system and could hear every word.

As she listened, it took every ounce of restraint she had not to burst into the room before her and stop what was now happening. Nick was lost, searching for anything and anyone who might possibly help him find his son. How could Parks allow this woman's influence? Couldn't he see the damage that was being done?

Her eyes found Parks. He looked so confident, so sure of himself. This was his promotion. At least that's how he saw it. More than likely, he would get it too.

Reaching out, she picked up the drawings Nick had left behind. Linda Cross. This woman claimed to be in contact with Nick's late wife. How convenient.

She looked up again, her gaze focusing in on Miriam. What did she want? What was her angle? Diane still did not know but she was determined to find out.

"My son is missing." Nick swallowed hard before continuing. "Can you find him? If you touch me again, is there a chance you could tell me where he is?" Desperation ate at his stomach. He didn't know how much he believed what he was now being told, but Jeff was gone, disappeared into thin air. He would try just about anything to get him back. He reached for Miriam's hand. "Please. Try."

She hesitated a moment before taking his hand in hers. Closing her eyes, she began breathing deeply. Her grip increased on his hand. He felt something, a tingling in his arm. For a moment, he wanted to pull away, frightened by the intensity of her concentration. But he didn't—he couldn't.

She released him suddenly. "I'm sorry," she said, taking several deep breaths. "I don't know where your son is." Tears stood out in her eyes. "I'm sorry."

"We can try again." Nick reached toward her. "Maybe you didn't hold on long enough."

She shook her head. "No. I'm sorry. This won't work." She wiped at her cheek as a stray tear slid down her face.

"But you don't kno—"

"Mr. Cross." Roger stepped forward. "It's late. Why don't we stop this for now."

Nick looked up at him. He could hear the worry in his voice, see the compassion in his face. He wanted to stop it before it went any further.

Nick looked back at Miriam. Her eyes were locked on the table, unable to meet his. "I'm sorry," he said. "I'm just ... I'm so ..." He felt his own emotions well up within him.

"It's late," Parks said. "Let's wrap this up. I think we'd all like to see an end to this day."

"Will you stay in town?" Nick asked Miriam. "I'd like to talk to you again."

Miriam nodded, seeming to have regained control of herself. "Yes. I will be staying for a few days."

CHAPTER THIRTEEN

ξ

Lieutenant Parks and Detective Clemens drove Nick back to his house. Some of the reporters had left, discouraged by the lack of information the police were supplying. Others were just tired. At three o'clock in the morning, when they pulled into his driveway, they drew little attention.

Nick trudged toward the house, his spirits low. Earlier, when he'd first realized Jeff was missing—really missing—he had hoped that they would find him, and find him quickly. But now . . . now he wondered if he'd ever see his son again.

Reaching the door, he fumbled for his keys, his brain having a hard time remembering which one opened the lock. Detective Clemens stayed behind, waiting in the car. Lieutenant Parks had started toward the house with Nick but he was no longer at his side. Nick glanced over his shoulder. Parks stood a few feet back, a small cluster of reporters around him. Nick could not hear what he was saying but he decided in that moment that he did not like the man.

Nick got the door open as Parks rejoined him.

"We're going to leave a unit parked in front of the house," he said, following Nick inside.

He nodded, stopping as his living room came fully into view. The room itself was in disarray. The carpet was stained from blood and some muddy tracks. The surfaces of most of the tables and door handles were covered in what Nick guessed was fingerprinting dust. And the furniture had been moved in several places as if someone had pulled it away and looked beneath and behind it.

His gaze stopped on a picture that hung sideways on the wall. It was the seascape, Linda's seascape. He walked to it and gently straightened it.

When they moved into their first house together, Nick had been in the moving van trying to figure out which room of furniture they should get out first when he heard hammering from inside the house. He'd rushed in just in time to see Linda hanging the seascape over the fireplace.

"What are you doing?" he'd asked, laughing at the sight of his wife reaching well over her head, nails clutched between her teeth, trying to hang the picture. "We haven't even gotten any furniture in here yet."

She had turned to him, dropping the nails into her hand. "I just can't stand to look at all these empty walls."

So it had become tradition. Whenever they moved, they hung the seascape first. Nick still did it, not wanting to give up that small part of her.

Parks walked up and stood behind him. "We'll need you to sleep in another room for tonight," he explained. "We've sealed your bedroom for right now."

"This was my wife's favorite painting," Nick said, still staring at the blues, greens, and golds on the canvas.

Parks nodded quickly, barely taking a breath before continuing with his explanation. "After we get a look at the evidence, we may want to come back and make another sweep of the house."

Nick walked away from the picture. "Whatever."

"Okay, then." Parks glanced at his watch. "I'll leave you to get some rest."

Nick sat down on the couch, rubbing his temples. "I don't think it'll be that easy."

"Give it a try." Parks's smile was wide and pleasant. "I think you'll be surprised." A moment later he was gone, leaving only the cloying scent of his cologne behind.

Nick closed his eyes, resting his head on the back of the couch. He needed to check the house himself, make sure there wasn't something the police had missed. But not now. He was just too damn tired.

Someone knocked heavily on the door, jarring him where he sat. He waited until the sound repeated itself before pushing himself up off the couch.

Reaching the door, he looked out the peephole and was surprised by who was standing on his porch.

"Detective Nolan," he said, pulling the door open. "I didn't expect you."

Diane walked past him, not waiting for an invitation inside. "I'm sorry. I know you're tired but I had to talk to you for just a few minutes." She surveyed the room. "They did a nice job on your house. I'm sorry. It's always a mess when they leave."

"It doesn't matter." But he was glad she had apologized, glad she had noticed.

"This won't take long. I came here to tell you one thing and then I'll leave." She stood with her feet slightly apart, her hands planted firmly on her hips. Her eyes were locked with his when she said, "Parks . . . the lieutenant and I do not see eye to eye on this case. I do not support his use of this supposedly psychic woman."

Moving to the couch, Nick sat down and leaned back. "Why not?"

Diane glanced at the door, then at her watch, hesitating. "I don't want to keep you up all night. I know you must be tired."

"You don't like Miriam Cramer," Nick said, trying to prompt her into talking. "You started to say why before Lieutenant Parks stopped you. I want to hear it now."

Slowly, she moved to the chair across from him and sat down. "I can give you my perspective as a police officer but it may not be what you want to hear."

Nick nodded. "I understand."

"I am speaking from experience," she began. "On two separate cases I've worked on, the family brought in a psychic. They didn't feel the department was doing enough for their particular case and they felt the psychic could do better."

"Did they?"

"In both cases, I would have to say no. To be honest, I don't think I've met one yet that's convinced me of anything. The visions they claim to have are no better than the clues we dig up. They're usually too vague to be of any real help."

"But the drawings—"

"She could easily get a picture of your wife. The rest of it is so vague. Watching any number of news broadcasts could give her enough information to pull that off."

"You're talking as if this is some sort of scam."

Diane licked her lips. "Mr. Cross, you're famous. Most people assume you are wealthy. This house . . ." She swept the room with her gaze. "One look at this house . . ." She stopped. "Let's just say, it would be a good opportunity for someone who thinks they can make some money off you."

"But she didn't ask me for any money," Nick said, hoping to convince the detective of Miriam's good intentions. He trusted her. He didn't know why but he felt she was genuinely concerned for him and Jeff. "She flew here from Chicago at her own expense just to talk to me. And there was no real guarantee that she'd even get to do that."

"She hasn't asked you for money yet," Diane said, emphasizing the last word, trying to make the point. "They start out that way but then they tell you how their expenses are adding up. Suddenly you're paying for the hotel bill, the air fare, the meals."

"It would be a small price to pay if she can help me find Jeff."

"But don't you see, that's the other part of it." Diane leaned forward in her chair, her voice fervent. "Right now, she claims to have some sort of link to your wife. Well, that's already a hell of a lot better than anything I can do."

Nick thought about the picture of Linda Miriam had drawn. He'd wanted to take it with him but she'd asked to keep it, claiming she might be able to zero in on her more if she held it and concentrated on her. That had given Nick hope—a great deal of hope, in fact. Now, he felt some of that hope dwindle. "So you think she's lying."

"I'm not saying that." She leaned back in her chair, more relaxed. She had obviously gotten through to Nick, hitting home her point, and she seemed satisfied. "I just want you to be aware of all the possibilities. I don't want you to pin all your hopes on her. She may be genuinely concerned but I just don't see how she can help at this point."

Nick leaned back, his head resting on the back of the couch. He stared up at the ceiling, letting it all sink in.

"I still want to keep in contact with her," he said after a time. "What if she can tell us what's happening? I can't afford to take that chance."

Diane nodded. "I won't rule out anyone's help. I just want you to go into this with your eyes open." She glanced at her watch and then stood up. "Listen, I think you should just get some rest. I'll stop by tomorrow, see if maybe we can nail this down a little more." She moved toward the door.

"Detective," Nick said, stopping her. "I just wanted to thank you. You've really helped me."

Her mouth turned up in the hint of a smile. "I'm glad, Mr. Cross."

"Nick," he said.

Her smile grew larger. "Not many people thank the police nowadays, Nick. I appreciate it." She left then, the door closing quietly behind her. Nick stared at it for several seconds until he heard the sound of her car start up outside and then pull away from the house.

His gaze shifted to the far wall. He was alone for the first time since Jeff's disappearance. He listened to the silence of the house, a feeling of loss settling over him, covering him like a shroud. Would this be it? Would he sit here night after night wondering what happened to his son? Never receiving an answer? Outrage crept over him, shaking his body, making him sick to his stomach. He felt as if he had been violated: his house invaded, his child snatched before his own eyes. He turned his head slightly and looked at the bloodstain on the floor, yellow police tape blocking off that end of the living room. How had things gotten to this point?

The man. Something about the man who had been in his house had been familiar to him. But what? Nick's thoughts drifted as he tried to remember. Exhaustion pulled at his mind. He couldn't think any longer, couldn't feel any more. He lay back, swinging his feet up on the couch. Old images flashed through his mind as he slipped into a restless sleep.

Diane was spent. She drove as if on automatic to her apartment, not seeing the roads and cars she passed. She was tired of thinking.

Pulling into her carport, she shut off the engine and stepped from her car. She stood in the parking lot, staring up at her second-floor apartment with its dark windows. Slowly, she walked toward the building, flipping through her keys until she found the one for the front door. She climbed the stairs, using the railing to pull herself upward, her legs feeling heavy and tired.

The living room was dark except for the light filtering through the blinds that was supplied by the security lamps on the outside of the building. It didn't matter. There really wasn't much to see. A small beige couch, two floor lamps set on either side of the couch, and a television with a bent aerial and broken volume knob. She spent little time at home. It seemed that most of her waking hours were spent on the job. It consumed her, giving her little time for anything else. Diane plopped down on the couch, dropping her head back and closing her eyes. She knew she should go straight to her bed or she'd end up sleeping on the couch, as she did so many nights.

But it was already too late. She couldn't get up. Reaching under her arm, she pulled her service pistol out and set it on the floor in front of her. Using her feet, she pushed her sneakers off and let them fall next to the gun. She swung her legs up and lay back, slipping one of the couch pillows under her head. She stared up at the ceiling, at the patterns the blinds made on the white expanse above her.

She should not have gone to see Nicholas Cross. She should have gone home as she was ordered. If Parks found out, she'd be written up for sure. But she couldn't let Nick believe everything that he was hearing. She could not let him think that this so-called psychic was going to find his son. It was the first time in her career that she felt an emotional connection to a case. Certainly, there had been other cases she felt strongly about. But with all of those, she had felt a desire to catch the bastard and put him behind bars or to prove she was as good a cop as any of the other male detectives.

This time was different. It was Nick, the victim, that concerned her the most. She could not let him go through it again. She would find his son for him and bring him home. She had to.

Miriam sat at her desk staring at her latest drawing, the one she had done for Nicholas Cross. With one touch of his hand, she had felt the depth of his loss, the intensity of his guilt and loneliness. She knew he was on the edge. His son had been the thread holding him together since his wife's death. Now, without him, the whole fabric of Nick's life was slowly unraveling.

But it was Linda Cross who had overwhelmed Miriam. She had come through strongly and clearly for the first time. Their life together flooded through Miriam, the love they felt for each other, the dreams they achieved together, the son they had shared.

And her fear.

Linda Cross was deathly afraid. And it was that fear that still coursed through Miriam's body.

It's happening again.

She finally understood what the warning meant. It was not just Nicholas Cross who was in danger but Miriam herself. The entity that had nearly killed her five years ago was back. Miriam had not told Nicholas Cross. She could not. Not yet.

Reaching for the phone, she dialed her home number. It rang three times before her husband answered.

"Hello?" His voice was gravelly with sleep.

"Bob," Miriam said, still staring at the paper. "I need you to bring a file with you tomorrow."

"What? A file? What are you talking about?"

"I saw Nicholas Cross earlier tonight," she said, trying to make sense to him.

"You got to see him?" Bob sounded surprised. "What happened?"

"I'll explain that to you tomorrow, honey." She did not want to get into it again tonight. She did not have it in her. "But I think what's happening to him now may be connected to what happened to me five years ago. I want you to bring my files with you. I need to check something."

"Are you okay?" Bob asked, his concern obvious.

"I'm fine," she said, wishing he were there with her.

"I'll be there first thing tomorrow."

Miriam relaxed slightly. "I'm glad." She paused. "I love you," she said, her mind once again turning to Nicholas Cross and his wife. They had loved each other dearly and something dark, something inexplicable had come between them and taken her away. She could not let that happen again.

Jeffrey Cross was cold, colder than he had ever been before in his life. He lay flat on his back. He could feel moisture soaking into his shirt and pants. His feet were numb. Slowly, he opened his eyes. His entire body ached as if he had fallen to the place he now lay.

It was night and he was outside. Soft, white snowflakes drifted around him, falling from the sky above, resting on the branches of the trees around him.

Turning his head to the side, he closed his eyes again as the blackness once more threatened to overwhelm him.

Where am I?

He could not remember how he had ended up in the woods in the middle of the night. Gently, he opened his eyes again, trying to focus on the world around him.

Maybe I'm dreaming.

But the numbness he felt from the cold told him he was not. Slowly, he pushed himself into a sitting position. Snow. The ground was covered in snow. The full moon reflected off the soft, white powder, lighting up the night.

What happened?

He stood with some effort, stumbling forward a few steps as the dizziness swept through him. He had no coat, just the sweatshirt and jeans he had pulled on in haste.

My father.

Someone in the house.

Jumbled memories flashed through his mind, out of sequence and blurred.

Where is my father?

In the distance, Jeff could see the outline of a house. Hugging himself for warmth, his teeth chattering noisily, he moved toward it. His exposed hands began to ache with the cold. He flexed his fingers, trying to keep the blood circulating, worrying about frostbite.

A knife. The attic. A tattoo.

Jeff glanced behind him, picking up his pace slightly. Someone had been in his house, someone who had wanted to hurt him. And suddenly, it all came flooding back, slamming into him with the force of a blow. He gasped, doubling over as the fear coursed through him. The man who had murdered his mother had been in his house tonight, chasing him.

He stood for a few minutes, trying to catch his breath, trying to figure out what was happening now. He looked around again. Visibility was poor; Jeff was only able to see a few feet in each direction. Was the man here now, watching, waiting, just out of sight? Jeff forged ahead, turning left, then right, feeling vulnerable and afraid.

In his new haste, he slipped several times, almost going down but somehow always managing to catch himself at the last second and stay on his feet. The snow increased, nearly blinding him. Jeff did not see the patch of ice until it was too late. He fell hard, rolling once, and ended up face down in the middle of the snow. The cold drifted away as the darkness returned.

CHAPTER
FOURTEEN

ξ

Nick sat at a table. The room around him was dark but a single light blazed above, outlining a two-foot area all around him. He could hear the noise of other people but could see no one. Looking down, he noticed a tray before him. Bugs crawled over the half-eaten food that spread across its surface, burrowing under a moldy bun and resting atop a small hunk of rotting meat. He shoved the tray away into the darkness. He heard the clatter of the dishes and metal hitting the ground. He tried to stand but found he could not.

"Do you like it?"

Nick turned sharply toward the voice that seemed to be talking directly into his ear.

"It would be a tattoo. A tattoo of a snake."

A man stood at the edge of the light that surrounded Nick. The lower half of his body was visible in the light. Nick strained to see his face but it was lost in the darkness.

The man extended his arms into the light, reaching toward Nick. "It would run up one arm." He traced a line up his left arm. "And wrap around his back before coming out the other side." He shoved his right arm forward.

"Who are you?" Nick's hands trembled. "What do you want?"

"It would be a tattoo. A tattoo of a snake."

Nick began shaking his head. "No. I don't like it." Something brushed against Nick's arm. He looked down. A snake wound itself up his biceps, moving toward his face, its forked tongue hissing at him.

"It's a tattoo. A tattoo of a snake."

Nick screamed, pushing away from the table, stumbling backward into the darkness. The snake bit at his arm, tearing out hunks of his flesh and devouring them whole.

"It's a tattoo. A tattoo of a snake."

Nick screamed again, swatting at his arm, crying out in pain as the teeth bit again and again. He was still slapping at his arms when he struggled up from sleep, gasping for air that would not come.

He sat up, rubbing his arms, trying to erase the feeling of the snakebite that was still so real to him.

"Shit," he muttered. Swinging his legs to the floor, he dropped his head forward and rubbed the back of his neck. A new goddamn nightmare. Just what he needed. When was the last time he'd had a good night's sleep? Only a couple of days ago, he thought, but it seemed like an eternity to him now.

He pushed himself up from the couch. He was done with sleep. Going to the window, he pulled back the blinds. The sunrise was just beginning to turn the sky a yellow-pink color. It was morning. Nick stared at the changing horizon, glad to be out of the darkness of night.

Turning from the window, he went to the stairs and walked slowly up them. He needed a shower or a change of clothes or something. He stopped in front of his son's room and looked inside. Everything was as it had been the night before. Jeff's blankets were half-off the bed, and the papers Nick had knocked from the desk were still scattered across the floor.

Nick bent down and began picking them up. Out of the corner of his eye, he noticed the photo album sitting beside Jeff's bed. Setting the papers down, he picked it up and began flipping through it.

Jeff's first birthday. His sixth Christmas. The day he learned to ride a bike. Each picture had a smiling, happy version of Jeff, usually held by his mother. Nick was very obviously missing from each one. The guilt settled itself more deeply.

Miriam sat on her hotel room bed staring at the morning paper, looking at the picture of father and son that topped the headlines.

A knock sounded on her door. She set the newspaper down and crossing the room in five steps, pulled the door wide. "Bob." She hugged him tightly, somehow feeling safer just having him near. "I've been waiting for you."

He dropped his bag at his feet and returned the hug. "I've missed you too."

They stood for a moment, half in the hall, half in the room just holding each other, glad to be together again.

"Did you bring the files?" she asked, leading him into the room. They sat on the bed together, Bob's bag left by the door.

"It's in my bag," he said, still holding onto her hands. "Tell me what's happening first."

"I'm not sure yet." She stood and crossed to the desk to retrieve the drawing of Linda Cross. Sitting back beside Bob, she handed him the picture.

"You know who she is." It was not a question. The detail of the picture told Bob that she did.

"It's his wife."

Bob looked at her. "Nicholas Cross? His wife?"

"Yes." She touched the drawing. "She's been trying to warn him but it was already too late." Rising from the bed, Miriam retrieved her morning edition of the *Detroit Free Press*. "Jeffrey Cross is missing." She handed the paper to Bob.

He scanned the story. "You think this is connected to what happened to you five years ago?"

"I'm not sure yet but it all seems too coincidental to not be connected in some way. I can't leave until I know for sure I've done everything I can to help these people."

"And the file I brought?"

She looked at her husband. "I want to go through it piece by piece. Maybe something inside will tell me what's happening now."

He sighed. "Then let's get to it."

Nick pulled a second photo album from Jeff's shelf. Sitting on his son's bed, he began flipping through the pictures. These were older shots. His and Linda's wedding, the first house they had owned, Nick's graduation from college, the first car they had purchased. He stopped, his brow furrowing. Turning back, he stared at the picture of himself standing in graduation garb, smiling like an idiot for the camera.

It's a tattoo. A tattoo of a snake.

And suddenly he knew.

Tossing the photo album aside, he made his way quickly to his bedroom. Yellow police tape crisscrossed the doorway, warning everyone not to enter. Nick tore it down without ceremony and going to the attic stairs, climbed up.

The boxes were stacked neatly against the far wall, CHICAGO stenciled in large block letters across the side of each one. He pulled the first one down and began digging through it. Clothes, books, and records were tossed aside in his frantic search.

"I know you're here," he whispered. And finally, he found it. His hands closed around the dingy green cover of his college freshman yearbook.

Flipping quickly through the pages, tearing them in his haste, he found the man. Tom L. Barker, his roommate for half of his freshman year. He held the picture closer, squinting down at the features. The photo showed a pudgy kid with greasy hair and a haphazard smile. But it was clearly Thomas Bevin.

Tom Barker. Nick had forgotten him completely. He had been such an insignificant part of his life. He had been glad when the introverted kid left his dorm room. Nick had made the mistake of telling him he was trying to write a novel and from that day forward he had been plagued by Tom L. Barker.

"Let me help you, Nickie." Tom looked over Nick's shoulder, trying to read the story Nick was writing.

"Tom, you can read it when it's done," Nick said with obvious annoyance.

They were in the cafeteria, Nick trying to get some writing done in between classes.

"We're supposed to be working on it together," Tom whined. "You said you'd let me help you and I came up with a great bad guy."

Nick sighed and turned toward his roommate. "Go ahead," he said as he had said so many times now. Each day, Tom came up with a new twist for Nick's book, a new hero, a new villain. He thought each one was better than the one before. But they were not and Nick simply humored him before turning back to his work.

"*Okay, this guy, he's a real bad ass biker type. With this huge tattoo on his arm.*"

"*A tattoo,*" Nick repeated.

"*Yeah.*" Tom nodded. "*It's a tattoo. A tattoo of a snake. It winds up one arm and around on his back.*" He turned around, showing his back to Nick to help illustrate his point. "*And then it coils out his other arm.*" He turned back to face him, his eyes wide with enthusiasm. "*Great, huh?*"

"*I don't know if that's going to fit into my story,*" Nick said, hedging away from the suggestion. "*Why don't you try and write your own book. You've got plenty of ideas.*"

"*I want us to be partners. I want us to write together.*"

Nick sighed. "*What's his name?*"

"*Whose?*"

"*This character. What's his name?*"

"*Bobby Tarp. Great, huh?*"

Sitting alone in his attic, staring down at the photo, Nick felt ill. "Bobby Tarp," he whispered. The tattoo had been so clearly defined on his arm that night. Even in the darkness, Nick had seen it. In that moment, Nick realized Diane was right. Bevin was playing a game with him, using that character from so long ago to terrorize him now.

Diane drove toward Nick's house. Two carryout containers from Yono's Family Restaurant sat on the passenger seat beside her. She knew from experience that in all likelihood, Nick would not eat unless she brought him the food herself and demanded he eat it. Reaching over, she flipped open the lid on the top container and pulled out a piece of toast. She was starving, and the smell of eggs and sausage was too much to endure without something, she reasoned, as she bit into the warm bread.

She glanced at the police reports tucked beneath the food containers. None of the physical evidence from the house had shown any connection to Bevin. And the information she'd found on Alan's desk regarding Bevin's name change hadn't gotten her anywhere either. As far as the department was concerned, the guy was clean.

Turning into Nick's driveway, she nearly hit several reporters that blocked her way. She tried to suppress the grin on her face as she watched them scatter frantically.

Harry Conner from Channel Three was the first one to approach her as she stepped from her car. "Detective, do you have any leads on the disappearance of Jeffrey Cross?"

Diane did not even bother to give out the usual "no comment." Instead, she gathered her reports and the breakfast she'd brought into her arms and walked past him, keeping her eyes coolly ahead. Reaching the front door, she shifted everything onto one arm, balancing carefully, and knocked.

Seconds ticked by.

She knocked again, this time trying to see in through the side windows. She felt her stomach muscles tighten. This was a repeat of the night before, the night someone had broken into the house and slain Alan.

She glanced around the front yard. Nick had to be here. If he had left, the reporters would have left with him, hounding his every move.

Something's wrong.

Setting her load down on the porch, she tried the door. "Mr. Cross," she called out. The door was locked. Panic swept through her. She should have left a uniformed officer inside. How could she be so stupid? She left the front door and went around to the back.

Harry Conner noticed her and followed closely behind. "What's going on, Detective? Where's Mr. Cross?"

"You're trespassing, Conner. Get back behind the police lines," she ordered, "or I'll arrest you right here."

Conner backed off but did not leave the yard. Instead, he watched her as she made her way carefully around the house to the sliding glass door at the back.

Diane could see it was slightly open even before she reached it. "Shit," she breathed, drawing her weapon as she approached. She glanced around the kitchen before pushing the door open with her foot and stepping inside. "Mr. Cross," she yelled, moving carefully through the room.

She didn't like this, going into an unknown situation without backup. But she could not afford to wait. Every corner she turned, she envisioned finding Nick's body gutted like Alan's, his eyes staring up into hers, blaming her. But as she moved through the house, she found nothing. She glanced toward the upstairs, her heart finding a new rhythm to beat in her chest.

"Nicholas Cross!" she yelled, moving up the stairs to the second floor, her back pressed against the wall. With every step she took, she expected to hear the loud blast of a gun going off, to see the barrel trained on her head. But she reached the second level without incident. The bedroom at the end of the hall came into view. The police tape had been ripped down from the doorway.

She licked her lips as she approached. Again, she had a sense of déjà vu as she reached the door and glanced quickly inside before moving over the threshold.

"Is someone here?"

The closet door stood open. She listened intently. But unlike the night before, she heard no noises from above. She moved inside and quietly climbed the steps, trying not to make a sound. She knew that as her head came level with the floor above she would be vulnerable. But she had no choice.

She rushed up the last few steps, her pistol held out in front of her, ready to fire. The attic was empty.

In the far corner, she noticed the boxes that were pulled down. She walked slowly over. CHICAGO was clearly stenciled on the side of each one. Kneeling down, she began looking through the junk that had been discarded.

"What were you looking for?" she muttered, holstering her gun. "What did you find?"

CHAPTER FIFTEEN

ξ

Nick drove toward the Bevin Institute for Psychic Learning, the address provided by the business card Thomas had given him three days earlier at the conference.

He'd managed to sneak out of his house that morning, avoiding the prying eyes of the press by jumping the back fence into his neighbor's yard. Then, borrowing the man's car and a well-worn hat, he'd simply driven away, just another face in the crowd.

Parking the small gray Honda in the lot, he pushed his door open and headed toward the large brick building.

He walked through the front doors of the Bevin Institute, the dingy green book he had brought with him tucked beneath his arm. After glancing briefly at the directory displayed on the wall, he continued down the hall.

"Nicholas Cross to see Thomas Bevin," he declared to the secretary in Bevin's outer office. "Thanks," he said, without stopping or waiting for her to announce him. He just pushed on through.

"Wait a minute." She followed closely behind. "You can't just go in there."

Bevin sat behind a large mahogany desk. He rose from his seat as Nick entered.

"Sandy," he said to his secretary, "Please call the police. I've had trouble with this man before."

Sandy left the office quickly. Nick could hear her on the phone. He closed the door.

"You don't have much time." Bevin took his seat again, his hands folded neatly in front of him. "Maybe you should leave before you get yourself into even more trouble."

"You're not quite as smooth as you like to think."

Bevin's gaze never wavered from Nick. "I'm sure I don't know what you mean." But the words were not sincere.

"Let's cut all this bullshit. I know who you are. So did Detective Howarth, although he had no idea at the time what it meant."

"And who am I?"

"Tom Barker." Nick slammed the book he had brought from home on top of the desk. It lay open to the page with Bevin's photo. "I remembered this morning."

Bevin picked up the book, staring at his own face. "I've come a long way since then, don't you think?"

"Where's my son," Nick said, his voice low.

"You are delusional." Bevin leaned casually back in his plush chair. "I was the one trying to warn you that something was going on, that your son was in danger. Or have you forgotten that?"

"Why are you doing this?" He had thought about that ever since he remembered who Thomas Bevin was. This man had no reason to hate him. He had been such a small and insignificant part of his life. But now, over twenty years later, he was back, trying to destroy what little Nick had left to live for. "I don't understand any of this."

And something in Bevin's face changed. His eyes sharpened slightly, and the set of his mouth became more firm. He rocked back in his chair, studying Nick. "I'm sorry you're having a hard time right now. But I cannot help you."

Nick felt the rage inside himself swell. He stared into the face of the man he knew was responsible for his son's disappearance and had to fight the urge to yank him out of his chair and beat him until he told him where his child was.

"Please leave now." Bevin turned his chair around to face the window behind his desk.

Nick stared at the back of the leather, his hands shaking at his sides. "Why are you doing this?" he said finally. "Jeff is only seventeen."

Bevin remained silent.

"Why didn't you leave him out of it? If you hate me, fine. Do something to me. Take your revenge out on me."

Slowly, Bevin turned around to face him again. A smile turned up the sides of his mouth. "Don't you see?" he whispered. "This is happening to you."

And Nick knew in that moment that he should not have come here. Thomas Bevin would never tell him where Jeff was.

"I saw the man you hired to be Bobby Tarp," Nick said. "We'll find him and he'll lead back to you. He'll give you up to save himself."

"So you do remember that story." He looked down at the yearbook on the desk before him. "I'm flattered."

"He's your weak link," Nick continued, hoping to intimidate him. "Once we have him, we have you."

Bevin's voice was faint when he spoke again. "He's a great character, don't you think? He should have been in your first novel." He turned his gaze on Nick. "But you

didn't use him. You never used any of my suggestions."
He stood and stared out at the grounds. "You know, I
didn't even know that Nicholas Cross, famous horror
writer, was my freshman roommate until I saw you inter-
viewed on one of the morning shows. There you were
looking so smug, talking about how you dedicated your
first novel to your pretty little wife."

"Linda," Nick whispered. He felt ill. His body began
to shake.

"I sent you a manuscript after that. I just wanted an
opinion." He sighed heavily. "I got it back unopened."

"My wife," Nick stammered, barely able to speak the
words. "You took my wife away from me."

Bevin shrugged noncommittally. "You stopped writing
after that." He turned to face him. "It's a shame you
started up again."

Nick did not speak. He could not. This man, standing
less than ten feet away from him, had murdered his wife.
Nick knew it, was sure of it. And he was in possession
of his son. There was no doubt in Nick's mind.

But why? Jealousy? No. Thomas Bevin could not have
destroyed Nick's life simply because twenty years ago
he wouldn't help him write a book.

"You know why I went to that conference?" Bevin
asked.

Nick shook his head, unable to speak.

"Because I wanted to see you face to face, see if you
would know your old friend." He sat back down in his
chair, glancing again at the picture of himself in the
yearbook. "Of course, you didn't." He leaned back in his
chair, rocking slightly, staring up at Nick. "When you
said it took a lot to scare you, I couldn't believe it. Twenty
years ago we sat in that same cafeteria and you told me
the same thing."

And suddenly the memory of that day flashed through Nick's mind. Eighteen years old, talking to his new roommate about his desire to be a horror novelist, bragging that nothing scared him.

"When I heard you say it again," Bevin continued, "I knew I had to prove to the world what a fraud you are."

"You've accomplished what you set out to do," Nick said, finding his voice. He tried to think of something more to say, something that would get him his child back. "I admit it. You've scared me. You've won. Is that what you wanted to hear?"

"Once, maybe, but not anymore." Bevin smiled. "You see, it's gone beyond that point, beyond anything I could have imagined."

"Where is Jeff?"

"I've been working on my own story based on the one we started together that freshman year." Opening his desk, Bevin pulled out a large notebook. "I remembered most of the details."

Nick stared at the stack of papers as Bevin began flipping through them. "What do you want?" he asked.

"The writing was going quite well," Bevin continued, ignoring Nick. "I just can't seem to get the ending though. I've tried several ways."

"You want an ending? I'll write you one."

Bevin looked up, smiling. "That's not necessary any more. I solved that problem. You see, Jeff is doing it for me."

It was the first time Bevin admitted any connection to Jeff. Nick's heart picked up its beat. "What are you talking about?"

"It's a shame your boy doesn't look more like you. This would all be so much more fun for me if he did."

"Where is he?"

"He's so polite." Bevin set his hands gently on the pages before him. "I liked him. It's a shame." He picked up the papers and began sorting through them. "Well, no matter."

"Tom," Nick whispered. His throat constricted. He was having trouble breathing. "What have you done?"

Bevin looked at Nick. "I'll have a best-seller when this is all over." He thought for a moment. "That is if Jeff survives, of course."

Nick lost control. He reached over the desk and gripping Bevin by the shirt, pulled him across the polished wood surface. "Where is Jeff!" he shouted.

The door to Bevin's office opened and Carl Neff rushed in. He gripped Nick by the back of the shoulders and pulled. Nick's shirt tore as he was yanked off Bevin and shoved away. He lost his balance and fell backward into the bookcase against the wall. Books showered down on him, knocking him in the head and shoulders.

"You're a fool," Bevin yelled. He slipped around his desk, putting it between himself and Nick. "Get him out of my office."

Carl Neff moved toward him.

"I'm not leaving without my son," Nick said, readying himself, his last unsuccessful encounter with Neff still fresh in his mind. But the punch came fast, too fast for Nick to react in time. He was hit high on the left side of his jaw. His head snapped to the side with the force of the blow.

Neff advanced again. Nick staggered backward, raising his hands in front of his face in an attempt to block the next punch. Neff was within inches when Nick lashed out. His fist hit Neff square in the nose. Instantly, blood began to pour down the big man's face. He backed off, his hands going to his nose, covering the wounded area.

Nick grinned, surprised that he was able to subdue him. He stumbled, a dizziness sweeping through him. He would have fallen if it were not for the arm that took his, supporting him.

"Are you all right?" Diane stood beside him and he realized it was she who was keeping him on his feet.

"Fine," he said.

But she led him to the couch in the corner and helped him sit down anyway. Neff sat on one of the chairs flanking Bevin's desk, holding his head back to try to stop the bleeding.

Bevin came around the front of his desk, jabbing a finger at Nick. "He barged in here shouting like a madman and when my associate tried to get him out, he assaulted him." He leaned against his desk and crossing his arms in front of his chest, said smugly, "I want him arrested."

Nick started to rise from the couch. "You bast—"

"Nick," Diane pushed him back into place. She kept her hands on his shoulders but it was her stare that held him in place. She leaned toward him and said very quietly, "Let me handle this."

Nick stared into her eyes. He saw the depth of her determination in her unwavering gaze. In that moment, he knew she was on his side—truly on his side—and he trusted her.

Straightening up, she turned to face Bevin. "If anyone is going to be arrested here, it's your associate." She eyed Neff. "He was the one on the attack when I walked in. Mr. Cross was simply defending himself."

"Mr. Neff," Bevin said, his voice terse, "was defending me. Mr. Cross attacked me a few moments before you arrived."

Diane turned to Nick. "Is that what happened?" she asked innocently.

"No." Nick's gaze locked on Bevin. "He called me and asked me to come down here. He said he had information about Jeff. Of course I came right here."

Bevin returned Nick's gaze. "You think you're clever don't you."

Nick did not answer. He stared at Bevin, waiting for him to make the next move.

Bevin's attention shifted to Diane. "You know he's lying but you don't care." He cocked his head to one side, his eyes narrowing slightly as he appraised her. It made Nick uncomfortable. "You're a surprise."

"I think," she said, as if she did not even notice the look, "we should all just lick our wounds and go home."

"What?" Nick stood. His jaw still ached slightly but the dizziness had passed. "I'm not going anywhere."

"Perhaps the police officer is right," Bevin said. He turned to Neff. "Are you going to be all right, Carl?"

The big man nodded. The bleeding had stopped but he continued to hold his head back. "I don't think he broke it," he said and his eyes found Nick. A new rage burned there. A new hatred for Nick.

"Well then," Bevin said. "I suppose this was just an unfortunate set of circumstances that escalated into something ugly."

"I'm glad we agree." Diane took Nick's arm.

"I'm not leaving." He wrenched free of her grip and took two steps toward Bevin. "I want my son back."

Bevin laughed. "I don't doubt that."

"Mr. Cross, please," Diane said, inserting herself between the two men. "I have to insist you leave with me."

Nick turned his gaze on her. Once again, he felt a connection to her. She had a plan and he was ruining it.

"You should get some rest," Bevin said. Nick looked

at him. A smug smile sliced across his handsome face. "This must all be so hard on you."

"Let's go," Diane urged.

And turning, they walked out together.

Jeff opened his eyes slowly, the lids feeling heavy. His body felt as if a million pins had been pressed into his flesh. He was on fire with pain.

Groaning, he pushed himself up. The snow which had been nearly covering him fell gently away. He tried to remember what happened and how he got there, but his mind could not focus.

Somehow, he managed to get his knees beneath him but found it impossible to stand. The harsh wind blew over him, cutting to the bone. He turned away from it, gasping, the breath yanked from within him. His body shaking uncontrollably, he crawled toward the nearest tree. Using it to lean on, he managed to get to his feet. His hands felt like frozen blocks of ice, the fingers stiff and useless. He tucked them beneath his arms, cringing at even the slightest touch against them.

His eyes focused on the house in the distance and he staggered toward it, using trees to guide him.

"One more step. One more step," he told himself over and over, coaxing himself closer and closer.

He fell against the front door of the house, barely able to hold himself upright. Raising a fist, he slammed it against the wood. Pain shot through his arm. "Please," he yelled. "I need help."

The wind gusted up, blowing loose snow all around. He turned away, pressing himself against the house, trying to shield himself from the bitter weather.

"Help me!" he yelled, banging on the door again. But as the seconds ticked by, Jeff knew there was no one inside. He staggered away from the door, using the house as support until he reached a window. Cupping his hands, his fingers protesting the simple movement, he peered inside. Dark. Still. Nothing moved. There was no one home.

He tried pulling the window up, straining against the locks that held it in place, his frozen fingers barely able to curl around the ledge of the windowpane. A strong gust of wind blew over him, swirling the snow all around, the bitter cold slicing through his clothes and biting at his flesh.

Raising his hand, he slammed a fist against the glass over and over, crying out in a combination of fear, frustration, and pain. Despite blow after blow, the pane of glass did not break. It did not even crack.

"I can't do this!" he screamed, collapsing to his knees. Crossing his arms over his chest, he tucked his hands beneath his arms and began rocking back and forth. "I can't do this," he whispered, squeezing his eyes shut, trying to block out the world around him.

But as the wind continued to howl around him, the snow grazing his body with its frigid touch, Jeff knew he had to get inside somehow. He staggered to his feet, his hands and feet painfully numb, the limbs barely functional anymore.

Stumbling back toward the front of the house, he scanned the ground, searching for something, anything that would get him inside. A heavy-looking pot sat next to the door as if waiting for the spring and the flowers that would be planted inside it. Dragging it to the nearest window, he heaved it up and tossed it through, turning his back as the glass shattered.

After removing the loose pieces of glass, he grabbed the ledge and tried to heave himself up. But he was unable to get a good grip, his fingers stiff from the cold. It took three attempts before he was able to pull himself up and inside. He fell onto the hardwood floor, landing on the glass fragments, crushing them beneath him. He lay there, breathing hard, unable to believe he was finally inside. Curling into a tight ball, he hugged himself against the cold that clung to his body and once again let the darkness take him.

CHAPTER SIXTEEN

ξ

Nick and Diane drove in silence for the first few moments, neither really knowing what to say to the other.

"I went to your house this morning," Diane began, slicing into the silence. "You must have left pretty early to go make your raid on Bevin."

Nick did not speak. Instead, he continued to stare ahead, his hands resting in his lap.

Diane glanced at him. He was wearing the same clothes he had had on the day before. He had not shaved, or, she guessed, showered. His hair was a tangled mess on his head. Whatever it was that made him rush out of his house that morning, she could only guess it was important. "You should have called me before going there."

"I know that now," he said quietly. "I appreciate what you did for me."

"Well, you're just lucky I heard the call or you might be sitting in a jail cell right now." They drove a few miles in silence. Diane tried to read Nick, tried to figure out what was going through his mind. She could not. His face was blank, giving up nothing. "So why did you go there?" she finally asked.

Nick took a deep breath and turning, stared out the side window. "I knew him in college," he said quietly. "I remembered this morning."

"Who was he?

"My freshman roommate. Dammit." He slammed his palm against the dashboard.

"What?" Diane asked, startled slightly by the sudden flash of anger.

"I left the yearbook behind. It had his picture in it." He ran a hand through his hair. He stopped several times, hitting the tangles on his head. He seemed not to notice. "I guess it doesn't matter now that I know."

"So you knew him before," Diane said, not understanding how this could help them. She stopped for a red light and turning toward him said, "That doesn't mean he had anything to do with Jeff's disappearance."

"He has my son." His eyes locked with hers. "I know he does." And in his eyes she saw a hatred she had not seen before.

The car behind her honked and she jumped slightly. The light was green. She accelerated away from the light, glad she no longer had to look into his eyes. She did not like what she saw. Whatever was happening, it was draining Nick of his humanity, of himself.

"Did he say he has Jeff?" she asked already knowing the answer before he spoke.

"Not in so many words."

Diane sighed. "In what words then. What exactly did he say."

In as few words as possible, Nick relayed his conversation with Bevin to her. As he spoke, Diane could hear the pain in his voice, the anger behind the words. In his mind, this information only helped to further his feelings of guilt. Now more than ever before, he blamed himself for what had happened to his wife and what was now happening to his son. She knew, sitting beside him, almost able to feel his misery, that she had to get his son back for him. She would not let him go through the agony of that loss. She did not think he could survive it.

"So you think," she said when he was finished, "that Bevin hired this tattoo guy to imitate the character from that story?" She mulled the scenario over in her mind, trying to make sense of everything he had just told her.

"Yes. He must have known that sooner or later I'd remember. He's playing a game just like you said."

"This is what we need," Diane said. "A link between the man who has been terrorizing you and Bevin himself."

"He has Jeff. I know he does."

"We need proof." She glanced at him. She could hear the excitement in his voice. She knew he thought they were close. "This helps, Nick, but it's still not enough."

"He said Jeff is playing out the ending of that book." He paused, turning it all over in his mind. "If he doesn't have him, why would he say that?"

"It's still not proof." She turned into his driveway, once more getting a small amount of pleasure watching the reporters scatter out of her way. "Let's just concentrate on the facts we have." She shut off the engine.

Nick looked out his window. A camera flashed in his face. He covered his eyes, turning away. "When are they going to leave?" he asked.

"Never," Diane mumbled. Pushing open her door, she made her way around to Nick's side of the car. The group of reporters moved closer, immediately beginning to call out questions. "We have no comment so just back off!"

As Nick stepped from the car, Diane caught sight of Miriam Cramer. She was getting out of a car parked two houses up the street. She walked with a man, their pace fast.

Gripping Nick's arm, Diane began pulling him toward the house, moving as quickly as was possible through the mob of reporters. She kept her eyes on Miriam, wanting to get Nick inside before she could approach him. His belief in her made Diane nervous. She did not trust the woman or her intentions.

"Mr. Cross!" Miriam called out as she drew near.

Nick turned. Diane could not stop him.

A moment later, Miriam stood before them, a man at her side. "I need to talk to you," she said, slightly out of breath from her attempt to catch them before they disappeared inside.

Diane opened her mouth to tell her this was not a good time, that Nick hadn't even showered yet. But he spoke first, inviting the pair inside.

Reluctantly, Diane followed.

"Jeffrey?"

He turned and scanned the darkness, squinting, searching for the source of the sound. A moment later his mother walked from the shadows and as she did, the room around her grew lighter and lighter. It was their house, but for some reason it was cold, so cold. She stood before him, hands on her hips, her face screwed into a look of disappointment.

"I'm sorry, Mom. I didn't hear you calling," he said, shuffling his feet, staring down at the floor.

She nodded. "I bet you didn't, young man." Grabbing him by the arm, she pulled him toward the stairs. "I want you to march up to your room and clean it up. And none of that stuffing everything into the closet and calling it clean."

As Jeff headed up the stairs, he heard the doorbell ring and stopped. Something tugged at his heart, something dark and bad. His body was racked with fear. It swept through him, shaking him to the bone, rocking him where he stood. He turned toward his mother.

"Don't open it!" he screamed. He shook where he stood, his mind screaming the warning over and over. Stop. Stop.

"Stop!"

But it was already too late.

Linda Cross smiled at her son and threw the door wide. The knife flashed, and blood stained the walls, the carpet, the furniture, and Jeffrey Cross.

"Mom!"

Jeff jolted awake, backpedaling across the floor, trying to escape the man from his dream and his mother's fate. In his panic, he did not see the table until he slammed into it, cracking his head against the hard wood of the leg. He fell forward then and landed on his hands. He panted, trying to get his bearings. Rubbing the back of his head, he looked around.

And then he remembered.

Closing his eyes, he fought back the tears that now threatened to overwhelm him. He wanted to go home. More than anything, he just wanted to go home.

Nick stood at the counter, slowly pouring water over the coffee grounds, watching the dark liquid fill the pot beneath. Miriam and her husband sat at the table with Diane. No one spoke. Nick could feel the tension in the room. He knew Diane did not like the idea of talking with Miriam but he was not ready to dismiss her yet.

The coffee finished, he brought the pot and four cups to the table. He was the only one who poured a cup. After taking a drink, he turned to Miriam and said, "What did you want to talk to me about?"

Reaching down, she lifted a small leather case onto the table. "My husband and I spent time this morning researching your background. I think our connection goes deeper than your recent troubles." She pulled out a set of papers. "Five years ago, I—"

"Five years ago?" Nick said, interrupting her. He glanced at Diane. She shot him a warning look he interpreted as, "Don't fall for this." When he spoke again, there was some hesitation to his voice. "My wife died five years ago." He leaned closer as Miriam spread the drawings out over the top of the table.

Each one was clearly of a man, the same man. But each drawing was progressively more clear, less shadowed. Nick picked up the most defined and stared at the face.

"Who is it supposed to be?" he asked. He handed the drawing to Diane before looking back at Miriam.

"When I drew these," Miriam said, gently laying a hand on each of the pictures. "I felt a strong presence. It sounds overly dramatic to say it was an evil presence but that's the only way to describe it."

"Five years ago," Nick said, sorting through some of the other drawings.

"A man came to me for a session. He claimed he wanted to make contact with his father. But when I touched him . . ." She paused, trying to think of the easiest way to explain it all. "Normally when I touch someone, I begin to feel a tingling from my shoulder to my hand as if the presence has come in through my body and is working through that hand. It usually takes several minutes before I can actually begin the drawing. But when this man touched me, I felt the presence the moment we touched—at the exact point his hand held onto mine."

"What are you saying?" Diane asked, picking up each drawing, looking at each face. "He gave you the presence?"

She nodded. "Yes. That's exactly what I'm saying. When he touched me, he sent something into me. In that moment, I felt as if a darkness had settled over my soul."

"And you drew these," Nick said.

"She only drew one," Bob corrected.

Miriam nodded her agreement. "It was very shadowy, very undefined. Usually when I'm drawing someone, their history floods through my mind. But not this time. I didn't receive any history, just bad, harmful feelings. Nothing about that session was normal. But none of that seemed to matter to the man. He was thrilled with the drawing." Her gaze darted down to the papers. "I was glad when he left."

"But you've got all these pictures," Diane said. "Did he come back for more?"

Miriam shook her head. "The presence never left me. Normally, I feel the person leave when I finish a session but that day I didn't." She smiled uncomfortably. "I told myself that I was just upset by the whole thing, that I'd missed the sign, the feeling he had gone. It bothered me, though, so much that I performed a cleansing ceremony that evening just to be sure that the atmosphere was clear. But that night . . ." She reached out and picked up one of the pictures. "That night was the first of many nights that I dreamed about him."

"The man in the drawings," Diane said.

"Yes," Miriam said, her voice cold. "He hounded me asleep and awake. It was as if he was trapped inside of me and was demanding to be heard." She no longer looked at the drawings, uneasy with the memories they brought back so clearly. "I couldn't continue with my other sessions because he would interrupt ... he kept ..." She fumbled over her words, unable to finish the sentence.

Reaching out, Bob took her hand in his and held tightly. "In essence," he said, continuing when she could not, "he began to push out any other presence that my wife felt. He began to take over."

Nick felt antsy. He did not know where Miriam was leading with any of this but he was suddenly uncomfortable. He could no longer sit at the table and look at the drawings. Getting up from his chair, he began pacing the room. "I don't understand what you're getting at. What does any of this have to do with me?"

Diane looked at Miriam. "Do you know the name of the man who came to see you that first day?"

She nodded. "Yes," she said, seeming to have regained control of herself. "But it was false."

"We tried to find him again," Bob said. "That's when we found out he never existed."

"What name did he give you?" Diane asked. "Maybe we can trace him somehow if it was an alias."

"He gave me the name Thomas Krausnicki."

"What?" Nick spun toward the woman, a flash of heat rising through his body.

Diane was out of her chair in an instant and by his side. "What is it? What's wrong?"

Nick gripped the back of the chair before him to support himself, afraid that without it, he might fall. "That's my name," he said, so quietly Diane had to ask him to repeat it. He turned toward her. "Krausnicki is my real name."

Diane guided Nick into a chair. "Okay. Now we have a real connection to you." She glanced at Miriam before looking back at Nick. "This is going somewhere. Who would know about that name?"

Nick shook his head. He felt overwhelmed, stunned. He couldn't think.

"Nick?" Diane touched his hand, gripping it tightly. He looked at her. "When did you change your name?"

It took him a moment to form the answer. "Not until I was published."

"Was it legally changed?" she asked.

"Yes. Before Jeff was born."

"So it was Krausnicki in college when you knew Bevin?"

Nick nodded. "He used to call me Nickie because of my last name. I should have put it together sooner," he said, his voice quiet, speaking more to himself than anyone else. "That's what Tarp's been calling me all along."

"You know this Krausnicki?" Bob asked. "You've seen him recently?"

"Yes," Nick said.

"We think so," Diane added.

"Then he must be using someone else this time," Miriam said, speaking directly to her husband. He nodded his agreement.

Nick turned to her. "What do you mean?"

"In order to catch this man, to stop him," Miriam said, "you have to first understand who he is, what he's capable of." She paused before continuing. "I think this man, whoever he is, is an occultist."

"That's what Bevin told me the first time we met," Nick said, nodding his agreement.

"So? What difference does it make what he calls himself?" Diane asked.

"An occultist," Miriam explained, "isn't necessarily psychic. He tends to be more of a directive force."

"What do you mean 'directive force'?" Nick asked. "He's in charge and that's all?"

"Possibly," Miriam said. "But personally, I believe this man has a limited amount of psychic ability. Just not enough to do what he's been doing."

"Which is?" Diane asked warily.

"When you work in the occult, you are actually manipulating cosmic forces, bending them to your demand. This can be taught to anyone. But an occultist cannot use these forces without also having a psychic or receptive side."

"And you were his receptive side five years ago?" Nick asked, trying to grasp what she was getting at.

Miriam nodded. "Yes. I believe so. He came to me because he wasn't able to release this presence on his own. He needed me to help him."

Diane's gaze bore into her. "So you're saying that Bevin has used and is continuing to use some kind of supernatural power against Nick." The tone in her voice made it clear she did not believe what Miriam was now saying.

"Yes," Miriam said, her voice serious. "That is what I believe."

"Makes perfect sense to me," Diane said with obvious sarcasm. "I'm so glad you've come here and explained all of this to us."

Bob turned toward her angrily. "Why don't you just hear what we have to say before dismissing us completely."

"Detective," Miriam began. "I don't really care if you believe me or not." She looked at Nick. "You know what I'm saying is true. I can feel it," she whispered.

"Give me a break." Diane crossed her arms over her chest. "You can spare us the theatrics."

Miriam continued, her eyes still locked with Nick's "I don't understand or even try to understand what I do."

"That's convenient," Diane inserted.

"But I know what I'm feeling," she continued, ignoring the detective. "You have to trust me for me to help you."

"I don't know," Nick said. He felt overwhelmed by it all. Was it possible? Could it be true?

"I think," Diane said, "Bevin wants us to believe he's using some kind of weird supernatural ability." She looked at Miriam and Bob. "I'll give you the benefit of the doubt and assume you're being used by Bevin to convince Nick, that you're not in this with him somehow."

"It's more—"

"But I don't believe any of it," Diane said, her voice loud, cutting Miriam off before she even had the chance to speak. "I think you hit it right the first time," she said to Nick. "Bevin is trying to scare you. You write horror and he's making a point."

"But what about Miriam?" he asked. "What about five years ago?" He stared down at the drawing he held, trying to sort through everything that was now flooding his mind. "We never met back then. Why would Bevin go to Miriam, use her, and then never bring the two of us together?"

Diane eyed Miriam. "You're assuming she's telling us the truth about all of that."

"That's it," Bob said, his voice angry. "We came here to help and you—"

"Bob, it's okay," Miriam said, her voice barely a whisper. She smiled at him reassuringly before turning to Nick. "Your wife came to me, trying to warn you through me. She kept telling me not to let it happen again. I didn't understand what she was talking about. I didn't understand why she was telling me this. Until this morning when I realized my connection to her."

Nick looked at her, his brow furrowing slightly. "What do you mean?"

"I told you I was drawing these." She held up one of the shadowy drawings of the man who had plagued her five years earlier.

Nick nodded. "Yes." He could feel the tension coming off of Miriam and it made him uneasy. What else could she tell him? What was she about to say?

"He was slowly draining me. I wasn't getting any sleep, I wasn't eating." She licked her lips, her eyes darting from the table back to Nick. "I became so weak. Nothing I did helped. I had no choice."

Nick's hands tightened on the drawing he held, the paper wrinkling in his fists. "What did you do?"

"I think this man, Bevin, I think you called him, came to me because he wasn't able to release this presence on his own." She paused. "He needed my help."

Nick was having trouble breathing. "And you helped him?" he managed.

"I think so," Miriam whispered. "I didn't know what was happening," she continued, her words coming out in a rush, sounding like a confession. "I couldn't keep it inside. It was killing me. I had to release it. I had to let it out."

"What the hell are you talking about?" Diane asked.

Reaching out, Nick picked up another drawing. "He killed my wife," he said, his voice low and emotionless. He looked at Miriam. "That's what you're telling me, isn't it?"

"Yes," she whispered.

"What?" Diane said, completely incredulous. "You think the man who murdered Linda Cross is actually an evil spirit of some sort conjured up by Bevin to do his dirty work?"

Nick stared at the face in the drawing for a long moment before speaking. "The man that came into my house was flesh and blood." His eyes found Miriam. "I saw him. He touched me."

"Many people have experienced phenomena such as poltergeists in their homes," Miriam explained. "These spirits open doors, throw dishes, turn on televisions. Some people claim they have been touched by these spirits, physically touched."

"Who really knows what's possible?" Bob added.

"No," Diane said. "Bevin did it then and he's doing it now. He's just very clever."

Nick did not speak. He sat staring at Miriam.

Diane leaned closer to him. "It's Bevin." She stressed the name, trying to convince him. "He's playing a very elaborate game for whatever sick reason. I know this all sounds good," she glanced at Miriam, "but believe me, it's not mystical."

"I'm sorry for any part I played in your wife's death," Miriam said.

Nick did not know who to believe. Looking at Miriam, he knew she was sincere in what she was saying. But could any of it really be true? He sighed, running a hand over his face. "So where do we go from here?"

Diane spoke first. "We have lab work to look over. I have the Chicago file on your wife's murder. I think—"

"We find your son," Miriam said, her words stopping Diane cold.

"Thank you for stating the obvious," Diane said. "What do you think we've been trying to do?"

Miriam turned on her angrily. "Don't you see? Linda has been telling me not to let it happen again. Bevin must be using someone else, working in conjunction with them to bring this spirit back."

"This is ridiculous!" Diane looked at Nick. "Don't you see where this is going? You end up hiring her to try and find this other mysterious person that Bevin is supposedly using. They convince you that without their help, you'll never find that missing link."

"You can afford to dismiss everything I've told you that easily?" Miriam asked, her own anger rising.

Diane's gaze was cold. "I can't afford not to."

The doorbell rang. No one at the table moved. It rang again. Slowly, Nick stood.

"No," Diane said. "Let me."

Nick sat back down. He waited until she left the room before speaking. "Can you tell me anything more about my son? Do you have any idea where he is?"

Miriam's face was sympathetic. "I wish I could. But nothing so far. I'm sorry."

Diane walked back in, followed by Roger. "Detective Clemens thinks he may have something," she said. Then, looking at Miriam and Bob, she said, "Could you please excuse us so we can—"

"No," Nick said, surprising himself. "I want them to hear this." He looked at the young detective. "What's happened?"

Roger eyed Miriam, obviously surprised to see her. "I got a call this morning from Ted Albin," he said, looking at each person in the room. His words came out slowly as if he were now reluctant to tell them what he had driven all the way over to Nick's to say. "He busted up a fight at a bar last night and had to take one of the guys down to Mercy to get stitched up. While he was there, a woman came up to him to ask about pressing charges against Thomas Bevin. She said Bevin put her grand-daughter in the hospital and she wanted him arrested."

"What?" Nick glanced at Diane. "How?"

"The girl, Ginny Lambert, has been working with Bevin at that institute of his. She apparently has some psychic ability and he's been trying to help her develop it and understand it."

"And now she's ill?" Miriam said.

"What's wrong with her?" Diane asked.

"That's the strange part," Roger said. "The girl has slipped into a coma for no apparent reason. The grand-mother says it's because of Bevin. He was having her do some kind of mind experiments that made her sick."

Nick looked at Miriam. "He's using her," he said.

Miriam nodded slowly. "It's a good possibility."

"Let's not get carried away with this," Diane said. "We have no idea at this point what's happening."

"But it fits with everything Miriam just told us. You can't deny that."

Diane looked at Roger. "Have you talked to Parks about any of this?"

"No. This is your case, this is your call."

After only a moment's hesitation, she said, "I want to see Ginny Lambert."

CHAPTER
SEVENTEEN

ξ

Jeff sat in the corner of the kitchen, trying to get himself under control. The feeling had begun to seep back into his limbs and with it came the searing agony of fingers and toes slowly thawing out. He flexed his hands and feet, waiting for it to pass.

Since waking outside, he had worked mostly from fear and panic. Now he wanted to clear his head, to try and think. Feeling reasonably stable, as stable as was possible under the circumstances, he attempted to stand.

His legs felt a bit shaky as he moved away from the window and the cold air that poured in through the hole he had made. But otherwise, he felt fine. The sound of his shoes crushing the broken glass that was scattered across the floor seemed to echo off the walls around him, unusually loud. Reaching for a light switch, he pushed it up. Nothing happened. He hadn't really expected anything. The house had a discarded, abandoned feel to it.

Walking through the downstairs, he opened closets and peeked inside cupboards. But each one, like the house itself, was bare. Not a single cup or plate or glass. Nothing hung in the closets, no old coats left behind by their owners waiting for them to return, no vacuum cleaner kept to use whenever people returned. Nothing, almost as if no one had ever lived here.

Standing in the middle of the living room, his arms wrapped around himself for warmth, Jeff felt an odd, queasy sensation begin in the pit of his stomach and quickly run through the rest of his body. It was the house. It seemed almost as if it were a set made to look like a house but without anything a real house contained. No pictures hung on the beige walls, the furniture was a drab uniform brown older in style, and the fireplace that sat in the far corner of the room looked completely unused, its utensils glistening like new, its bricks untouched by fire.

How had he gotten here? He couldn't remember. His last clear thoughts before awakening outside were hiding from the man who had killed his mother.

And then something caught his eye, something odd in the sparse room. He hadn't noticed it at first, tucked against the farthest wall, hidden within the shadows. He walked slowly toward the small bookcase, squinting through the darkness at the titles. As he read each one, he felt his heart slam against his chest. They were his father's books, every one he had ever written, in order of the dates that they had been published.

Suddenly this house, which had seemed like a safe haven against the cold, frightened him. Someone had led him here, knowing it was the only place he could go.

He backed away from the books, his eyes scanning the room all around him. Was someone watching him even now? He had checked this floor but as his gaze swept upward, he felt a new chill race through him, a chill not from the cold.

Upstairs.

He rushed toward the front door, his escape, but he stopped before reaching it. Where could he go? He didn't know where he was, he had no protection from the cold, and he had no way of defending himself if someone did decide to chase after him.

He scanned the room, his eyes stopping on the fireplace. Moving quickly to it, he snatched up the poker, holding it tightly in his grip. If he was going to get out of there, he needed something to keep him warm from the cold.

Blankets. He needed blankets.

Holding the poker out in front of him, moving as quietly as possible, Jeff started up the stairs.

"You three wait out here." Diane's gaze swept over Nick, Miriam and Bob. They stood outside the hospital room of Ginny Lambert. "Roger and I will go in first and talk to this woman, see what's what."

"No," Nick said, not happy with the arrangements that were being presented to him. "I want to hear what she has to say."

"She's not going to say anything yet," Diane said. "All I want to do is feel her out, see if she's even willing to talk to us about this. If we all tramp in there, we're just going to scare her. Let us smooth the way, get the idea of what we want first."

Nick hesitated. But ultimately, he knew she was right. "Okay," he said. "We'll wait right here."

Diane and Roger disappeared inside the private room.

"She doesn't believe me," Miriam said as soon as Diane was gone. "She thinks I'm making all this up."

"She's a police officer," Bob said. "What do you expect?"

Nick turned toward them. "She's just being cautious."

Miriam nodded. "What about you? What do you think?"

"My son is missing," whispered Nick. "That makes me more open-minded to listen to just about anything that might help find him."

A moment later Diane pushed the door open and stepped out into the hall. "She wants to talk to Miriam." She eyed the psychic, her voice less than enthusiastic.

"Did you explain what's happening?" Nick asked.

Diane shook her head. "Never got the chance. The minute I said I had a psychic out here, she wanted her inside." Her eyes bore into Miriam. "This woman is obviously desperate," she said, her voice taking on a warning tone. "She seems almost on the verge of a breakdown. I don't want anyone doing anything that might push her over the edge."

Miriam's gaze was unwavering. "You have nothing to worry about." And in her voice, Nick could hear a confidence he himself did not feel.

Diane opened the door, allowing them inside.

Roger stood to one side, watching as the others slowly approached the bed.

"Mrs. Lambert?" Diane said as they drew near. "I'd like you to meet a few people."

The woman rose slowly, as if having difficulty doing so. She turned, her eyes red-rimmed from crying. The bed came fully into view behind her.

Nick was stunned by the small frame in the bed.

She can't be twelve years old.

He hadn't expected her to be quite so young.

"This is Miriam Cramer, the psychic I was telling you about," Diane said.

"Can you help my granddaughter?" Evelyn Lambert

wrung her frail hands together, her eyes never leaving Miriam's face. "She's all I have left."

"I hope so," Miriam said, her voice kind and soothing. Going to the side of Ginny's bed, she sat down. The others crowded around her, staring at the small, still form. Ginny's face was drawn and pale. Her eyes were closed. There was no movement behind the lids.

"Has she been having nightmares?" Miriam asked.

Evelyn nodded hesitantly. "I think so but she wouldn't talk to me about them."

Reaching out, seeming to be somewhat reluctant about it, Miriam took one of the girl's small hands in her own. Her breathing deepened as she closed her eyes, her head bent slightly forward.

The room fell unnaturally silent, each person seeming not to breathe. Nick watched, his body shaking with anticipation. What was she feeling?

A moment later, Miriam released the hand, shoving it away. She stood up, the chair she sat in moving back several inches. She began backing away. Tears stood out in her eyes. She was having trouble catching her breath, and her hands shook at her sides.

"What is it?" Nick could barely voice the question. He could feel her fear. It was coming off her in waves, washing over him, shaking him. "What's wrong?"

She turned toward her husband. "It's the same." She was breathless when she spoke.

Moving forward, Bob took her in his arms, hugging her tightly against himself. "I knew this was a mistake," he said. "I knew we shouldn't have come here."

"What's going on?" Nick said more loudly than before. "What did you feel?"

Miriam's eyes found Nick. She shook violently in her

husband's arms. Finally, in a voice that was barely audible, she said, "I felt your son."

Jeff moved to the first door on the second floor and positioning himself, threw it wide, the poker held high. The room was empty. Inside was a bed, a bedside table with a lamp on it, and a dresser. Moving to the bed, he stripped off the bedspread. The mattress was bare beneath it. No other blankets, no sheets, just the bedspread.

Pulling the thin material around his shoulders, happy for any extra warmth, he moved to the dresser. He pulled out the drawers one by one, discovering each to be as empty as the one before.

He stepped toward the closet, not expecting to find anything inside but needing to be sure just the same. Swinging the doors wide, he took a startled step backward, raising the poker again as the body came into view.

An instant later he realized it was a little girl, curled into a tight ball and pressed against the far wall. Her hands covered her face, muffling her crying.

Jeff knelt down in front of her, setting the poker aside. "Hey, are you okay?" he asked, not getting too close, not wanting to scare her.

She peeked out at him from between her fingers, her eyes wide with fear.

"I won't hurt you." He held his hands out in front of him, showing her he wasn't concealing anything.

She shivered where she sat, her small body convulsing.

"Are you cold?" Pulling the blanket from around his shoulders, he held it out to her, offering it. She did not move. Jeff laid it on the floor before her and backed away, sitting cross-legged outside the closet. He didn't know what else to do. Who was this little girl? Why was she here all alone in this house?

Slowly, she reached forward and snatched up the blanket, wrapping it around herself. The crying had stopped. "Thank you," she whispered, her eyes darting to Jeff.

"You're welcome," he said, pleased she had spoken to him. "Is this your house?" he asked when she seemed to be comfortable with him.

She shook her head.

"Are you here visiting someone?" he tried next.

"No." She began crying again.

"Don't cry. I don't know how I got here either so we'll just have to figure it out together, okay?" He smiled. "My name's Jeff."

She wiped her nose with the blanket. "I'm Ginny."

"What are you talking about?" Diane moved forward. "How can you 'feel' Jeff?"

Miriam disentangled herself from her husband's arms. Wiping a shaking hand across her eyes, she said, "I'm not sure yet. But I definitely felt his presence when I touched her." She looked down at the young girl again. "Wherever this child's conscious is, Jeff is with her."

"That's impossible," Diane said.

Miriam turned to Evelyn. "When did she have her first nightmare? What night?"

"Sunday. I kept her home from school on Monday she was so ill."

"That was the night that young boy died," Miriam said looking toward Diane. "I'm right aren't I?"

It was a moment before Diane answered. "Yes."

"Five years ago, when I had my nightmares, Linda Cross died." She looked back down at Ginny's still form. "And last night, the police officer was killed." Gripping Ginny's hand again, she held on, gritting her teeth. It was only a moment before she released it again. "But he's not with them now."

"Who?" Diane stepped closer.

Miriam turned to Nick. "You saw him, the man in your house. You said he touched you."

Nick nodded and then looking at Diane, he said, "We chased him."

"And Jeff was missing." Miriam's gaze shifted from Nick to Diane and back to Nick. "Don't you see what's happened?"

"What?" Diane asked.

She turned to her. "Bevin used me to release this thing that killed Nick's wife. Now he's using Ginny for the same thing except this time he's taken it one step further. It didn't just kill last night."

"I'm still not following you," Diane said, glancing at Nick.

He still stood by the door but now his eyes were locked with Miriam's as understanding sank in. The reality of Bevin's words hit him, the meaning suddenly becoming very clear. He doubled over, his stomach convulsing with fear. "Oh, God," he muttered.

Diane went to him. "Nick, are you going to be sick?"

He stumbled forward in the room. "You feel Jeff," he said, staring down at Ginny. "When you touch her, you feel Jeff."

"Yes," Miriam whispered.

He closed his eyes, letting it all sink in. "He told me . . . He told me when I went to see him but I didn't understand."

"Understand what?" Diane asked.

Nick stumbled forward, talking directly to Miriam. "He said that Jeff is playing out the end of a book . . . Bobby

Tarp . . . oh, God . . ." He needed to sit down before he fell over. "Bobby Tarp is real."

"Nick, what are you talking about?" Diane asked.

He did not answer. Instead, he found a chair and sat down, leaning back heavily. "This isn't happening."

Diane knelt down in front of him and took his hands in hers. "Tell us what you're talking about."

But it was Miriam who answered. "Jeff is literally playing out the ending of that book." Her gaze returned to the young girl in the bed. "And Ginny is with him."

Diane turned to her. "What are you saying?"

"I believe that with Ginny's help Bevin has somehow created an alternate reality. He has managed to take a character out of it and put Jeff inside."

"What?" Diane thought she misunderstood. "You can't be serious."

"I'm very serious," Miriam said, her gaze unwavering.

Nick sat slightly forward, his hands rubbing the side of his head. "This is crazy," he whispered, trying to recall the details of that first story.

"This is crazy," Diane looked at him. "You can't believe this?" He looked steadily at her, his feelings clearly displayed in his eyes. "You do, don't you? You believe this."

"Something is happening. Something strange."

"But not this." She looked back at Miriam. "Come on. Bevin wants us to believe he has these powers. But it's simply not possible."

"Why? Because you don't think it is?" Miriam said. "You have to try and believe it because if we don't work under the assumption that Jeff is in that new reality, we may never get him back."

Slowly, Jeff was able to coax Ginny from the closet. He retrieved two more bedspreads from the other bedrooms on the floor but nothing more. The rooms were empty beyond that. No one was inside the house except himself and this small girl. He gave two of the thin blankets to Ginny and kept one for himself.

They sat downstairs in front of the small fire Jeff had managed to build by breaking up a flimsy coffee table beside the couch. The warmth from the fire felt good.

"Ginny," Jeff said when he felt she was comfortable with him. "Can you tell me how you got here?" He kept the poker at his side, still unsure of his safety, and now, the safety of this little girl as well. "Did your parents come with you?"

"No." She stared into the fireplace. Her next words were barely audible. "They died a few years ago."

"I'm sorry," Jeff whispered. Great beginning, he thought. Then, in a flash of insight, he added, "My mother died too."

She looked at him, her eyes wide. "She did?"

Jeff nodded.

"Do you still miss her? 'Cause I miss my mom and dad all the time still."

Jeff smiled sadly. He had not really thought about it but yes, he did miss his mother. "I try and remember good things about her," he said. "It helps me not feel sad."

Ginny thought about that for a moment. "That's a good idea." Then she caught Jeff off guard by asking, "What about your dad? You still have him, right?"

"Yeah," Jeff said, hoping it was true. "He's probably wondering what happened to me." He stared at the flames in the fire in front of him, thinking about his dad. He had blamed his father for so much. He had hated him for not being there to save his mother, hated him for not being his mother, hated him for being the one left alive.

"I didn't think you'd have parents," Ginny said suddenly.

Jeff turned to face her, his brow furrowing. "You didn't," he said, confused by the statement.

She shook her head and then said, "Which one are you? I've been trying to figure it out for myself but I can't. Is it okay if you just tell me?"

"Which one?" Jeff said, trying to make sense of what she was saying. "I don't know what you're talking about."

"Which guide." Ginny stressed her words as if Jeff should know already and was just acting stupid.

"I'm not a guide." Then a new thought struck him. "Did someone bring you here, a guide of some sort?" he asked, hoping this person would come back and lead both of them home.

Ginny sighed, clearly exasperated with Jeff's misunderstanding of the situation. "You're the guide. Mr. Bevin told me—"

"Bevin." Jeff tensed. "Thomas Bevin," he asked, his voice harsh.

Ginny shrank away from his sudden anger, sinking further into her blankets, trying to disappear beneath them. "Yes," she whispered. "He said the other man would be gone the next time I came here."

Jeff gripped the poker more tightly. "What other man?" He glanced around. "I thought we were alone." But now he wondered if he had checked every room in the house. Could someone be upstairs? In an attic? A hidden room?

"I didn't like him," Ginny said, still cowering beneath her blankets. "So I got you instead."

Jeff stared at her, trying to sort through what she was telling him. He could not. "Ginny," he said, making sure to keep his voice as calm as possible. "Why don't you explain to me what you're talking about. How do you know Thomas Bevin and why are you here?"

"How do we get Jeff back?" Nick asked.

Miriam thought for a moment. "I'm not sure yet. I have to try and make contact with him, see what it's like where he is."

"This is ridiculous," Diane said. "Nick, I'm not going to let you get sucked into this nonsense."

"At this point," he said, turning on her angrily, "what can you do to help me?"

She fumbled for an answer. "We can try and find evidence that proves Bevin is involved."

"We've been trying to do that. We've come up blank. Miriam is suggesting a real plan."

Diane nodded. "Fine. You believe her all you want. But to get Bevin, even if this is really happening, we're going to need solid proof."

"She's right," Miriam added.

Nick looked at her, confused by her sudden change of attitude. "I thought you and I were on the same team here."

"We are. But the detective is still right. You'll need evidence, solid proof for a court of law if you want him to pay for what he's done to you."

Nick was torn. He looked from Miriam to Diane. "I don't know what to do," he said finally.

"I think," Diane began, "we should go back to your house and try to find something that will link Bevin to all of this."

"Bob and I will stay here," Miriam said. "I'm going to try and somehow break the hold Bevin has on Ginny. Maybe if it breaks, Jeff will be returned."

"I don't like it," Bob said, his voice firm.

Miriam turned toward her husband. "I'll be fine. This isn't the same."

Bob looked at Nick. "I'm sorry about your son. I really am. But I don't want to risk my wife for you or anyone else."

"I'm not asking her to risk herself," Nick said, confused by the man's sudden apprehension.

"But you are." His body stiffened and his voice tensed. ·

"Bob, this isn't the same," Miriam said again.

He turned toward her. "Yes, it is. You know it is. You just won't admit it because of the boy. You're so worried about what might happen to him that you're not even thinking about yourself."

"I know what I'm doing," she insisted.

Bob turned to Nick. "Five years ago, my wife nearly died. This thing, whatever it is, got a hold of her and wouldn't let go." He glanced at Miriam before looking back to Nick again. "You know what it's like to lose a wife."

"Bob, stop," Miriam said, stepping in front of him.

"No," Nick said. "He's right. Why should you risk yourself again?"

Miriam turned to him. "Because it's my choice and I want to do this."

"I can't ask you—"

"You're not asking," Miriam interrupted. "I'm volunteering."

"Miriam—"

"No, Bob," she turned to him. "You can't stop me."

Husband and wife stared at each other, neither one speaking. An obvious strain hung between them. It was apparent to everyone in the room that this was not the first time they had had this particular fight.

"Well, now that that's settled," Diane said, trying to

break the tension in the room. "I think we should go back to your house," she said to Nick, "and see what we can find."

"Like what?" he asked without much enthusiasm. He had a feeling she was just trying to give him something to do, some kind of busy work.

"I won't know until I see it. But we need something that will link Bevin to all of this. Your house seems as good a place to start as any."

Miriam waited until Nick and Diane had left before turning to her husband. Bob was angry with her, angry that she had agreed to do this, and angry at himself for allowing it to go this far.

He stood in front of the window, silently stroking his beard and staring outside. But she knew he was not seeing the bright sunshine of the day beyond the glass. He was trapped back in time, five years earlier, watching her struggle for her life. Somehow, Miriam had to find a way of pulling him forward, of making him understand.

Evelyn Lambert remained beside her granddaughter's bed as Miriam stood and crossed the room to her husband.

"Bob," she said, stopping behind him. "I have to do this."

"No, you don't," he said, keeping his back to her.

"I didn't tell Nick the whole truth. I couldn't."

Slowly, Bob turned to face her. "What do you mean?"

She turned, her gaze fixed on Ginny. "She's weak. And she's getting weaker all the time."

"The way you did." Bob stood behind Miriam. His hands came to rest on her shoulders and began to massage gently.

She nodded. "Ginny is with Jeff, trapped in that other

world. But she's also the reason that world exists. If she dies, then that world ceases to exist."

Bob's hand tightened on her shoulders and she knew he finally understood. "And so would Jeff," he whispered.

Diane sat on the floor of the bedroom going through the boxes marked CHICAGO. She and Nick had carried them down together, but she had suggested he get a shower and a new set of clothes while she started looking. He needed the break and the time to catch his breath.

As she pulled out each item, she thought about the life stored in the boxes, a life neither Nick nor Jeff had glimpsed for five years. The search was going slower than she anticipated.

JEFF was stenciled across the top of the box now before her. She pulled off the lid, realizing for the first time that she had never met the boy she was so desperate to find. When she saw the box with its neat letters on top, she had thought it would have recent items from his past: cassette tapes, old jeans, maybe even a catcher's mitt. But as she stared in at his baby clothes and toys, she realized it was full of things from his first years. None of it would help them now, yet she did not immediately put the box aside. Instead, she reached in and pulled out a small, blue, checked baby blanket. A tiny stuffed clown sat beneath it. The face smiled up at her. She lifted him out, the body soft against her fingers. On the back, she found a key. She turned it slowly and the soft sound of the Brahms lullaby drifted through the room. Its tune still playing, she set the clown aside. Pulling out some clothes, she stopped to look at each little shirt and pair of pants. A book lay at the bottom of the box, the words Baby's First Year scrawled across the front in cursive letters. She lifted it out and slowly began turning through the pages.

Jeff's first word, first step, and first laugh were all diligently recorded inside. But it was the choice of Jeff's favorite toy that made Diane smile. "Sopping wet washcloth" was written beside the heading with a large smiley face.

Diane closed the book, hugging it against her chest. For the first time since taking on this case, she felt a connection to Jeff, a connection that up until this point she had only felt with Nick. She was more determined than ever to bring him home safely.

As she began to carefully pack up his baby items, the bathroom door opened. She glanced up. Nick walked out. His hair was still wet, but combed back into place. He wore a dark blue robe.

"I forgot to bring in a change of clothes," he said, moving to the dresser and pulling open the drawers.

Diane watched him as he pulled out a pair of jeans and a shirt. She couldn't help herself. She had told herself over and over that she needed to keep her mind on the case, not Mr. Nicholas Cross, but time and again, she found herself staring at him, wanting to touch him, hold him, comfort him.

"Any luck?" He faced her again and caught her watching him.

"No, not yet." She looked away quickly and began to pack the box again. "I'm sure we'll find something, though." But she wasn't sure if she was reassuring him or herself.

Nick leaned against the dresser, staring at all the half empty boxes with their contents spread around her on the floor. "I don't even remember that story," he said quietly.

"What?" She glanced toward him.

"Bevin wanted to finish the story I was writing in college. I don't remember what it was about."

"It doesn't matter."

"But it does." Nick walked forward and leaning down, picked up a small stuffed giraffe she had not yet put back in the box. Diane could hear the rattle inside moving around. He touched its face, running his fingers over the material. "Don't you see, if Miriam is right and Jeff is in that story, then whatever is happening to him is my fault."

"Miriam is not right," she said, watching him and knowing he believed the garbage Miriam was spewing.

"I didn't think of that before." He held the giraffe against his chest. "I created that place he's in. I created the danger. All this stuff . . ." Reaching down, he picked up one of the boxes and threw it across the room. "None of this is helping." The box smashed against the wall, the contents spilling out.

Diane was on her feet in an instant. "Nick, stop it," she said, going to him as he picked up another box. "Stop it!" she shouted, trying to wrestle the box out of his hands. He pulled free.

"Get your hands off me!" He shoved her away before slamming the box against the far wall, knocking over a lamp and sending it crashing to the floor. He wiped an arm across the dresser, sending cologne bottles and change across the floor.

"Goddammit, Nick!" Diane shouted, grabbing him again. "Stop this. You're not helping. Jeff needs you—"

Nick pulled out of her grip. "That's a laugh," he said, his anger swelling. "He needs me to what? Get him killed?"

"He needs you to help him. He's out there—"

"Don't you see, Diane, I'm the reason this is all happening. I've brought this to my son and laid it in his lap."

"You've done nothing. It was—"

"Bevin," Nick finished for her. "But why? Because of me. Jeff is God knows where because of who his father is." He turned away from her.

Diane reached out, wanting to set a hand on his shoulder, to support him in some way. Her hand hesitated before falling back to her side. "Are you okay?" she asked.

He shook his head, unable to face her.

"Nick, we can win. We just have to be smarter than he is."

"I don't think I am." He took a deep, rattling breath, his back still to her. "I can't do it again."

"Do what again?" she asked, her voice soft.

"I went by myself," he said, shaking his head slowly back and forth. "I thought I could handle it."

Diane's brow furrowed. "Handle what? I don't know what you're talking about."

"I was so sure they were wrong. I thought I'd see the body and it wouldn't be Linda. But it was. She . . . she . . ." A sob escaped his lips.

"This isn't the same," Diane whispered, trying to imagine what it must have been like for him. Praying she could stop it from happening again, she said, "I won't let it be the same."

It was a moment before Nick could speak again. "You were right about one thing. This is all a game. But I don't know how to play."

Diane reached out but this time she touched his shoulder, squeezing gently. "No," she whispered. "We'll win. We'll beat him."

"I can't do it again. I can't go down to that place and look at my child's body the way I did Linda's." He turned toward her and gripped her upper arms, holding on tightly. "Tell me what I'm supposed to do." He shook her slightly as he talked. Tears stood out in his eyes. "I have to do something. Tell me. Help me." The last two words came out as a choked plea. He pulled her against himself, hugging her tightly. Diane was taken off guard. After only a moment's hesitation she reached out and began stroking his hair, trying to calm him, hoping to soothe him.

He buried his face in her shoulder, openly crying. She supported him as he wept, releasing his pain and frustration. Her hands rubbed his back, moving slowly, reassuringly.

Eventually, he pulled away. His eyes were red and swollen. His face was wet with tears. She wiped his cheek with her hand and then, leaning forward, she gently kissed him. It was an innocent, comforting kiss meant to make him feel better.

But as their lips touched, she felt something else, she felt a deeper need. And soon the kiss turned hungry. His hands traveled over her body, through her hair. She could almost feel his heart in her chest, the two beating in perfect rhythm.

And then he pulled away. His face registered a combination of shock and embarrassment. He took a step back. "I'm sorry. I didn't—"

"Shhh." She put a finger to his lips, quieting him. Pulling her gun out from the holster under the arm, she placed it on the dresser. Nick watched as she pulled her T-shirt over her head and tossed it aside. She then unbuttoned her jeans, slipping them down over her hips. And still he watched. She moved toward him then, her eyes locked with his. As she touched the front of his robe, she felt him shudder beneath the terry cloth. Running her hands down his chest, she let her fingers work through the knot at his waist.

Nick's breathing became labored. She kissed him, pushing the robe over his shoulders and pulling it off his body. He stood naked before her. She looked at him, her eyes traveling slowly over his body. Her own breath came in gasps as he reached toward her, removing first her bra and then her panties. His hand trembled as he cupped her breast. She placed her own hand over his, steadying him.

"It's all right," she whispered, her free hand gently touching the side of his face. "Everything will be all right."

The blankets were soft as Nick lowered her onto the bed.

CHAPTER EIGHTEEN

ξ

Thomas stood in front of the large window in his office, staring out as dusk slowly overtook the day. Things were going so well. He could not have imagined how easy it would all be.

The door behind him clicked quietly open. "Carl?" he said, turning. But there was no one there. He moved around his desk and reaching the door, opened it. He stepped out into the reception area. Carl was seated at Sandy's desk, his back to Thomas.

"Carl," he said, moving around the desk to face the big man. "I asked you—" The words died on his lips as Carl came into full view. His wrists and throat had been neatly sliced. His wrists, which rested in his lap, had stained his pants and the chair a bright red. His white shirt seemed to be dyed the same color.

Thomas backed away, his eyes scanning the room continuously. He dashed into his office and slammed the door shut.

"I've been waiting."

Thomas spun toward the voice. Bobby Tarp sat in his chair, leaning back slightly. A large, blood-covered knife sat on the desk. Thomas's eyes locked on it. "What are you doing here?"

"We've never met formally," Tarp said, his dark eyes boring into Thomas. "I just wanted to introduce myself." He nodded toward the door. "Your friend out there was not very cooperative."

Thomas felt as if his feet were glued to the floor. He could not move. This man should not be here. Thomas was in control. Always in control. Yet here he was. "I haven't called for you."

Tarp laughed. "You still think you're in charge?"

"I am," Thomas insisted. "You would not be here at all if it weren't for me. I gave you this existence."

"Yes, I understand that." Tarp nodded slowly. "That's why I'm here." He stood. The chair he was sitting in slammed back against the wall.

Thomas stepped back, startled by the sudden movement. "You have to leave." He tried to make it sound like a command but failed miserably.

"I like this world." Tarp stepped around the desk, moving toward Thomas. "I think I'll stay."

Thomas's heart beat an irregular rhythm in his chest. He wasn't quite sure but he thought he detected a threat in the man's voice. "You think I can't just end this now?" he said, still trying to hang onto his control. "You are only here by my good graces. Don't forget that."

Tarp plucked the knife off the desk. "You are only partially to blame for that place I'm from." Placing the tip of the blade against the palm of his hand, he began turning it ever so slowly. "But you must pay the same as the other." Blood began to pool in his hand where the tip sliced neatly into his flesh. He glanced up. "Do you understand me?"

Thomas was pressed up against the wall, trying to lose

himself in the wallpaper. This was wrong, terribly wrong. "You can't," he started to say but in the next instant, before he could finish his sentence, the room around him began to shake. Papers spilled off his desk, the lamp on the end table tumbled over, and the large window behind his desk cracked, the glass resembling a large spider web.

Wind whipped up, blowing loose papers from the desk-top and swirling Thomas's hair wildly around his head. Cold air curled up his body, wrapping itself around him, tugging at his clothes, his skin.

"Stop this!" Thomas shouted, gripping the chair before him, afraid that without it he might lose his footing.

A loud sound ripped through the office. Thomas covered his ears as it increased in intensity. He stared wide-eyed at the far wall, the wall behind Bobby Tarp. Slowly, another landscape came into view. Snow and ice tumbled into the office, wetting the desk and chairs.

Thomas lowered his hands from his ears. His heart thundered in his chest. He found breathing difficult. A high-pitched howl emanated from within that world. The sound washed over Thomas, sending a different kind of chill through his body.

Tarp stepped forward, his eyes locked on Thomas.

Diane lay in bed, her body pressed against Nick. He was breathing deeply and she knew he was asleep. Rolling gently over, she looked at his face. She traced lightly down his cheek over his mouth. A good mouth, strong. She liked his mouth, his nose, his jawline. He was a handsome man, a gentle lover.

Letting her shoulder fall back, she lay staring up at the ceiling, listening to his soft intake of breath beside her. She shouldn't be doing this. Every fiber of her body told her that. Yet she couldn't bring herself to leave.

Nick mumbled quietly in his sleep, an unintelligible sound, and then was silent again. She liked where she was, lying in this man's bed, being with him.

She found herself wondering what it would be like to wake beside him every day. She had never met a man who had made her ponder that question. Love, relationships, commitment. Those were not words in Diane's vocabulary. Not until today.

Out of the corner of her eye, she caught sight of the picture that sat on his bedside table next to the alarm clock. Reaching over slowly so as not to wake Nick, she picked it up.

Linda's smiling face looked out at her.

It was an old photograph. One with Nick, Linda, and Jeff posed together, each smiling for the camera. Diane stared at the face of Nick's late wife. She had had this man, loved this man, and was now lost to him. And he still missed her gravely.

She glanced at Nick as he murmured again in his sleep. Reaching out, she brushed his hair away from his forehead. She longed to wake him and tell him how she felt, that she never wanted to leave him, that she wanted to help him, to love him. Instead, she set the picture back on the table next to the clock and snuggling close to Nick's body, closed her eyes and drifted into the fantasy world of sleep.

The nightmare again.

Nick stood before the stainless steel table, staring down at the figure beneath the bloody sheet. He did not want to see, did not want to know.

He blinked and the sheet was gone.

Screams poured from him as he stared down at his son's bloated corpse. The skin across his chest and face hung away, raw and peeling, chunks of his flesh gone. Each hand was missing at least two fingers, the bloody stumps oozing onto the white sheet around him. But it was his eyes that made Nick scream. The same clear eyes that had been Linda's, still perfect, forever frozen in death.

He backed away. But a hand shot out, the remaining fingers grabbing at him. He swatted the hand away, repulsed by the feel of the skin.

Jeff sat up, skin peeling from his back. "You were supposed to protect me," the corpse said, his eyes finding Nick's.

Nick continued to back away, twisting and pulling. He screamed, struggling backward. The hands held on, pulling him closer and closer.

"Nick."

His name formed on the dead lips. Fetid breath blew in his face.

"Nick."

"Don't touch me!" he yelled, pulling away.

"Nick, wake up."

He did, bolting straight up in bed.

"Relax. You're fine. Everything's fine," Diane said, her voice softly reassuring.

Nick stared at her, unsure of where he was and who she was. And then he remembered and relaxed. A little.

"Nightmare?" she whispered.

He nodded, trying to slow his pounding heart.

"Bad one, huh?" She pushed his hair away from his eyes, easing him back to the pillow. Leaning on one elbow, she looked down into his face. "How often does that happen?"

He rubbed a hand over his eyes and then through his hair. "Just started again this week," he said after a moment. "Haven't had nightmares for years."

She lay next to him, her head resting against his chest, her arms tucked protectively around him. He felt safe. For the first time in years, he felt safe.

"Diane." He touched her shoulder before running his hand down her smooth back. Her skin was like satin. "I don't know where this will lead."

"It doesn't have to lead anywhere," she said. But despite the casual nature of her words, he felt her tense in his arms.

"I'm not saying it won't lead anywhere," he said, trying to explain himself. "I'm just saying, I don't know where it will lead. I haven't been with anyone . . ." He broke off, not wanting to finish the sentence. "I've been alone a long time," he said instead.

"I understand," she whispered.

Nick liked how she felt in his arms, liked the feeling of being with someone again. She was just so different from Linda. "It just occurred to me that I don't know anything about you. You could have a husband and three kids waiting for you at home."

She looked at him. "You really think that?" And he could hear the hurt in her voice.

He hugged her closer. "No," he whispered. "I was kidding. It wasn't funny. I apologize."

She relaxed slightly. "I've never been married," she said after a moment. "It's not part of my life plan."

"You don't want to get married?"

"I don't plan on it." She traced a finger over his chest. "I don't think I'm cut out for a husband and kids."

"Why not?"

"Why are we talking about this?" she asked.

He looked at her. "Because I'm curious about the woman I just slept with." He turned her face to his. "Is it because you're a policewoman? You don't think you could have a family with that kind of work?"

She hesitated and he knew she was deciding if she should reveal herself to him or not. "My father . . ." She let out a long sigh before continuing. "My father left my mother when I was only seven. It was very abrupt, very unexpected. My mother had no job, no car. We were left with pretty much nothing," she said. "But she was determined to make it on her own. I think at first it was more of an 'I'll show him' attitude but it got us through." Diane's body language changed as she spoke. At first it was subtle, a slight shift to the side, a hand moving away from his body. But as she continued to speak, Nick realized she was no longer touching him. Instead she lay stiffly beside him, her eyes fixed on the ceiling, her arms crossed in front of her chest. "She went to work, below minimum wage, and I got clothes and sometimes even shoes, from our neighbors. Hand-me-downs." She paused for a moment. "We struggled for a lot of years."

"Your mother never remarried?" Nick asked when it seemed she was not going to continue. He knew there had to be more to the story, something she hadn't revealed.

"My mother . . . she was so strong after my father left. She never seemed afraid to me, never seemed without a plan. But she was through with men. She told me once that she never wanted to be under a man's thumb the way she was my father's." She looked at Nick. "I've never forgotten that."

"Did you ever see your father again?"

"Yes," she whispered, shaking slightly as if caught off guard by a sudden chill.

"What happened?" Nick asked when she did not continue. He had to resist the urge to take her in his arms, afraid she might push him away if he tried.

"It was maybe seven years later. He showed up one day out of the blue. I was at school. . . . He was drunk." She glanced sideways at Nick. He could see the pain in her eyes, the hatred that still burned there. "I think he was just passing through town and he stopped to see if we still lived in the same house. We should have moved, should have left so he could never find us again." She was talking faster now, the words pouring from her. "He came to the door and my mother refused to let him in. So he kicked in the door . . . and attacked her." Her lips trembled. She stopped talking, taking a moment to compose herself again. "I found her when I got home," she said when she was able to continue. "She was . . . she was in so much pain." Again, the words choked off in her throat.

Nick took her in his arms and then pulled her close. She resisted at first, trying to push him away. But he persisted and it was only a matter of moments before he was able to pull her close. She buried her face against him, her tears wetting his chest. Running his hands over her hair, he spoke quietly, reassuringly to her.

"My mother," Diane said when she was able to continue, "never told me what happened that day. I think my father . . . he may have raped her." She seemed more together now, more in charge of her emotions. The change was abrupt and a little unsettling. "Looking back now I believe he did." And Nick realized it was now the cop in her speaking, looking at her mother as a victim of rape, able to distance herself from it.

"Did she report him to the police?"

Diane nodded slowly. "But they didn't do anything. She wanted him arrested. After talking to my father, they basically had the attitude that she got what she deserved. They humiliated her the same way my father did.

"After that, my mother was never the same. She was always afraid. We moved away but it didn't help."

"Is that why you became a police officer?"

"A lot of the reason. I wanted to change things for women, wanted to make it better."

"Is it better?"

She sighed again. "I don't know. I think it all comes down to each individual. Some of the guys I work with treat me like every other cop. But with others . . . I'll always be the woman."

"Is that the problem you have with your lieutenant?" He sat up, pulling her with him. They leaned against the headboard, Nick wrapping his arms around her and holding her close.

She leaned against his shoulder. Her voice was quiet when she spoke. "That's part of it. Yes."

"Why put up with it?"

"I've got over fifteen years on the job. I make a pretty good buck and I have some seniority." She closed her eyes. "It's my job. I don't know what else I'd do."

"Your mother must be very proud," Nick said.

"She was." Diane's words were soft. "She died about three years ago. Cervical cancer."

"I'm sorry," Nick said and meant it. He sat there with her, holding her close, listening to her soft breathing. "So," he said, leaning down and speaking directly into her ear. "You hate men because of your father?" He nibbled playfully on her lobe.

"Not when they do that," she said, smiling. "But you have to understand . . ." she paused as Nick's lips traveled from her ear to her throat. "I had a poor example as the only male figure in my life." He was now to her shoulder, kissing her exposed skin. "It left me with a bitter taste in my mouth." He moved down her arm. He couldn't believe she was still talking. "My idea of marriage is oppression of the woman under the man's will."

Nick stopped, pulling back slightly. She turned to look at him. "You really have a low opinion of men," he said. And for the first time he realized just how deeply her father had hurt her.

"I'm trying to change that." Turning, she brushed his lips lightly with her own, the kiss fleeting. "You've helped," she whispered.

"Me?" He was surprised.

"Seeing you, the way you feel about your son."

His heart picked up slightly in his chest at the mention of Jeff. "I'm a poor example of a good father."

"You love your son," she said simply. "I've met a lot of people on this job who can't say that."

"For all the good it's done him."

"You're too hard on yourself."

"After Linda died," he began, "I talked about it a lot. So much that my friends got sick of hearing it." He took a deep breath. "Can you imagine? My wife is murdered and after a while, my friends are bored with it, they don't want to hear it anymore." He touched her hair, running his hands through it. It felt soft between his fingers. "I shut them out after that, stopped seeing everyone."

"You can't hide from the world," she whispered.

"I tried to. For a long time I tried too. But Jeff . . . Jeff wanted out. He wanted a life." He stopped then, the thought of his son too painful.

"You can't expect forgiveness from your son when you can't even forgive yourself," Diane said.

Nick looked at her. How could she possibly understand what he felt? Not a day went by that he didn't think about Linda. Not a day went by that he didn't wonder if the murderer would come back. "You have no idea what my life has been like since my wife died."

"That's true. But all I hear from you is blame and guilt. That's all you're feeling about the past, about your wife. If that's the attitude you're projecting to your son . . ." she trailed off. "You can't try to make sense of your wife's death. There is none. But you can accept it and move on. You have to."

"You make it sound so simple." The tone in Nick's voice was stinging.

"The man that murdered your wife has been controlling your life ever since. Can't you see that?" She looked at him. "You have to take control back."

Nick laughed then, a bitter, angry sound. "He has taken my son from me the same way he took Linda," he said, his voice harsh. "There's nothing left to get back."

Diane was silent. They were no longer lying in each other's arms. Somehow, during the course of the conversation they had separated. They now sat apart, each on a separate side of the bed.

"I'm sorry." She began gathering a sheet around herself, suddenly self-conscious. "This was probably a mistake. I should leave."

Nick watched her, unsure of what to say, only knowing he did not want her to leave. How did things go so wrong, so fast? "Please." He moved closer to her. "Don't go."

She stopped but did not look at him. "Nick," she said and he could hear the regret in her voice. "I can't be with you as long as you hold on to the past so tightly. You're not ready to deal with it. You may never be."

Nick touched her shoulders, rubbing gently. "Please don't leave," he said again. "You're the first person, the first woman . . . I don't want to be alone anymore. I don't—"

The phone beside the bed rang, cutting him off before he could finish. Diane got out of the bed as he reached for the receiver.

"Hello?" Nick watched her as she began to gather her clothes.

"Mr. Cross. This is Detective Clemens. Is Detective Nolan still there?"

"Hold on." He held the receiver out toward her. "It's Clemens."

Moving to the bed, she took the phone, pulling her shirt over her head. "Yeah, Roger?" she said, zipping her pants. "You're kidding." A pause. "No. I'll be right there."

She handed the phone back to Nick. "What's going on?" he asked.

She replaced the weapon and the holster under her arm. "Something's come up. I've got to go."

Nick watched her. She was moving faster now, in a bigger hurry than she had been only a moment before. "What is it? What's happening?" His heart sank. "It's Jeff, isn't it?" He pushed the blankets back. "What are we doing? We were supposed to be trying to find—"

"It's not Jeff." She pushed him back into bed. "You can't do anything right now." She looked into his eyes for a long moment, searching them. Nick stared back, hoping she could see the depth of his need for her. "Just stay in bed." She sat on the edge of the mattress and pulled on one shoe, her eyes scanning the floor for the other one. "You need the rest." Her voice was detached, emotionless.

"Diane—"

"I'll call you when I know what's going on," she said, cutting him off.

"You're not coming back here, are you?"

She turned and Nick could see the hurt in her eyes.

She had trusted him, told him things about herself that she didn't easily share and he had blown it.

"Everything's going to be fine," she said, her tone softer. "I promise you." She reached toward him, running a hand gently down the side of his cheek. "This will all work out." And after only a moment's hesitation, she leaned toward him and kissed him. Her lips were warm and moist against his.

He reached for her but she stood and moved quickly to the door. It closed quietly behind her.

Nick lay back against the pillows.

What am I doing?

His son was missing and what was he doing? Sleeping with the detective who was supposed to be working on the case, worrying that she might not come back to him.

Turning, he looked at the photograph that sat on the bedside table. What had he done to his family? He lifted the picture from the table and hugging it to his chest, closed his eyes, trying to remember what his life had once been.

CHAPTER NINETEEN

ξ

Diane pulled up in front of the Bevin Institute. She flashed her badge at the uniformed officer stationed at the door.

Stepping inside, she stopped as Lieutenant Parks turned to face her. "Shit," she mumbled, not expecting to run into him.

Parks walked toward her. "I've been waiting for you." His voice was loud and demanding, heads turning at the sound.

Diane glanced around. "I came as soon as I got the call."

Parks stopped in front of her. "You must think I'm an idiot."

Several possible replies came to mind but Diane decided to stay with the safest one. "I don't know what you're talking about."

Taking her arm, he pulled her aside. "I don't appreciate being kept in the dark," he said between gritted teeth. "I've been chasing your shadow all day trying to catch up." He paused. "I don't want you screwing this up."

"Sir," she began, grinding the word out. "I have

handled this case in the same manner I handle all my cases. I—"

"Where is Mr. Cross right now?" Parks asked, ignoring her.

"He's home. Sleeping," she added.

One eyebrow went up. "You've seen him recently." It was not a question. "Does he know what's happened?"

"Not yet. I thought I'd see what—"

"Stop." He held up his hand. Diane wanted to reach out and break each finger. "Who's with him right now?"

"I left Williams outside."

He nodded. "I think I'll go over there myself."

"Sir, he's finally resting. I don't thin—"

"Stop." Once more, the hand came up.

Diane stared at it.

I'd start at the pinky. It'd snap easy. Then I'd just work my way over slowly, one by one until I reached the thumb.

"I didn't ask for your opinion on this," Parks said. "Right now, I want you to go inside and do your job. If you get any new information, call me at Cross's. Is that clear enough for you?"

"Yes, sir," she said when she realized Parks was waiting for a reply.

"Good." With a satisfied grin slowly spreading across his face, he turned and walked away.

Diane stood for a moment watching the commotion outside the building. Reporters were being kept back by police. The whine of an ambulance siren could be heard in the distance. This was her life. Murder, dishonesty, every horrible act mankind could think to do to itself. She turned away. For the first time, she wanted more. Tonight had confirmed that in her mind. Nick made her feel. . . . made her want another kind of existence. Up until this time, she had devoted herself to making it in a male-dominated profession. And she had done it, sacrificing everything else along the way. But no more. Now it was time for a life. She hoped it would be a life with Nick.

"Roger," she said, reaching Bevin's outer office. She stared down at Carl Neff's blood covered corpse.

Please, God, let Jeff be okay.

"What's going on?" she asked, her heart beating a heavy rhythm in her ears.

Roger glanced at her. "Who the hell knows? This is some weird shit."

"What about Jeffrey Cross? Did you find him?" But she was already sure of that answer. He was still gone, his location still a mystery.

"We're searching the place. But so far, nothing. The kid's not here and we haven't found anything that would indicate he ever was here."

"Dammit." Diane ran a hand through her hair. She had told Nick everything would be fine, but now she had her doubts. Those doubts gnawed at her stomach. Would Nick blame her when his son did not turn up safe and sound as she promised?

Looking down at the blood-covered desk, she said, "What've you got so far? Was this suicide?"

"You tell me." Roger led the way into Bevin's private office as the photographer arrived to take pictures of Carl Neff. "The office has been trashed," he said, walking through. "But there's not a trace of Bevin in here."

"Any blood found?" Diane surveyed the damage. "Anything that would indicate Bevin was involved in a struggle of some sort."

"Nothing. It's a mess but it's a clean mess."

Diane stood in the middle of the room, trying to let

everything sink in. But as she added it up in her mind, she realized that none of it made sense.

Bevin kidnaps Jeffrey Cross and gets away with it. Then he takes off for no reason whatsoever, leaving his right hand man behind to kill himself?

No. That didn't make sense. Bevin was holding all the cards. They couldn't touch him. Why this?

"What about Bevin's house?" she asked. "Have you got anyone over there yet?"

Roger began nodding even before she could finish. "The same. A big zero."

"None of this fits," she muttered more to herself than to Roger.

"Wanna hear Parks's theory," Roger said. She could hear the contempt he had for the lieutenant in his voice.

She turned to face him. "That bad?"

Roger glanced around the room. "He thinks Bevin killed the kid and left town, leaving the stiff out front behind. Now his thinking is that Neff gets all mad about this and trashes the office. Then, and this is where it really gets good, then he regrets it and kills himself either because he doesn't want to go back to prison or because he's afraid he disappointed Bevin in some way."

"You've got to be kidding," Diane said, her gaze taking in the whole room. "First off, we had nothing on Bevin. He had absolutely no reason to run. We couldn't even search this place if we wanted to. And second, this guy Neff was already in prison. I don't think the idea of going back would push him this far over the edge."

"I pointed that out. But Parks seems to think that Bevin's conscience was getting the better of him and he would have confessed had he not fled."

"Yeah, right."

"Personally," Roger said. "I think Bevin's doing it all for drama."

Diane's brow furrowed. "What do you mean by that?"

"It's all a show to him. He mysteriously disappears, his closest assistant is found dead, Jeffrey Cross is never found. Great exit and it would all drive Nicholas Cross crazy."

Diane tried to picture it all in her mind. "You really think he could convince this guy to kill himself just for effect?" She shook her head. "I don't buy it. Why would they do it? They were winning."

Roger shrugged one shoulder. "Who knows, Diane. Maybe we're giving the guy too much credit. He was a nut. Why did he do any of it?"

"No, something's wrong about all this." And then suddenly, it dawned on her, the thing that had been eating at her since she arrived. "The third man," she said slowly.

Roger leaned against Bevin's desk, arms crossed. "What third man?"

"The guy with the tattoo," she said. "What happened to him? He's not here."

"I thought he was just hired to play a part."

"That's what we thought but now I'm not so sure. Maybe he was much more involved." Her gaze took in the room. "Maybe he's responsible for this."

"You think he killed Neff and made it look like suicide?" Roger said. His tone of voice told her he was not buying it.

"We thought Daniel was a suicide at first."

"He was a kid. We're talking about a grown man. A very large man at that. I think if someone were to try and force him to kill himself, we'd see some broken furniture, a few overturned chairs, some signs of a struggle."

"What do you think all this is?" Diane said, indicating the mess around them. "Maybe it started in here but ended out there." She pointed to the other office.

"The body's too clean for that. Did you look at him? The only damage is to his throat and his wrists."

Diane knew what Roger was saying made sense but still she could not get the idea out of her mind. The man with the tattoo had not yet been found and neither had Jeffrey Cross. Maybe if she found one, she'd find the other. A new thought occurred to her. "Was there a knife found?"

Roger sighed. "I was hoping you wouldn't ask me that."

"So there wasn't one," she said, smiling.

"I still think it's a show," Roger insisted. "If Bevin were here, supervising Neff, he could have taken the knife with him when he left. Again, the drama. A suicide without the knife."

"Thin, Roger, very thin," Diane said, liking her own theory more and more.

"Let me show you something else." Walking to the television in the corner, Roger turned it on. He pushed the play button on the VCR beside it. Nick's face appeared on the screen.

"What is this?" Diane walked over to the television and turned up the volume. It was a press conference and from the look of Nick, it was several years old. "This was here?" she asked, looking back at Roger.

He nodded, pulling other tapes out from a shelf beside the television. "There's more." He put in another tape at random. Again, Nick appeared on the screen.

Diane watched as Nick discussed his writing career with the host of *Good Morning America*. She turned it off after only a few moments.

"This guy was obsessed with Cross," Roger said. "He was a nutball, that's all."

Diane glanced at the other tapes on the shelf. None of them were labeled, but there were at least ten more. She shuddered as she realized the extent of Bevin's hatred for Nick.

"I'm going to take a quick trip over to the hospital," she said after a time.

Roger's brow furrowed in confusion. "Why?"

"Because," Diane said. "I still have my doubts about Miriam Cramer. And with this new development, I think it's time to cut her loose."

Lieutenant Steven Parks pulled up in front of Nick's house. Shutting off the engine, he turned the rearview mirror toward himself. His hair had gotten slightly mussed on the drive over and he patted it back into place before stepping from the car.

He crossed the street and walked directly into the heart of the group of reporters. He looked good on television, he had decided earlier, as he watched himself fielding questions. Maybe he'd run for a political seat when this was all over.

"Lieutenant Parks," Harry Conner from Channel Three walked beside him. "Have there been any new developments in this case?"

Parks put on his concerned look. "I do have some news but I must talk with Mr. Cross before revealing any information."

"Is it about his son?" another reporter asked.

Parks held up his hands. "Please." He stepped up on the porch before turning to face them. He flashed a toothy grin. "I will make a statement after I have talked with Mr. Cross."

Turning, he prepared to knock on the door but stopped before his knuckles actually rapped on the hard wood surface. Nolan had said he was sleeping. He hated to get him out of bed. Reaching out, he tried the door. It was open. Parks slipped inside.

He strode toward the stairs, surprised at how cold the house was.

"What are you doing here?"

He turned toward the deep voice. "Mr. Cross?" he said, trying to see through the darkness of the room. A man much larger than Nicholas Cross stepped from the shadows. "Officer Williams?" he said, his hand resting on the butt of his gun. He still could not see this man clearly and he didn't want to take any chances.

The man walked out of the shadows, a sly smile cutting across his face. "You're not supposed to be here."

Parks could see the tattoo on his arm. He reached for his weapon. But even as his hand connected with the cool steel, the large man tossed a length of rope toward him, the thick cord landing near his feet.

Parks took a step back, startled by the unexpected movement. But as he stared down, it suddenly was not just a bland length of rope anymore but a snake, slithering closer and closer. Parks smiled. It looked just like the one on the man's arm. He watched it, hypnotized, as it glided across the floor, moving closer to him. It wrapped itself around his ankle and he gasped, a surge of electricity shooting through his body with every movement the snake made.

"It's a gift," the man whispered, his voice throaty and low. "With it, you can get all the attention you crave."

Parks closed his eyes as the snake wound its way around his body, slithering over his chest and arms until it reached his throat. It stopped then and Parks waited.

But it was no longer moving and the tingling sensation was slowly slipping away. Reaching up, he touched it but it was now only a rope again. It hung around his neck, trailing down his back.

"It's all up to you now," the stranger said, still smiling. "You know what must be done to bring the people."

Parks touched the rope, the tingling sensation returning. "Yes," he gasped.

Diane pushed through the door of Ginny Lambert's hospital room. Miriam sat beside the girl's bed, her eyes closed in concentration, her hands wrapped tightly around Ginny's.

"They're together," she said, still not opening her eyes. "I think they're all right for now."

Her husband sat beside her, watching tensely. "Can you see where they are? Can you describe the place?"

"Bevin is gone," Diane said watching the show that was being performed for her benefit. "He's skipped town. So whatever link you think he has to this girl is fiction. I'm not buying any of it."

Miriam released Ginny's hand, gently placing it back on the girl's chest. Taking a deep breath before speaking, she said, "Bevin is gone?"

"Yes." Diane remained beside the door.

Miriam looked at her husband. "If Bevin's no longer in control, then things are worse than I originally thought."

"How convenient," Diane said. "You're proven wrong so naturally, things are just worse."

Miriam ignored Diane and, instead, continued speaking directly to Bob. "The entity must not need Bevin to survive. He's stronger than we thought."

"Can we stop him?" he asked.

"I'm not sure." She focused once again on the young girl in the bed. "But for her sake, we have to try."

"Where is Evelyn Lambert?" Diane asked.

For the first time since Diane entered the room, Miriam looked at her. "We convinced her to get something to eat. She's at the cafeteria."

Diane nodded. "Good. I want you gone by the time she gets back."

"What?" Miriam said, clearly shocked. "You can't be serious. You don't know what you're dealing with. You need my help—"

"Nick isn't here right now," Diane said, her voice loud, overriding Miriam's protest. "You won't convince me so just stop trying."

Miriam's expression softened and became passive. "Did you find Jeff?" she asked calmly.

Diane shifted where she stood. "Not yet. But we will."

"No, you won't," Miriam said in that same patient tone. "You won't ever find him. Not a trace of him because he's not here."

"Just stop. You're not hitting your target audience any more."

Miriam stood suddenly and crossing the room, took Diane's hand in hers before the detective realized what she was doing. It was only a second before Miriam released her and moved back to the bed. Snatching up a pad of paper, she began to draw.

Diane remained at the door, shaken slightly by Miriam's behavior. She did not want to see what Miriam was drawing and told herself once again that this woman was a fake. "I don't want you to contact Nick again," she said.

Miriam's hand continued to move across the paper. "He thinks you're in over your head." She shot a glance toward Diane. "He says 'You need to open your mind to all the possibilities, Dee.'"

"What?" Diane crossed the room in three long strides. Only one person called her Dee and then only when they were alone together. No one else. No one. She looked over Miriam's shoulder at the drawing. "Stop this," she said, staring into Alan's eyes.

Miriam continued to work, her hand moving over the jawline. "He says like always, you're being stubborn. He—"

"Stop it!" Diane yelled, snatching the drawing away from Miriam. "I don't know how you did this." She waved the paper in front of her. "But I'm not buying it."

Miriam's clear eyes looked into Diane's. When she spoke, her voice was firm. "I am telling you the truth. Jeff is trapped within that other world and if we don't do something . . . think of some way to bring him back, then he will never come home."

Diane looked at the picture in her hand. She thought of Nick lying in the bed.

I promise it'll be all right. I promise.

But she was no longer sure if it would ever be all right again. She had nothing to go on, no idea where Jeff was, no idea of what had happened to him. And she was beginning to wonder if she ever would.

"What can we do?" she asked. There was a desperation to her voice that had not been there before. The clock was ticking and they were quickly running out of time. She was still skeptical of Miriam and her abilities but she could no longer dismiss her outright. Too much had happened, too much Miriam seemed to understand when no one else did.

"I have a theory," Miriam began. "In order to send Jeff

inside, Bevin had to create a portal of some kind between these two worlds."

"Like a doorway," Diane said, trying to grasp what she was saying. "So we find this doorway and bring him out?" That sounded plausible to her, even possible.

"No. If the doorway were still open, we'd know it and Jeff would already be home."

Diane was frustrated. "So what are you telling me?"

"We need to find a way to open that portal again."

"In theory, that's what you believe," Diane said. "What if you're wrong? What if there is no portal?"

Miriam's eyes bore into Diane. "Then Jeffrey Cross will never come home."

Diane's stomach tightened. He had to come home. Nick could not go on without him. "Once this portal opens, can we go inside and get him out?"

"No. Under no circumstances should anyone go inside. That world is unstable." She sat down beside Ginny. "This little girl is keeping that world alive. But she's weak. I don't know how long she can sustain it."

Diane moved forward. She looked down at the small girl in the bed. "What are you saying?"

Miriam's look was hard. "She's dying and so is that world."

Chapter Twenty

ξ

Nick lay in bed listening to the sound of the wind against the house. Where did she go? What had happened? Now he wished he had insisted on going with Diane instead of staying behind. The waiting was driving him crazy.

He closed his eyes, trying to clear his mind of all thoughts. It seemed as if he had not been able to shut out the world for weeks.

But his thoughts drifted back to his son, as they had been doing constantly for the last two days. In his heart, Nick wanted to believe that Jeff was still all right, that he would come home again. But in his mind, Nick could not be so certain. He had read books about kidnapping and the percentage of people who make it back alive.

He couldn't stand the waiting any longer. Throwing back the blankets, he stood and pulled on a pair of jeans. He was zipping them up when he heard . . . footsteps.

In the stillness of the house, in the quiet of the night, he could hear the slow, deliberate steps of someone coming up the stairs.

She's back, he thought. Grabbing a shirt, he slipped it

on, not bothering to button it closed, and stepped out into the hallway.

"Diane?" His breath fogged out in front of him. He hugged himself for warmth.

Why is it so damned cold out here?

"Diane?" No answer. He stood, listening. He could hear the clock ticking in the kitchen and the ice maker in the freezer of the refrigerator dumping ice into its bin. But nothing more.

He shivered, glancing over his shoulder at the empty hallway behind him, then back to the stairs in front of him. Still he heard nothing. But he no longer felt alone.

Someone is here. Someone is watching me.

He stood in the hallway, unsure of what to do. The hair on the back of his neck prickled, standing on end.

Is he behind me?

Nick looked over his shoulder again. The end of the hallway was lost in shadow. As he watched, the shadow seemed to shift, sliding away from the wall. Nick took a step back. The shadow grew larger, moving forward. Nick pressed himself against the wall, his breath escaping in small gasps. He wanted to turn and flee but he felt compelled to watch, his eyes locked on the hypnotic movement of the shadow as it grew and reshaped itself. He blinked. And in that split second of time, that instant when his eyes were not locked on the shape, the shadow withdrew. It no longer moved. Instead, it was tucked back in the corner of the hallway, nothing more than a shadow.

Did it move at all?

Nick did not want to find out. He started toward the stairs again, no longer wanting to remain on the second floor, or in the house alone, for that matter. He was three steps down when he saw the body.

"My God," he breathed. He froze where he stood, his

eyes locked on the legs as they swung ever so slightly back and forth. The rope made a slight creaking sound as it rubbed against the wooden ceiling beam it was tied to. It was too dark to see the man's face, but in Nick's mind, he could see the bulging eyes, the protruding tongue, the blue tint to the skin.

He began to shake. It started in his legs, a slight trembling that threatened to spill him down the stairs but it quickly moved through his entire body. Turning, he fled upstairs. He headed toward his bedroom.

A phone. He needed a phone.

He never reached his room. The shadows at the end of the hall shifted again but this time Bobby Tarp emerged.

Nick came to an abrupt halt only a few feet from him. His belly tightened with fear as the knife Tarp held came into view. But Nick did not back away.

"Where is my son?"

Tarp laughed and the sound of it made Nick's knees go weak. "You gave me life. In a sense, I am your son."

"Where's Jeff?" Nick demanded. He took a step toward Tarp. But the flash of the knife stopped him.

"Little Jeffy," Tarp said, studying the knife while running its sharp edge against the palm of his hand and drawing blood, "is in a place I do not intend to return to." His gaze left the blade and came to rest on Nick. "Do you understand me?"

"Are they safe for now?" Diane asked. "Can you tell me that?"

Miriam took a deep breath. "I'll try." Reaching out, she took Ginny's hand again. Closing her eyes, she began breathing deeply, trying to release herself into Ginny's subconscious. "Something's changed." Her body shuddered with the cold she felt each time she touched the girl. "Someone else is inside. Someone . . ."

Diane moved toward her as her voice trailed off. "Is it Tarp?" she prompted. "Is Tarp with them?"

"No." Miriam was having trouble catching her breath. She felt herself slip deeper inside. "It's someone else, someone . . . I don't know." Images drifted through her mind.

A house. Snow. Night.

"Can you see the place they are?" Bob asked. "Can you lead them away, protect them somehow?"

"No," Miriam said, straining to see.

A house. Snow. Night.

"It's too vague. I can't get inside. I can't—"

Jeff stood and crossed over to the window, hoping to see dawn cutting across the horizon. But only the solid darkness of night stared back.

He turned and looked at Ginny. The small girl sat before the fireplace warming herself. Did she really believe that this place was not real, that he was some kind of spiritual guide sent here for her? But Jeff knew she did. The way she relayed the details to him, the strength behind her words. *Bevin.* He had convinced her. Somehow he had made her believe. But why? Why is she here? What does he want? Jeff did not want to find out. Now more than ever, he wanted to get out of this house and find his way back home.

His gaze traveled over the snow-swept landscape. Snow? And for the first time, he realized how wrong that was. He caught movement out of the corner of his eye. He strained to see outside, trying to discern something out of the darkness and the shadows.

A tree branch blowing in the wind? Snow sweeping

across the ground? He squinted. No. It was something else, something that was moving slowly, steadily toward the house, low to the ground.

"What are you looking at?"

He jumped slightly, startled. Ginny stood beside him. He had not heard her approach.

"Nothing," he said, glancing back outside.

Ginny put her face up to the window, cupping her hands around them to see.

"Move back," Jeff said, taking a step away from the window, suddenly afraid to let the thing that crept so slowly forward see them.

"I found you."

Jeff gasped, spinning toward the voice behind him. Thomas Bevin stood only a few feet away. His hair was wild on his head, and his clothes were wet through. He had obviously been outside for some length of time.

"I found you," he said again. But he was not looking at Jeff when he spoke. Instead, his eyes were locked on Ginny.

"Thomas?" she said and Jeff could hear the uncertainty in her voice. This was not the man she knew. There was a rage in his eyes, an anger she did not recognize.

Jeff's gaze shifted to the poker he had left leaning up against the couch. He wished now that he had kept it with him.

Bevin took a step toward them.

"What are we doing here?" Jeff blurted out. "How do we get home?"

And at the sound of Jeff's voice, Bevin stopped. Slowly, he shifted his gaze to Jeff. His eyes flickered over the length of his body. "You won't ever go home." The words were angry and bitter. Then, indicating the room around him with a sweep of his arms, he said, "This is it for you, kid. Forever and always, this is your home now."

Jeff's heart picked up its beat at Bevin's words. His limbs felt suddenly weak. "What—" he started to say but could not finish the sentence, the question choking him. In that moment, Jeff realized he did not want to know what the man meant.

Bevin's gaze darted back down to Ginny. Quickly, he crossed the room and knelt before her. Jeff took a few steps back, not wanting to get anywhere near Bevin, afraid of what he might do.

Reaching out, Bevin gripped Ginny by the shoulders and said, "You have to send me home." His voice was low, almost a whisper. But there was no mistaking the panic behind those words, the desperation that seemed to be consuming Thomas Bevin.

Ginny began crying, a soft, muted sound.

"Stop crying!" he shouted, shaking her. "Stop crying. You have to concentrate. Think!"

Tears streamed down her face as her crying increased.

Jeff watched as Bevin continued to shout in her face, demanding help, his hands squeezing tighter and tighter against her soft flesh.

Anger welled up inside him. "Get your hands off her!" Lunging forward, Jeff wrapped an arm around Bevin's throat and tried to drag him backward, away from Ginny.

Bevin cried out in shock, releasing the little girl as his air supply was cut off. The two men stumbled backward, knocking over an end table and sending a lamp crashing to the floor.

Ginny screamed, squeezing her eyes shut. Covering her ears with her hands, she tried to block out the sounds of the fight.

* * *

Miriam released Ginny's hand, she had to. Her body continued to shake. "Bevin," she said. "Thomas Bevin is with them."

"What?" Diane knelt down beside Miriam, her body tense. "How can that be?"

The images faded, the house, the cold, the night—they were all gone. Miriam's eyes fluttered open. "I've lost them again." Her body quivered. Sweat stood out on her brow. She gulped for air, feeling short of breath. "I can't hang on. I can't get through."

"Try again," Diane said.

"No." Bob sat beside his wife. "This is taking too much of you. I want you to stop."

Diane turned on him angrily. "She's all we've got."

"A few minutes ago, you thought she was lying," Bob shot back. "You have no idea what you're asking, no idea what the risk to my wife is."

"You're right. I don't." Diane's eyes flashed hot anger. "I only know the risk to those two kids." She turned to Miriam. "I've got to know what's happening. There has to be a way to reach them, a way to help them."

Miriam struggled with her emotions. Her fear kept her from reaching as deeply into the young girl's subconscious as she knew she could. But her compassion made her reach toward the girl's hand again. She breathed deeply, closing her eyes. Images flashed before her eyes, emotions flooded through her.

Miriam strained to hold on to that place, strained to keep her bond. But again it slipped away. "I'm sorry."

Diane stood and began pacing before her. "This doesn't make sense. Why would Bevin go inside? Why risk it?"

Miriam shook as a chill passed through her. "Maybe he had no choice."

Diane looked at her. "What do you mean?"

"Maybe he was forced inside."

"By who?" Diane puzzled. But an instant later the only logical answer to that question came to her. "Tarp," she breathed. "But why?"

"Revenge," Bob suggested. "Maybe Tarp wanted revenge on the person who put him in that world.

"It's a cold, dark place," Miriam said. "Not one I would choose to live in."

Diane's eyebrows furrowed as she thought about it. "But then—" And a sudden look of dread crossed her face. "No," she muttered. Crossing to the bedside table, she snatched up the phone.

"What's wrong?" Miriam asked watching her dial frantically.

"Nick is responsible for that world too." She stood, winding the cord between her fingers, nervously tapping her foot. "He's not answering. Dammit, how could I be so stupid!" She slammed the phone down, heading for the door.

"Detective," Miriam called, her voice stopping Diane before she could leave. "I don't know what Tarp's limitations are. Please, be careful."

"Don't worry about me," she said. "You just find a way of contacting those kids and bringing them home."

Jeff snatched up the poker and came toward Bevin again. "Leave us alone!" he shouted. "Get out of here!" A new anger burned inside him, anger at the life he had lost when his mother died, anger at the years of bitterness toward his father that he could not erase, and anger at his current captivity. He wanted control of his life back. "Get out," he screamed, swinging toward the man he blamed for everything.

Bevin avoided the swing, easily dodging the poker. "You little shit," he muttered, managing to elude another blow. "I'm going to teach you who is in control here." And as Jeff swung again, Bevin reached out and grabbed the end of the poker and held on.

Jeff pulled hard, desperately trying to keep his grip, afraid of what Bevin would do if he gained control of this weapon.

And then in an instant everything changed.

Out of the corner of his eye, Jeff saw the large dark shape loom outside the window seconds before it crashed through the glass. Ginny screamed. Jeff released the poker. He lunged toward her, covering her body with his own as the shards rained down on them.

He cried out as stray pieces of flying glass cut into his flesh. He heard a thud as something large landed near them. Chancing a look up, he saw a dark shape moving slowly toward them. Half dragging, half carrying Ginny, he scrambled forward. He caught sight of Thomas Bevin as he charged into the kitchen, slamming the door shut behind him. Jeff opened his mouth, ready to call for help. But his foot caught on the edge of the carpeting and he tripped, sprawling forward, Ginny tumbling away across the floor.

"Get upstairs!" he screamed as she came to a stop.

She was crying, covering her face with her hands, trying to pull herself into a tight ball.

Jeff rolled over and caught sight of the poker. It lay only a few feet away. He was reaching for it even as three more dark shapes leapt through the new opening.

His heart jackhammered against his chest. Wolves. They had to be wolves. Scooping up the poker, he got to his feet and turned. He held the metal utensil out in front of him, slowly swinging it from side to side. He backed toward Ginny, keeping himself between her and the animals. Four sets of eyes glowed at him through the darkness, caught in the light of the full moon pouring into the house. Four sets of eyes shifted in the darkness, each moving in a different direction, circling him, stalking him.

"Ginny, get up!" He jerked left, then right, swinging hard each time, trying to keep all four in view at all times. "Go to the stairs!" he ordered.

She looked around, whimpering softly and crawled forward on all fours. He was almost to her when the largest animal began to growl deep in his throat. Jeff's stomach tightened and his breathing became tense. It moved forward more aggressively and growled again.

Taking a deep breath, Miriam gripped Ginny's hand.

Panic. Hysteria.

Cold. Weak.

Hide. Help.

"No!" she cried, releasing the hand. She gasped for breath. "Something's happening. Something's changed." She swayed where she sat.

Bob took her in his arms, steadying her. "You can't keep doing this. You're not strong enough."

"They're afraid now, Bob." She shuddered again, unable to shake the cold and fear that hung on her. "Blind panic. That's what I felt. My God, I have to get them out. I have—" She stopped mid-sentence.

"What is it?" Bob said as she pulled away from his strong embrace.

Miriam felt another presence hovering nearby, wanting to help, waiting to be heard. She reached toward it with her mind. A tingling sensation ran down her shoulder to her arm. Miriam grunted as Linda Cross slammed into her. She fell forward, shaken by the force of the presence now within her.

"Miriam!" Bob grabbed his wife's shoulders, keeping her from falling from her chair. "What's happening?"

"Get me some paper." Her hand was jumping and twitching. "It's Linda," she said, breathless. "Get me some paper!"

Bob handed her what she needed.

Miriam's hand scribbled on the page, tearing it. "She's going to help. She thinks ... if we both try ... if we work as one ... we can do it." Miriam's voice came out in short choppy phrases. She was having trouble catching her breath. Linda's emotions were so strong, so protective. "Together ... we're going to try and get inside." Her hand stopped the frantic pace of its work. Her breathing became normal. Miriam's gaze found Bob. "I think I can send Linda inside the same way Bevin sent Ginny in," she explained. "I can take over for Ginny, essentially take her place."

"You're going to keep that world alive?" he asked.

"Ginny is weak. I don't think she can do it much longer."

"Can you? Are you up to it?" And she could hear the doubt in his voice.

"With Linda's help, I think I can." Miriam touched Ginny's forehead. It was cold. "Linda's going to try and bring her son home."

Jeff chanced a look over his shoulder and saw Ginny just reach the stairs behind him and begin up.

"Foooood."

He spun back around as the word reverberated off the walls around him. He held his breath, his eyes searching.

Had he just heard that? But he could find no one hiding in the shadows, just the animals still moving forward.

"Hungrrrry."

Jeff's mouth went dry. His eyes focused on the animal before him.

"Starrrrving," it growled.

Jeff's limbs felt weak, and the poker nearly fell from his grip. He wasn't hearing this. But at the far end of the room, he could hear quiet growls mixed with words. His gaze darted around, looking for the other animals, his heart beating a heavy rhythm in his ears.

The animal before him arched up, its body rippling and stretching. Jeff watched, unable to move, unable to take his eyes from the beast before him. Slowly, the fur changed to flesh and the limbs lengthened. The creature took on the shape of a man.

"This isn't happening," he whispered, trying to convince himself he was not seeing what he knew was there. *It's a dream. I'm lying in my bed at home and I can't wake up.*

"So hungrrrry." The man-thing licked its lips, taking a step forward.

"Wake up!" Jeff screamed. He swung hard, striking the beast on the side of the head. It howled as the poker ripped into its ear, tearing it in half. The other three animals growled, their own transformations beginning.

"This is a nightmare," Jeff said aloud, needing to hear his own voice, wanting its reassurance. But as the creatures slinked forward, panic overtook logic. Turning, he fled up the stairs behind him.

Diane pushed Nick's front door open, her hand resting on the butt of the gun strapped to her side. The body hanging from the living room ceiling quickly confirmed the feeling that was knotting her stomach.

Pulling her weapon from under her arm, she approached it. "Parks," she breathed as the lieutenant's corpse came fully into view.

"I'll take his place." Nick's voice filtered down from the second floor. "Just bring him back."

A wave of relief swept through Diane. Nick was alive.

"Why do you think I'm here?"

Diane froze as she heard the second voice taunting him. She moved quietly toward the stairs.

"Just let Jeff—" Nick's words cut off abruptly. There was a loud thud. Diane froze, her breath coming in short harsh gasps. She wanted to call out and make sure Nick was still all right, still alive. But instead she stood where she was, listening, trying to decide what had happened.

"You are the second half of my equation."

She could hear Tarp's voice, deep and resonant.

Diane started toward the stairs again. He would not continue to talk to Nick if he were dead.

"I will continue my life here. You are sentenced to exist in the hell you created."

Diane tested each step before actually moving, trying to judge if they would squeak. The two men came into view as she stepped on the fourth step from the top.

The light from Nick's room filtered into the hall, back-lighting the men in an eerie glow.

Tarp held Nick by the throat, pressing him against the hall behind him. The knife he held flashed briefly in the waning light. Nick's shirt hung open, exposing his chest. As Diane watched, Tarp pressed the blade to Nick's bare chest and slowly drew it downward toward his belly. The knife made small cuts along his skin, leaving droplets of blood in its trail. Nick gasped for breath, his hands pulling on Tarp's, trying to free himself from the choking grip.

Diane moved up the remaining steps but stopped several feet away from the two men. "Let him go," she said, her arms locked before her, the barrel of the gun aimed at Tarp.

He turned to face her and slowly, a smile spread across his face. A darkness passed through Diane as she stared at him. He was walking death, an incurable disease, pure evil.

His gaze, hypnotic in its intensity, took her in. She had to force herself to look away. Instead, she focused on Nick. His eyes locked with hers. She could see the panic behind them as he was forced to gasp for every breath.

"Who is this, Nickie?" Tarp asked, the knife wavering in front of Nick's eyes. "Do you have a new friend?"

"Let him go." Diane took two steps closer.

Tarp sighed. "You certainly have a great deal of friends." And before Diane could react, he yanked Nick forward and slammed him back into the wall. Nick's head snapped backward with the blow, cracking against the wall behind him. Tarp released him and Nick crumpled to the floor, dazed.

Tarp turned to Diane.

"Move back," she ordered, trying to angle Tarp away from Nick and herself closer to him.

Tarp seemed amused as he stepped backward.

"Drop the knife," she said, still making her way closer to Nick.

"What knife?" he said. And Diane realized it was gone. Clutched in his fist, held out for her inspection, was a rope.

"Drop that," she said, her voice less sure.

He shrugged. "Okay." He tossed the rope toward her.

She flinched back, startled. As the rope connected with her hands, it changed. Her eyes widened as she watched it squirm and writhe against her skin. Within seconds it was a snake, winding and twisting around her hand and the gun she held. She cried out in pain as it squeezed. The gun fell from her grip. Diane pulled against the snake's body as it wound more tightly around her arm and moved toward her body. She felt the sharp edge of its teeth as it bit again and again into her exposed flesh.

Jeff darted toward the open bedroom door, a high keening sound escaping from his lips. As he slid past it, slamming it shut behind him, he caught sight of the thing racing after him.

This is not happening. This is not happening.

But as the beast hurled itself against the door, rattling it in its frame, Jeff realized it was all too true.

Ginny sat in the corner curled into a tight ball, rocking slowly back and forth. Jeff crossed the room and kneeling down in front of her, began talking softly.

"Ginny, we have to leave here. You have to be strong."

She continued to rock, ignoring him.

Reaching out, he gripped her by the shoulders and shook lightly. "Ginny, listen to me."

She covered her ears with her hands, humming loudly, trying to drown out his voice.

"I'm not going to let anything happen to you," he said, his voice determined. Then using her own logic said, "I'm your guardian. You asked me what guide I was, well that's it. I'm your guardian."

The humming stopped. Slowly, her hands lowered from her ears. She looked at him. Her eyes were wide pools of fear reflecting back his own feelings of dread. "You are?" she asked, her voice timid.

"Of course I am." Then added, "This is all just a test . . . a test for me . . . of my abilities." He floundered for the right thing to say. In reality, Jeff was no longer sure what he believed. He knew he was not this little girl's guide but this place, those things . . . Could they harm him if none of this was real?

The beast slammed against the door again, this time cracking the wooden frame with the force of its blow.

Jeff glanced over his shoulder, his heart thundering in his chest. How many more blows before that door opened? Three? Two? Or just one? Jeff no longer wondered if any of this was possible, if the animals outside his door could harm him or not. Only one thought filled his mind, blocking out all others—they had to get out—and they had to do it fast.

Jeff's gaze swept the room, which was as barren as the rest of the house. Escape. He focused on that word, his mind running through the possibilities.

Snow pelted the window above Ginny's head as the storm outside intensified. The beast hit the door again. The lower hinge came loose and the door bulged slightly inward.

Reaching up, Jeff pushed the window open. Wind and snow slammed into him, blowing him backward with force. He clung to the windowpane, trying to catch his breath. He leaned forward, but the overhang was too large and he could not see the ground below.

"Ginny," he said, pulling back inside. "I'm going to crawl outside on the roof and see if there's any way we can get out of here from there."

"Don't leave me," Ginny cried. "Please, don't leave me." And her tears began again.

"Ginny." Jeff hugged her, trying to calm her. "Nothing

is going to happen to you. I'm only going to look." He patted her back. "It'll take five seconds."

She looked up at him, sniffing loudly. "You promise?"

"I promise," Jeff said, wiping the tears from her cheeks. "Would your guardian let anything happen to you? I'd get fired for sure."

She smiled and then nodded. "Okay. I trust you."

Jeff climbed over the ledge onto the roof overhang. It was covered in ice and more slippery than he had anticipated. Crawling carefully, he moved to the edge of the roof and looked over the side. Unbroken snow covered the ground below. No animals were in sight.

Miriam sat alone in the room with Ginny. A few minutes earlier, she'd sent Bob to retrieve Evelyn Lambert. They would need her help if they were to succeed with this new plan.

Miriam stood and crossed to the window. She looked up at the crescent moon and the stars. *Infinity.* Would Jeff be lost forever within that world? If Miriam went inside, would she? *Infinity.* The word frightened her. She had been wrong about Bevin and his control over Tarp. She couldn't help but wonder how many other miscalculations she might make. Was this whole plan a mistake? She had no way of knowing. But she could still feel Linda Cross within her, giving her confidence, so sure they were doing the right thing. And Miriam trusted her.

The door opened and she turned as Bob and Evelyn entered the room. Miriam quickly explained what they were about to attempt.

"When Ginny comes back," Miriam said, talking directly to Evelyn. "I need you to keep her here. Don't let her slip back inside."

"How can I do that?"

"If I'm right, she'll come awake. You keep her awake, you keep her here with you. If she goes back inside, I'm afraid I'll lose my grip on that world and my grip on Jeff."

Evelyn nodded, her brow crinkled with worry. "I understand."

"What happens once you're inside?" Bob asked.

"I'm not really sure," Miriam confessed. "If we can do this, then our main objective will be to find Jeff and explain what's happening to him. He needs to understand where he is and how he can get out." Taking a deep breath and looking first to Evelyn before turning to Bob, she said, "I guess that's all. We're ready to try this."

"Are you sure?" Bob whispered.

Leaning forward, Miriam kissed her husband. Pulling back slightly, she looked deeply into his eyes. "This will work," she said, trying to reassure him. "I know it will."

He nodded. "I believe in you."

Miriam smiled. "And I in you."

Taking a deep breath, Miriam reached toward Ginny, closing her eyes. She concentrated on the cold, dark place within Ginny. Linda gave her strength, helping her reach through, helping her find her son.

And suddenly, she was there.

A thunderous boom split open the night. The house shook, seeming to heave up on its foundation. Jeff cried out as he lost his balance and tumbled over the side of the roof.

Ginny gasped, convulsing upward in the bed. Her eyes were open as she fell back down.

"Ginny." Evelyn was on her feet immediately, leaning down over her granddaughter, gripping her by the shoul-

ders. "Stay with me, Ginny," she coaxed. "Stay with me
honey."

Ginny's eyes filled with tears as she looked around the
room. "Gram," she whispered. "Gram, what's happening?
Where am I?"

"Thank God," Evelyn breathed. Leaning down, she
took Ginny in her arms and held her close.

Miriam moaned. Her hand slipped from Ginny's, spilling off the bed. She began to slide from her chair as her
body went slack. Bob caught her and held her against
himself, bracing her upright. She twitched in his arms,
her skin cold to the touch, her breathing almost nonexistent. And he knew she was there.

Nick watched as the snake moved toward Diane's shoulders, slowly making its way to her throat. She struggled
against it as it wrapped itself around her neck and began
to squeeze.

"Diane," he breathed, crawling toward her, his own
body alive with pain.

A long low rumble shook the house. Wind whipped
up and washed over Nick, knocking him backward with
its force. He looked up. Tarp stood above him, glaring
down.

"Time to visit your sonny boy," he said. Behind him
a whirling cyclone of air began to twist clockwise against
the wall. The wind sounded like a freight train whistling
through the house. And then Nick saw it.

Against the wall, at the place where the storm raged,
Nick could see what looked like another world. Trees,
stars, a snow-swept landscape.

Diane cried out. Nick jerked toward the sound. She
was on her knees, the snake tightening around her neck.

He crawled toward her. But before he could reach her, he felt strong hands on him, pulling him away.

His eyes caught the glint of her gun, lying only a few feet away. He lunged toward it, his hands grazing the cool steel. But before he could get a good grip on it, he was pulled away. He managed to catch the barrel in two fingers, barely holding on as he was slammed backward into the wall again.

A large hand tightened around his throat. He gasped, the gun slipping from his left hand to his right, almost falling. He fumbled with it as his air supply was savagely cut off.

"You'll watch her die. Then I'll cut out your heart." He jerked Nick around to face Diane. The knife found a home against Nick's chest, the point breaking his skin and drawing blood. True to his word, Tarp rested the tip of the blade just above Nick's heart.

The ground shook beneath Jeff. Opening his eyes, he pushed himself up. His body ached from the simple movement but he did not think anything was broken. His gaze swept the snow around him but he was alone.

"Ginny," he gasped, glancing over his shoulder at the house behind him. She was nowhere in sight.

Crawling forward, still unable to stand, he began to make his way back to the house. His hands grew numb as he was forced to submerge them in the snow time and time again. The storm increased, the wind sending stinging pellets of ice against his skin. He turned his face away, trying to shelter himself against the weather's torturous ways.

The ground beneath him trembled again.

Reaching the house, he used the wall to pull himself

upright, his legs barely able to support him. He leaned against the wooden frame trying to catch his breath.

Still Ginny did not lean out the window and call to him. Jeff feared the worst.

I promised to protect her. But I don't think I can.

Movement caught his eye and he turned as the dark shape of an animal came around the side of the house.

"No," he whispered, shaking his head back and forth. He could not do this. The animals were too strong, and it was too cold outside. He needed help. "Go away!" he screamed.

Another man-beast stepped from the shadows of the house, and this one stood directly in front of Jeff.

"Meat," it growled, taking a step closer, swinging its powerful hands toward him.

Rage swept through Jeff, savage and uncontrollable. He stepped forward and curling his hand into a fist, he screamed, "Get away!" and swung hard.

He missed. And as the animal side-stepped the blow, its paw caught Jeff high on the back of his left shoulder, the claws slicing neatly into his flesh. Jeff cried out in a combination of frustration and pain and spun around to face the creature again. But his feet hit a patch of ice and he went down. The beast was on him in an instant, clawing and biting.

Diane fell on her side, still struggling as Nick found the trigger of the gun. He pumped it twice, sending two slugs into Tarp at point-blank range. Tarp screamed and the knife arched upward. Nick fired again and felt a flash of pain. The gun tumbled from his hands. For an instant, he wondered if somehow he had shot himself. Then the knife drew up again.

* * *

Jeff struggled with the animal. Its claws racked down the side of his arm, shredding his shirt and his skin at the same time.

His arms ached with the force it took to keep the animal at bay. "Help!" he screamed, his arms shaking and about to collapse. He didn't know who he was calling to, who he expected to come to his aid, but he could not stop the words from escaping his lips. "Someone! Please!"

Another animal loped through the snow toward them. An instant later it attacked, knocking the animal from atop him. He scrambled away as the two fought, each wanting the boy for his own. Jeff felt his warm blood trickling down his arm, wetting his hand.

He was crying. He had not been aware when it started but now he could not stop it. It was hopeless. He was going to die out here in this cold, dark place and never know what had happened to him.

In the darkness, he saw more shapes moving toward him.

On the floor, Diane screamed. She clawed at her pant leg, pulling desperately, trying to get to the small caliber gun she kept strapped to her ankle. Her fingers brushed the cool metal as the snake tightened its choking grip. Her vision began to grow dim. Her ears rang. She yanked the gun from its small holster and fired as the knife arched downward.

Tarp jerked spasmodically as the bullet penetrated his back. The knife sliced within inches of Nick's face before slashing his leg on its downward descent. Nick buckled and fell with Tarp, the man's hand still clutching Nick's shirt, tearing the material. The knife clattered away down the hall as their bodies hit the floor.

* * *

Jeff held his bleeding arm and limped away from the two animals, leaving a trail of his own blood in the snow behind him. A flash of movement at the edge of the woods caught his eye. He turned, afraid he'd see more of the beasts slinking toward him. But it was a woman. She stood at the edge of the trees beckoning to him, calling him closer.

"Mom," he said, barely able to believe what he was seeing. He took a hesitant step forward and swayed, dizzy from the blood that dripped from his hands and stained the snow.

"I'm hallucinating," he told himself. But mind trick or not, he needed his mother. He rushed toward her, making quick strides across the snow-covered ground.

Her arms opened to embrace him as he drew near. She engulfed him in her arms, wrapping him in warmth and security.

"Mom," he sobbed.

She rubbed his back, stroking his hair. "It's all right, baby. Everything's all right."

This was his mother. Her touch, her feel, her smell. He was washed with her love, rejuvenated by her touch. This was what he wanted, where he wanted to be.

"I'm here to help you get home," she whispered close to his ear.

Home.

Jeff could not believe it could happen, that he could actually go home again. He looked back at the house behind him. "Ginny's inside. I can't—"

"She's safe," Linda said. "Just like you will be soon." She took his face in her warm hands, turning him to her again. "There are so many people helping, so many people trying to find a way to bring you home."

A new sense of optimism flooded through Jeff. Maybe t was possible, maybe he would get home.

Behind them, a deep growling suddenly filled the night. They turned in unison, Jeff gulping for air. He had forgoten. For a moment, he had forgotten.

"Run, Jeff," Linda urged, pushing him in front of her.

"Come with me," he pleaded.

"Run," she said. "I'll help you get home but you must un. Now!"

Nick pushed Tarp away and crawled toward Diane. The snake was now only a rope again, hanging loosely around her neck. She pulled it free and greedily sucked in air.

Shoving the rope aside, Nick pulled her into his arms. He needed to hold her, needed to feel the life in her, needed to know she was still alive.

The portal raged behind them, spitting snow and cold air into the hallway. They both turned and looked, unable o believe what they were seeing. Another world, existing within their own.

"Jeff's in there," Nick said. The snow piled up in the hallway, drifting high against the wall.

Diane nodded. "Yes," she whispered.

The house rumbled again, the floor beneath them shaking. "I'm going inside."

"No, you can't." Diane pulled away from his grip. "Miriam said no. She doesn't know how much longer hat world will exist. You can't risk going inside."

"Don't you see my choice?" He felt calm, at peace somehow. His son was within his reach; he had found him. All he had to do was bring him home. "I can stay here, hoping Jeff finds his way to us before this thing disappears or I can go inside and bring him out myself."

He looked toward the portal again. "I don't want to live in this world without him. I have to go."

"We'll both go," she said.

Nick returned his gaze to her. "I need you here," he said. She opened her mouth to protest but he spoke before she could get a word in. "I don't know what it'll be like in there. I need you to stay here and guide me out once I find my son." He began to stand.

Diane saw the blood soaking the side of his pants. She gripped his hand, stopping him. "You're not going anywhere until we wrap that up and you change into the appropriate clothes."

"There's no time for that," Nick protested. "We don't know how long that thing's going to stay open."

"You go inside now, in the shape you're in and it won't matter," she argued. "You and Jeff will both be lost for good."

It took only a moment for Nick to see her logic. They moved quickly. Diane bandaged his leg as Nick changed into a heavy sweater, slipped on a pair of boots, and pulled a heavy coat over his shoulders. Going to his closet, he retrieved his hat and gloves, and at the last minute, grabbed the flashlight he kept there. In less than ten minutes, he was ready to go.

On the floor where they had left him, Tarp moaned. The house shook, the portal blurring for a moment.

Nick stared down at him. "He can't die," he said as a sudden realization struck him.

"What are you talking about?"

"He opened this doorway," he explained. "If he dies, it might close."

Diane knelt down. "I'll keep him alive. Just hurry."

Nick moved toward the portal.

"Nick!" Diane yelled. He turned toward her. She stood

facing him, the wind rippling her clothes and blowing her hair. "Take this." She held her gun toward him. "You might need it."

He accepted it and leaning toward her, kissed her one last time. "I'll come back. You'll see." And with that, he stepped inside and was quickly swallowed up by the swirling mass of white.

Jeff made quick strides in the snow. Home. He was going home. But as he ran on blindly, he realized he did not know where home was. He stopped. His breath heaved in and out from the pace he had been keeping. He clutched his arm. It still ached where the animal had cut him but the bleeding had stopped.

"Mom?" he said, turning left, then right, no longer certain if she had been there at all. "Which way?" he yelled.

He could hear the animals in pursuit, the growling, hungry sounds coming from all sides. The ground shook beneath his feet. He fell against a tree, holding on as the ground continued to rumble.

"Jeff." His name drifted on the wind. "Jeff!"

But it was not his mother who called to him through the darkness. His heart picked up its beat as he recognized the voice. "Dad," he whispered, searching for his father, needing to see him and know he was near. "Dad!" he yelled.

A man stepped from behind a tree only a few feet from Jeff. His face was lost in the darkness of the woods but Jeff knew instinctively that this was not his father. He took a step back.

"Where are you going, Jeffrey?" Thomas Bevin plunged through the snow toward him. His face reflected the rage that coursed through his body. "Come here," he shouted. "Come here!"

The words stabbed through Jeff. He turned and began to run. But he stumbled in his panic, the snow suddenly giving him trouble. He did not realize how close Bevin was until his hand closed around the back of his shirt and yanked.

"Jeff!" Nick yelled again. For an instant, he had thought he heard a voice, very faint, answering back. Now he was not sure.

The snow was deep, going halfway up Nick's calf. Diane had been right. He wouldn't have lasted five minutes without protection from the bitter cold. He wondered how Jeff could. He swung the light around again, searching. But even with the high-powered beam, he could not see more than a few feet in front of him. The landscape seemed to go on endlessly. Trees, snow, and nothing else.

The wind pushed at his back, nudging him on, farther away from Diane. He glanced back over his shoulder but could no longer see the portal opening.

From far away, he heard a howl, long and plaintive. He stopped and listened. But the animal was quite a distance away.

"Jeff!" he yelled again. The word was snatched from his mouth and tossed away. This was useless. Jeff could be anywhere. He swept the light to the side. Was someone there?

Two bright points glowed at him from the darkness of the trees. Two bright points moved toward him. Nick took a step back as an animal emerged from the shelter of the woods.

* * *

"You'll pay for your father's arrogance!" Bevin shouted above the noise of the raging storm. Snow and wind ripped at them, tearing at their clothes and bodies. Pulling his arm back, he struck Jeff, sending him sprawling against the snow. An instant later he reached down and yanked Jeff to his feet and hit him again.

Jeff felt dazed as he lay in the snow. But as Bevin approached him, he drew a leg back and kicked out. He struck Bevin square in the stomach, doubling him over. Then he scrambled to his feet and scurried away.

Which way? Which way?

He knew the creatures that had been chasing him couldn't be that far behind. He didn't know which death would be worse. Being beaten to death by Thomas Bevin or being ripped apart by the powerful beasts. He decided he did not like either choice.

He staggered toward the haven of a thick grove of trees.

The beast growled deep in its throat, taking two more slow steps toward Nick. He raised the gun, ready to fire. The animal leapt without warning, catching him off guard. Nick managed to fire twice, actually hitting the animal high on the left shoulder once. It went down.

But it did not stay down for long.

It struggled to its feet. Nick moved closer, wanting to shoot at point-blank range. But as the animal came into view, he stopped, his breath catching in his throat.

In a flash, he remembered the story.

These were his shape-shifters: half-man, half-animal, able to change form at will. As he watched, the beast's snout grew short, becoming human in shape. The paws reshaped themselves into hands, the hair withdrew, the skin became human. Locking his arms in front of him, Nick pulled the trigger three more times.

The animal lay still. Nick nudged it with his foot to make sure it was dead. He never saw the second one. It hit him from behind, knocking him to the ground and rolling with him. Nick lost his flashlight and the gun and was left with only his fists to combat the beast. He managed to hold it at arm's length. As he stared up into its face, he realized this one was more human than animal.

It began to change even as it struggled with Nick. The hands that were gripping so tightly became powerful paws that swatted, the sharp claws easily slicing his flesh. It snarled down at him with razor-sharp fangs as the mouth and nose lost their human form.

Drawing his leg up between himself and the beast, Nick managed to get some leverage. With one powerful push, he shoved up and away, throwing the beast from him. He searched the area, scrambling on all fours, desperately digging through the snow, for the gun, his breathing heaving in and out from the battle already fought.

The animal loomed up before him.

"So hungrrrrr . . ." It growled deep in its throat, unable to finish the word as it became more animal than human. A long tongue protruded from its mouth, licking its lips in anticipation of the feast. It took a step toward him, the feet bending, twisting, becoming paws. Nick crab-walked backward in the snow, unable to take his eyes from the beast, caught by its gaze, mesmerized by its changing form.

Another step closer, still snarling, it was now down on all fours.

Nick could not catch his breath. He felt his heart pounding against his chest as he struggled to get air into his lungs.

The animal leapt.

A single shot rang out, striking the beast in the side of the head. It was dead before it hit the ground.

Nick spun to his left. A dark figure stood in the shadow of the trees, the gun still held out before him. He strained to see past the shades of darkness that shrouded the figure.

Jeff staggered forward two steps before his legs gave out. He went down on his knees, his body visibly shaking. Slowly, he slumped forward into the cold wetness of the snow.

Nick rushed to him, sweeping him into his arms and hugging him close. "Jeff," he whispered, touching his face, his hair, making sure he was real. After all the worry, all the fear, he was here, right here. "Thank God," he cried with the joy of holding his son again.

Jeff shook uncontrollably in Nick's grasp, overwhelmed by the cold. His eyes were hooded slits that stared up at nothing. His lips were tinged a pale blue. Nick slipped out of his coat and wrapped it around his son.

"Jeff," he said again, this time more forcefully. "Jeff, look at me." He gripped Jeff's face in his hands, turning it to his. "Look at me!" he yelled.

Slowly, Jeff blinked. He struggled to focus on Nick, his eyes rolling around for a moment before coming to stop on his father. "Dad," he whispered, his lips giving him trouble from the cold.

"You're all right. Everything's going to be fine."

Jeff managed a smile. Moving slowly, his hands curled into painful fists, he greedily pulled the coat closed over his body. "T-t-take me home," he uttered.

"Gladly," he said, ready to lead the way out. But as Nick

looked around, he was no longer sure which direction to go.

Diane stood in the hallway, hugging herself for warmth. she had heard the gunshots and was barely able to keep herself from following Nick inside.

"What is taking so long?" she muttered. More than once she had thought she detected dark shapes inside, moving between the trees, black against the white snow. Diane could not make out the shapes but she did not think they were human.

On the floor where he lay, Tarp moaned. The opening before Diane blurred momentarily, seeming to dim in intensity.

Diane knelt beside Tarp. "Damn you, don't die," she said, checking the bandage she had wrapped around his wounds. The bleeding had stopped . . . for now.

Standing again, she moved to the portal, straining to see inside. Nothing. Just the endless snow.

Setting one foot inside, not daring to go further, she cupped her hands around her mouth and yelled, "Nick!"

She waited, listening as the word blew away on the wind, echoing through the night. No answer.

She cupped her hand and tried again.

"Nick!"

Nick jerked toward the sound of Diane's voice calling him.

"Who's that?" Jeff asked.

"That's who's going to get us out of here," he said with some relief. Closing his eyes, he listened. "Come on, Diane," he whispered.

"Nick!"

Opening his eyes, he looked left. "This way," he said,

some of his confidence returning. He pulled Jeff up, supporting him as he got to his feet. "Let's go." .

They staggered together through the snow, following the sound of Diane's voice, trying desperately to find their way out. In the distance, Nick saw it. The doorway home.

"Nick! Hurry!"

At the sight of the exit, Jeff began running, making quick strides through the snow. Nick followed, only a few feet behind his son. A loud rumbling rolled across the ground, shaking the earth where they stood and throwing them slightly off balance. Jeff managed to stay on his feet but Nick stumbled, going down on one knee. He kept his gaze forward though, keeping the portal in sight, too afraid of losing the doorway home. But as he stared, his eyes fixed forward, the portal seemed to blur for a moment, the image of the doorway fading before locking solidly back into place.

"Hurry!"

A thread of panic ran through Nick's body at the sound of Diane's voice. He could hear her fear and knew what it meant—it was going to be close.

Jeff ran ahead, getting farther and farther away until he was just a dark shape in the distance. Nick got to his feet with some difficulty, his body beginning to ache from the continued cold. The wind blew over him, shoving its frigid air down his throat, robbing him of every breath he took. He started forward again, following his son's path in the snow. But he never reached the portal.

Diane watched as Jeff raced toward her. He stumbled through the opening, collapsing on the floor in a heap, shaking all over. Diane went to him, covering him with one of the blankets she had prepared for their arrival.

She pulled it around his shoulders and began rubbing his arms. "You're safe," she said.

He looked up at her. His lips had a slightly blue tinge to them and he had trouble forming the word. But after a moment of trying, he managed it. "Thanks."

Diane smiled. "My pleasure."

"D-d-dad?" he said, staring over her shoulder.

And Diane realized Nick had not come out yet. She glanced back. Snow and wind whirled around the opening. But still Nick did not emerge. Standing, she walked back to the portal and looked inside.

Nick was nowhere in sight. She glanced back at Jeff. He sat watching her, his face anxious. Diane bit her lip. *Where the hell is he?*

Thomas Bevin tackled Nick from the side, and the two men tumbled over several times in the snow before coming to a stop.

Bevin was on his feet almost immediately. And as Nick struggled to get up, Bevin kicked out, his foot finding Nick's rib cage. Nick grunted, falling on his side. Bevin kicked again, this time striking Nick in the left temple and sending him rolling.

The second blow left Nick dazed. He lay on his back, staring up into the swirling snow. Within seconds, he felt rough hands grab at him and drag him to his feet.

"You're not going anywhere!" Bevin shouted. Then indicating the area all around him, he said, "This is your new home, Nickie. Haven't you got that yet?"

For the first time, Nick realized the depth of Bevin's loathing for him. He could hear the pure hatred behind each word.

Bevin leaned close to Nick, a wild look on his face. "You're going to die here."

"So will you," Nick whispered back. And pulling his hand into a fist, he slammed it into Bevin's stomach. He doubled over, releasing Nick, who crumpled to the ground.

Immediately, Nick began a visual search of the area, looking for the exit, once again unsure of which way led out. A long, low howl drifted toward him, closer than Nick would have liked. He spun toward the sound, now hunting for the animal. He saw nothing but the swirling snow.

With some difficulty, he struggled to get to his feet. He braced himself against a tree, needing it to stand. Bevin was also up. He lunged at Nick again, a savage cry escaping from his lips.

Nick dodged sideways, striking Bevin on the back and knocking him to the ground. "Stop!" he screamed, taking a step backward. "Stop," he said again, this time the word barely a whisper. And as he stared at Bevin, struggling to get up on all fours, images flashed through Nick's mind with crystal clarity.

Jeff, left out here to die with no protection against the cold, no way of defending himself against the beasts that live here.

Bevin got to his knees.

Linda, screaming for help, so alone, so afraid, ripped from her family, lost forever.

Bevin staggered to his feet and turned toward Nick, breathing hard. He came at Nick again.

"No more." Nick's hands closed into tight fists at his sides. "No more!" he screamed and pulling back, he hit Bevin in the jaw. He staggered backward but did not fall. Nick struck again, this time in the stomach, forcing air from his lungs. Bevin went down on his knees. Nick drew up a knee, knocking him in the nose and sending him sprawling backward, blood covering his face. He walked forward and lifting his left foot high, held his boot over Thomas's head.

"Nick!"

He jerked as if slapped. Bevin lay beneath him, gasping for breath, a loud wheezing escaping him. Flecks of blood stained the snow around his head. Nick took a step back horrified by what he had almost done.

Bevin laughed, spitting blood. Slowly, with obvious pain, he managed to sit up. "What's the matter, Nickie? This is what you want, isn't it?" he taunted. Opening his arms wide, he indicated the world around him. "You made this violent place. There's nothing here to stop you, so go ahead!" He stared up at Nick, the challenge hanging between them.

The ground trembled and the storm intensified.

"Nick!"

He looked behind him, toward the direction Diane's voice was coming from. He saw it then, a dark hole, darker than the rest of the area around it. He was almost home. He turned back to Bevin. He still sat in the snow, coughing up blood. "There's still time!" Nick shouted above the sound of the storm. "You can still get out!"

Bevin shook his head. "Don't worry about me." Wiping at his mouth, he pushed himself up from the ground. "I'll get out of here." He cringed, doubling over in pain. "But you won't." He came at Nick again, forcing Nick to strike him one last time. Again, he fell in the snow.

"Nick! Hurry!"

After looking one last time at Bevin, Nick turned and fled toward Diane's voice. Behind him he heard the growl of animals. A moment later Bevin screamed. Nick stopped and turned. He immediately regretted it. Bevin lay on the ground, two animals ripping at his flesh, tearing it out in large chunks as he screamed, uselessly struggling against them.

Nick took a step toward him.

"No." The single word stopped him. At his side, less than ten feet away, stood Linda. "You can't help. You must go home," she pleaded.

"Linda," he breathed, unable to believe his eyes. He reached toward her. A wave of warmth washed over him, bathing him in the glow of her love.

"Go to our son," she said, moving backward and fading away.

"Please," he said, beginning to follow. But she was already gone, evaporating before his eyes, dissipating into the darkness around her. Nick took one more unsteady step toward the place she had been.

And Bevin screamed again.

Nick jerked toward the sound in time to see one of the animals tear Bevin's throat out, silencing him forever. Nick took an involuntary step backward, nauseated. His stomach convulsed in a combination of fear and disgust. And then he realized that only one animal stood over Bevin's inert body.

Only one.

His gaze swept the area, his heart picking up its beat. Where? But then he found it. The animal slinked toward him, low to the ground, its pace slow as it stalked its prey.

Panic overwhelmed him. Turning, Nick fled in the opposite direction, silently praying he was heading the right way. The animal let out a earsplitting howl, the sound filled with a deep need, a hunger that seemed almost palpable. A moment later it began its pursuit, making easy strides in the deep snow.

Nick glanced over his shoulder as he ran, needing to

know where it was, how close . . . He stumbled and almost went down. He caught himself and ran on. Ahead, less than twenty feet away, he saw it—the portal. Diane stood just beyond the doorway, calling frantically and waving her arms, guiding him home.

As Nick fell through, Diane heaved Tarp up and shoved him inside. The portal immediately began to close. The animal charged forward. Diane cried out, stepping back as it leapt. The portal snapped shut around it, cutting it in two. A head, half-human, half-animal, landed with a thud on the floor before her. She kicked it aside.

Nick was on all fours, his breath heaving in and out. Jeff crawled toward him and Nick, seeing his son, clung to him. Diane leaned down and draped a blanket over Nick and then stepped back, giving father and son time to be together. Nick held Jeff against him. Tears flowed down his cheeks. He had done it.

His son was home.

And they were safe.

EPILOGUE

ξ

Nick woke alone. He looked around the bedroom but like every other day, Diane was up long before him. Getting out of bed, pulling his robe around himself, he headed downstairs.

"Good morning," he said, entering the kitchen.

Diane and Jeff sat at the table eating breakfast. As usual, Diane had already showered and dressed. She was still uncomfortable about staying the night, worried about what Jeff would think. But Nick knew Jeff liked her and it would only be a matter of time before she realized it too.

"Morning," Jeff said, spooning eggs into his mouth.

Nick filled a plate for himself and sat down beside Diane. Leaning over, he kissed her on the side of the neck.

"I thought you'd sleep all morning," she said, smiling.

Nick took a bite of his toast. "You could have gotten me up."

"And disturb your beauty rest? Never."

"Is there any coffee?" Nick asked. He glanced at the empty pot and began to rise.

Diane pushed him back into his chair. "I'll make it," she said. "You eat."

"Thanks," he said as she got up and moved to the counter.

"Miriam called," Jeff said suddenly. "She's going home today. Wants to see us, say good-bye."

It had been two weeks since Jeff and Nick emerged from the portal. Since then, Miriam had worked with both of them, helping them get over the pain of Linda's loss. For the first time in five years, Nick felt as if he could begin life again, a life he now planned to spend with Diane.

"She's over at Ginny's right now," Jeff continued. "I thought maybe we could drive over and see both of them."

Nick nodded. "Sounds good but why don't we offer to drive her to the airport." Then he looked at Diane and added, "Can you go?"

She shook her head. "Gotta work today."

Nick shrugged. "Okay, but you're going to miss all the fun." He turned back to Jeff. "Maybe afterward you and I can make a run into Ann Arbor."

Jeff's face screwed up in confusion. "Why?"

Nick took another bite of his breakfast and said as casually as he could, "I just thought maybe we could take a walk through the U of M campus."

"What?" Jeff's eyes grew wide.

"Well, I want to see the place where my son plans to spend the next four years."

Jeff's smile was wide. "Are you serious, Dad?"

"Of course I am."

Jeff rose from his chair and hugged Nick, holding on tight. "Thanks, Dad," he whispered in his ear.

Nick held his son, grateful for the growing closeness between them. They were given a new beginning. At

ast that's how it felt to Nick. They were given a new
ɛginning and he was going to make the most of it.

"I'm gonna catch a shower," Jeff said, releasing his
ther and straightening up again. "We probably should
ɔ pretty soon, don't you think?"

"Within the hour," Nick said, his son's excitement
ɔntagious.

"Great!"

After he left the room, Diane spoke from behind him.
You know you made his day."

Nick sighed. "It was long overdue. I guess I—"

"Dammit, Nick."

He turned toward Diane's angry voice, his words falling
f. She stood in front of the coffee pot, wet grinds
ɔvering the counter.

"What'd you do?" he asked, standing and going to her.

"I have had it with this thing." She dumped the ruined
lter into the garbage. "I'm going to put it out of my
isery."

"You overfilled it again," he said, helping her clean
ɔ.

"Tonight when you guys get back," Diane said, grab-
ng a sponge and scooping the mess toward the sink,
'm taking you both out to dinner and then we're going
buy a new coffee maker. Maybe a nice Mr. Coffee."

Nick took the sponge from her hand and dropped it
to the sink. Wrapping his arms around her waist, he
lled her close. "That's sounds good to me," he whis-
ɛred in her ear. "I think I'm about due." And he kissed
ɛr long and hard.

The Dollmaker was a serial killer who stalked Los Angeles and left a grisly calling card on the faces of his female victims. With a single faultless shot, Detective Harry Bosch thought he had ended the city's nightmare.

Now, the dead man's widow is suing Harry and the LAPD for killing the wrong man—an accusation that rings terrifyingly true when a new victim is discovered with the Dollmaker's macabre signature.

Now, for the second time, Harry must hunt down a death dealer who is very much alive, before he strikes again. It's a blood-tracked quest that will take Harry from the hard edges of the L.A. night to the last place he ever wanted to go—the darkness of his own heart.

THE CONCRETE BLONDE

"Exceptional...A stylish blend of grit and elegance."
—Nelson DeMille

THE CONCRETE BLONDE
Michael Connelly
_____ 95500-6 $5.99 U.S./$6.99 Can.